TRASH MOUNTAIN

TRASH MOUN-TAIN

Winner
Red Hen Press
Fiction Award

a novel by

Bradley Bazzle

Red Hen Press | *Pasadena, CA*

Cover artwork by Nikita Shulgovich @sevsilver
Book design by Selena Trager

Library of Congress Cataloging-in-Publication Data
Names: Bazzle, Bradley, author.
Title: Trash mountain: a novel / by Bradley Bazzle.
Description: First edition. | Pasadena, CA : Red Hen Press, [2018] |
  "Winner/Red Hen Press/Fiction Award 2016"—ECIP galley.
Identifiers: LCCN 2017051268 | ISBN 9781597099103 |
  ISBN 9781597096232 (ebook)
Subjects: LCSH: Young men—Fiction. | Southern States—Fiction. | GSAFD:
  Black humor (Literature)
Classification: LCC PS3602.A9994 T73 2018 | DDC 813/.6—dc23
LC record available at https://lccn.loc.gov/2017051268

The National Endowment for the Arts, the Los Angeles County Arts Commission,
the Ahmanson Foundation, the Dwight Stuart Youth Fund, the Max Factor
Family Foundation, the Pasadena Tournament of Roses Foundation, the Pasadena
Arts & Culture Commission and the City of Pasadena Cultural Affairs Division,
the City of Los Angeles Department of Cultural Affairs, the Audrey & Sydney
Irmas Charitable Foundation, the Kinder Morgan Foundation, the Allergan
Foundation, the Riordan Foundation, and the Amazon Literary Partnership
partially support Red Hen Press.

First Edition
Published by Red Hen Press
www.redhen.org

for Mom & Dad

TRASH MOUNTAIN

Chapter 1

IN THE BEGINNING I had two parents and a sister. The parents weren't much, but the sister was pretty good. Her name was Ruthanne. She had a weird spine because of the dump next to our house, where there was a big pile of trash we called Trash Mountain.

Trash Mountain loomed outside Ruthanne's bedroom window, on the other side of a fence. Trash Mountain was so unstable that the fence was lined with razor wire so kids wouldn't climb around on it. Trash Mountain didn't smell like trash, weirdly, but like this spray they sprayed on it that smelled like bowling shoe spray, times a million. Trash Mountain was always changing: a flattened fridge on top one day, pieces of car the next, couch cushions, a dried-up houseplant. Trash Mountain grew and grew until it was literally a mountain, meaning taller than one thousand feet. Ruthanne and I could tell how tall it was because we approached the issue scientifically. What we did was put our eyes in the exact same spot, at the bottom left corner of Ruthanne's bed, and use an old key to scratch a mark on Ruthanne's window where the top of Trash Mountain was. Then we measured Trash Mountain with a special technique I learned at school to measure trees using the tree's shadow and a pencil. It was trigonometry, basically. I was a genius at it. Maybe I could have done it for a living, but instead I had to destroy Trash Mountain.

One day Carl, who drove us to school, was hanging around our house while he waited for my parents, who hadn't paid him, and he saw me marking the window with the key. Ruthanne was in the bathroom, maybe hiding. Carl asked what I was doing, and I told him. He laughed, which pissed me off, but then he got serious. He said, "Yeah, man, it's fucked up y'all live right next to that thing. Could be worse, though. On the other side, in Haislip, they don't even spray it down. But those Haislip people don't complain."

"Pretty soon they won't have to complain," I said, and I laid out for Carl a plan that had been germinating inside me. My plan was to tunnel into the base of Trash Mountain and plant a nuclear bomb inside it, then escape just in time to roll under the porch while the bomb went off and incinerated the whole dump.

Carl nodded. He knew a good plan when he heard it.

"And then," I said, "they won't put another dump there because they learned their lesson. If we're lucky it'll be a super fun site."

"Superfund site?"

"Whatever. There'll be a playground and stuff. And a football field where the goal posts are also soccer goals so you can play soccer too."

Carl said it sounded like a pretty good plan. I asked him where could I get plutonium and he said he didn't know. Then Ruthanne came out of the bathroom and Carl said he liked her new brace. "Can I sign it?" he asked.

"It's not a cast, you idiot," she said.

"My bad," he said. Then Ruthanne went into the kitchen, and Carl whispered to me, "Your sister's got a nice little body but man is she a bitch."

"Don't call my sister a bitch," I said. Then my parents came home and scraped together twenty of the fifty dollars they owed Carl and he left.

That night, after my parents' light went out, I crept out of my bedroom and down the hall to Ruthanne's room. She was reading a book under the sheets. I asked her what book it was, and she said it was none of my business. But I saw the cover and it had a picture of a shirtless guy with long hair and shiny boob muscles. I told her about my plan to set off the bomb, since she hadn't heard it before, and it felt wrong to me that Carl was the first person I told instead of her. She said it was a pretty good plan but maybe too ambitious. She had just turned fifteen and was becoming levelheaded.

"Better just to light it here and there, strategically," she said, "and watch the fucker burn. The fumes will be noxious so we'll probably die, but we'll have sacrificed ourselves for the greater good. They'll do a monument about us."

Ruthanne was right, I decided, but I didn't tell her so she wouldn't get a big head. I started imagining the monument they'd do about us. Ruthanne's would look like the peaceful version of Jesus where he's raising two fingers and tilting his head, except the head would be Ruthanne's head instead of Jesus's head. Mine would be a worm-dragon shooting out of the ground with a ferocious scowl and a beard-and-mustache combo like flames and also tiny powerful claws tucked under my chin, for fighting.

The next day in computer class I read about lighting things on fire and found out the cops could tell when you did it on purpose and put you in jail. The jail was a building by the highway with tiny windows and razor wire around it where sometimes, when we drove by, I could see guys playing basketball and smoking cigarettes. There was a big gray bus like a school bus that took those guys places. They always had their heads leaning against the windows with their eyes open, like they were really tired but couldn't fall asleep.

Jail wasn't for me, I decided. I would either succeed or be killed. So I opened my notebook and wrote down the names of the most combustible chemicals I could find: chlorine trifluoride, cellulose nitrate, phosphorus heptasulfide, phosphorus sesquisulfide. I had no idea where I could get any of those chemicals. Eventually Mr. B saw me writing stuff and said, "Hey there, Ben, whatcha working on?"

"Nothing," I said, covering my notebook with my forearm.

"Mind if I have a look?"

"It's private."

"Totally cool, Ben. I respect your privacy. Just let me know if you have any questions, okay? The internet is an unfiltered source of information, and sometimes a parent or teacher can help put things in perspective. But will you do me a favor?"

I shrugged.

"Try to finish the internet treasure hunt before period ends?"

I said I would.

The internet treasure hunt wasn't a treasure hunt at all, just a list of lame facts we were supposed to find on the internet. This one was Alaska themed, like how tall Mount McKinley was and why Alaska was called Seward's Ice Box. The questions took about ten seconds so I did them all, to keep Mr. B off my back, then I took my paper to him and he graded it right in front of me and gave me an A-plus. I was a genius at geography, he said. Geography was another thing I could have done for a living if it wasn't for Trash Mountain.

I stayed on the lookout for chemicals, but by the time Saturday came I hadn't found any so I decided to proceed to stage two of my plan: canvassing the target area. I told my parents I was going to the empty school where I liked to kick a ball against a brick wall, but instead of going there I started walking the perimeter of the dump, probing for weaknesses.

The wire fence went along the other side of an alley behind our house. It was ten feet tall with planks of wood that went up maybe six feet, and on the very top was a stretched out coil of razor wire. I had climbed the fence before and knew there was no getting through that razor wire, which was woven through the chain-links so you couldn't lift it up. I kept walking.

Where roads dead-ended into the fence, there were little guard-rails to keep drunk drivers from crashing through. Beer cans and soda bottles and fast food wrappers were all around the guardrails, like maybe people had been sitting there during a party. There were clothes hanging in backyards, and sometimes rusted-out cars and appliances that looked pretty cool. I saw an old man watering what looked like a sandbox except there were plants in it. He waved his cigarette at me but I didn't wave back. I was on a mission.

In half a mile the alley hit an empty six-lane road with a dead grass median, and the fence took a sharp right. There wasn't any sidewalk so I walked along the median, kicking trash as I went. The sun was up high by then and stung my neck. I wished I'd worn a hat, but I didn't like wearing hats because I had a big head and hats made it look weird. Eventually the road veered left and the fence kept going straight. Between the fence and the road was a patch of shitty looking forest. The trees had flaky bark and some were dead. The ground between the trees was slick and smelled like the bowling shoe stuff they sprayed at the dump. I wondered what would happen if a person breathed the smell too long. Would he pass out and never be found again?

I saw an empty plastic vodka bottle and some wadded up clothes, what Grandpa would have called a hobo bed. The vodka bottle scared me because the person who had drunk it might be crazed. We saw an educational movie about it at school. The movie was in black and white and the people talked like idiots, but the drunk character made a shocking impression on me. His eyes were bugged out and he had drool all over his lips, and he tried to grab a lady's boobs with both hands.

I started walking faster but not too fast, hoping to look casual. Then I heard something that sounded like a crow but I decided in my head was a crazed drunkard making crow sounds to signal his crazed partners that there was a kid in their midst, because they preyed on kids like me for who knows what, so I started to run.

When the forest ended I stopped to hunch over and catch my breath, and I saw that the fence looked different. The razor wire had turned into a droopy coil of barbed wire, which any self-respecting thief could get over with a heavy blanket or scrap of old carpet. But I had neither. I thought about climbing the fence to get a good look at the trash, but I was too tired. Thirsty, too. Lucky for me, there were some houses in the distance. I crept towards them along the fence, hoping to find a hose or something (I would have drunk out of a dirty kiddy pool by that point), but before I got to the houses I heard some kids. I followed their cries to a big, empty lot where crumbling asphalt was being overtaken by weeds. Some black boys a few years older than me were drinking beer and playing catch with a football. I watched them for a while, waiting for a break in the action to test my courage and ask them about the water situation, then I noticed a boy standing apart. He was a little younger and was digging in the dirt with a stick. When he saw me his stick went still. He glanced over his shoulder, like he was deciding whether or not to holler at the older boys, then he resumed poking around with his stick. When I got closer, I saw he was working loose some kind of soiled garment from the rocky dirt.

"That yours?" I asked.

"Hell no," he said. "Look like I wear teal?"

I laughed. The garment had indeed been teal at one time, and had fringes like a lady's shirt. I told the boy my name was Ben, and he said his was Demarcus. I never heard that name before so I said, "Like Marcus?"

"*Of* Marcus."

"So your dad's named Marcus?"

"Gerald." On the subject of Gerald, his dad, Demarcus opened up considerably. Demarcus's dad owned a bar outside Haislip that kids weren't allowed to go to. He came home early each morning to have breakfast with Demarcus and his brother, Daryl, but by the time they came into the kitchen he was usually hunched over the table sleeping.

Now that Demarcus was warmed up I asked him about maybe getting some water, and he glanced back at the older boys before leading me across the overgrown lot to a tin building painted white.

Behind the building was a hose faucet. Demarcus turned the spigot and each of us drank some water.

The water was superb. I felt like it was going straight from my stomach into my blood and the skin on my arms, and my eyes too. Everything was bluer and greener now, somehow more hopeful. Demarcus's face was shiny with sweat. He had a bald spot on his head, and when I asked him about it he said he fell off the monkey bars and they shaved it to give him stitches but when they took out the stitches the hair didn't grow back. It was lumpy, he said, and he let me feel it. It *was* lumpy, and I told him it was cool. He said he didn't think so. But I told him that when he was older and had more muscles it would make him look hard, like a guy in an action movie. He agreed.

I had a notion I couldn't ask Demarcus directly about Trash Mountain, couldn't let him know what I was after in case he thought differently and told the police on me, or maybe even the FBI, since I was basically a terrorist by this point, so what I did was ask him what he thought about "that old trash pile over there," tilting my head in the direction of Trash Mountain without looking at it so the overall effect was, I hoped, nonchalant.

"There's pretty interesting stuff in there," Demarcus said.

I was shocked. "You've *been* in there?"

Demarcus shrugged.

"How'd you get in?"

Demarcus led me across the street and between some houses to the fence. Here, the fence didn't even have barbed wire, let alone razor wire, so I thought we were going to climb it, but Demarcus kept walking along the fence until we came to a spot where the fence seemed to have popped up from the ground. There was a divot in the dirt beneath it where some boys or dogs had dug it out. I watched with reverence as Demarcus took off his shirt, balled it up and stuffed it into his pocket, then slid on his back under the fence. I did the same and slid after him pretty easy. By the time I put my shirt back on, Demarcus had found a chrome-sided toaster and was inspecting it. All around us were tin cans and plastic bottles and scraps of wood and trash bags, some closed and some ripped open with their guts hanging out: coffee filters, banana peels, wadded up Kleenex. Some furniture was arranged in a ring nearby, and some faded beer cans were stacked in a pyramid. I was so dazzled by the spread that it took me a while to remember we were at the base of Trash Mountain. When I did remember, I looked up from the junk furniture and ripped trash bags, up from the dried grass clippings and dirty plastic toys, up and up until the surface of the mountain was so far away it looked like pieces of a colorful jigsaw puzzle spilled in a big, tall pile. I was overwhelmed. It was like when we went to this lake one time and I was sitting on the dock, not really thinking about anything, just staring at the calm, dark water, when suddenly I thought about how deep the water might be, and the thought of all that cold, dark hidden space made me dizzy. That feeling by the lake had been frightening, but this, I decided, in the shadows of Trash Mountain, was the greatest and most frightening feeling of my life.

Demarcus acted real casual, though. He said he and his friends messed around in there all the time. That made me sore. I guess I felt like a softie for being so moved. "You and your friends, huh?" I said in a needling way. "Were those boys playing ball without you your friends?"

"They aren't my friends," Demarcus said. He had popped the chrome shell off the toaster and was inspecting the inside. "They're older. My brother's with them."

"Where are *your* friends?"

Demarcus didn't say anything, and in the silence I pictured a bunch of black boys lying in bed wearing braces, like Ruthanne. That made me feel bad for saying what I did. Demarcus was a good man, I decided. He could be trusted. So I told him Trash Mountain made my sister's spine weird and was poisoning the rest of us and stinging Jesus's eyes worse than sin. Demarcus nodded in a serious way that made me think he had suspected this all along. Then he said, "But we don't eat it or nothing."

"You don't gotta eat it," I said. "It's in the air. It's all around. We're breathing it right now and getting it into our skin. Don't worry, though. I'm gonna blow it all up."

Demarcus squinted at me. "What?"

"Well, maybe not all of it, but part of it." I didn't have time to go into more detail. The sun was just over top of the trees, which meant I wouldn't get home before dark. I was scared, not of the scolding I might get from my parents but of that stretch through the forest, with the hobo beds. The crazed hobos came out at night, I suspected, to do their perversions. I decided to call Carl. I asked Demarcus if I could use his phone. He said of course and led me back under the fence, then a few blocks away to a little wooden house with a sagging front porch. The screen door was latched to keep a gray cat inside. We slipped in sideways, using our feet to block the cat, whose name was Ghost.

Demarcus said "Hey Dad" as we passed through the front room. Demarcus's dad was wearing a bathrobe and sitting in a lounge chair, reading a newspaper. He eyed us over the paper as we went into the kitchen. After Demarcus showed me the phone and I took it off the cradle, Demarcus's dad called to his son in the warm yet commanding voice I associated with dads on TV. I was convinced that he, unlike Demarcus, knew at a glance I was a terrorist. So after I called Carl, who was startled by my request to be picked up in Haislip and said he'd come right over, I walked boldly into the living room. I had decided I would introduce myself to this man in a friendly way that suggested I had nothing to hide.

"Hello, sir," I said, "I'm Ben. Pleased to meet you."

The father, who was very tall and had graying puffs of hair over his ears, shook my hand and introduced himself as Mr. Caruthers. He asked what brought me to Haislip, and I surprised myself by telling the truth: that I was following along the fence until I found a way inside the dump.

"Why on Earth do you want to go inside that nasty old dump?" Mr. Caruthers asked.

"To see it," I said, which was true, though I left out the part about strategizing to destroy it by firebomb.

"Can't you see it from over there in Komer?"

"There's razor wire to keep us out."

He shook his head. "Figures," he muttered, then told us we shouldn't be playing in that dump, though he admitted the temptation to be irresistible. He told us about a creek where he grew up and how they built forts out of old tires and driftwood that floated down the muddy water. "Simpler times," he said.

When Carl showed up, he looked stoned. Mr. Caruthers shook his hand in a stiff way and asked if he was here for his brother. I'm not sure why Mr. Caruthers thought Carl and I were brothers—we looked nothing alike—but for some reason I blurted, "Yeah, he's my brother. He's gonna take me home." Then I shook hands with Mr. Caruthers and on my way out I whispered to Demarcus that I would be back to finish the job.

In the car, Carl started making a speech about how I shouldn't wander so far away, but I told him to fuck off. He said he was doing me a favor and I should be more respectful. I said I was sorry. Then I asked him about Haislip. Carl said he sometimes delivered pizzas over there but it was scary at night because the empty houses had vagrants inside. I had no idea what a vagrant was but assumed it to be a sort of creature.

We went back the opposite way that I came, completing my loop around the dump. Turns out I had walked the long way before, and Haislip and Komer were only a mile or so apart. I made note of this for later.

When I got home, Ruthanne was washing dishes and asked me where I'd been. I told her the whole story, leaving out the particulars of my plot but allowing that I had been casing the dump. It was important to tell at least part of the truth to Ruthanne because she had a nose for lies.

"I swear, Ben," she said, "sometimes you just don't think."

"I think all the time," I said. "Pretty hard, too."

She snorted like it was ridiculous, the idea of me thinking. That made me mad. It also made me mad she had the energy to stand there washing dishes but hadn't told me before, because if I knew she felt strong we could have rode bikes. So I went into my room and didn't sneak into hers even once that night.

During computer class the next day I tried to find out more about Haislip. I wanted to know if it was worthy of my sacrifice, if saving Haislip, in addition to Komer, would doubly glorify me. The internet said Haislip was named after a Civil War guy and was known as Flag City, USA. I was confused. I thought Komer was Flag City, USA. Then the internet said Haislip was the hometown of mountaineer Bob Bilger, who was the first man to videotape climbing Mount Everest and wrote a book about it, but I thought Bob Bilger was from Komer. Then the internet said Haislip was the birthplace of the frozen hamburger even though everybody knew Komer was the birthplace of the frozen hamburger, so when Mr. B came over to bug me about staying on task I asked him where was the birthplace of the frozen hamburger.

"I don't know," he said. "Is that question on the internet treasure hunt?"

"I finished that. You know anything about Haislip?"

"Haislip is a very interesting city, full of history and hardworking people, not unlike Komer. You'll learn more about Haislip in high school, where half the students will have gone to Truckee."

He meant John R. Truckee, the middle school in Haislip. I was at Milford Perkins, the one in Komer, which people said was better but had sloppy joes made of rat meat.

"Why the curiosity about Haislip?" Mr. B asked.

"No reason." I didn't want to let anything slip that might be a clue when the FBI questioned everybody who knew me. "I gotta finish my internet treasure hunt now."

Mr. B walked away, looking confused.

I knew Mr. B wouldn't bug me for a while so I turned my attention to the actual firebombing. I learned that firebombs, aka incendiary weapons, looked like rusty logs and were thrown from planes during World War I to light towns on fire. Since I couldn't get my hands on one of those logs, I would have to settle on an "improvised" incendiary weapon such as a Molotov cocktail. Molotov cocktails were easy to make. All you needed was gasoline and a glass bottle and some fabric for a wick.

The beer Dad drank came in cans, so late that night I snuck out my window to check the alley for glass bottles. The bottles in the alley were all broken, though. Then I heard a distant clang and saw a dark shape lurching down the alley. At first I thought it was a junk monster of some sort, born from the dump, but it turned out to be a lady hobo pushing a grocery cart. I watched her lift the top off a trashcan and root around in there until she pulled out some bottles, so I did the same thing and found some nice clean bottles of my own. She noticed me and muttered something, probably a hex.

Next, I got the big red jug of gasoline Dad kept by the side of the house for his mower. The jug was almost empty (he had used it to top off his car) but there was just enough gas in there to fill three bottles halfway, which was how much you were supposed to fill them for Molotov cocktails. It was dark outside and hard to see so the gas went all over the bottles and my hands and shorts. I rinsed the bottles in the kitchen sink then balled up my shorts and hid them under the stairs in front of the house. They were my favorite shorts so this was a terrible sacrifice, but it felt good to feel the feeling of sacrifice.

Next came the wicks. I looked under the sink for a dishrag but got nervous because Mom had a peculiar memory. I opened my closet and got my worst, most skid-marked underwear, but the underwear was so threadbare that I worried it might burn too fast. So what I did was cut a strip from the bottom of my bed sheets. If I cut cleanly enough, I reasoned, no one would notice that my top sheet was a few inches shorter. I cut the long thin strip into three and tied each strip as tight as I could around the side of each bottle. (The internet said most people stick the wick directly into the bottle, but the wick can get too much gas on it and explode in your hand so it's better to do it on the side.)

I kept the Molotov cocktails under my bed until five o'clock Saturday morning, when I stuck them in my backpack and crept out the door before Mom and Dad woke up. It was still dark outside, which was good. I needed to commit my act of terror under cover of darkness. But as I walked down the alley I started thinking about Ruthanne, because what if I died? Wouldn't she want to know what I died for? I was still sore at her for what she said about me not thinking, but I didn't want to leave things bad between us in case I was blown up by my own firebomb. I decided to write a note.

Back at the house I got a piece of paper and puzzled for a while over what to write. It had to be somewhat vague in case the FBI questioned her, but also heroic and majestic and memorable. Finally I wrote, *"Dearest Ruthanne, You're the best sister a boy could have. What I do today I do for you, for all of us, and for the galaxy. Your ever loving brother, Ben."* I folded up the note and was going to put it in her favorite shoes, but then I heard Dad banging around in the kitchen looking for something to eat. I thought about sneaking out, but I knew I shouldn't risk it. He had eagle eyes like me, and it was getting light outside anyway. I didn't want to spoil my plan out of hastiness.

I spent the whole day fidgeting alone in my bedroom until the sun was just over the treetops, then I grabbed my backpack and told my parents I was sleeping over at a friend's house. What friend, they asked, which was a reasonable question since I didn't have friends. I told them Timothy McCoughtrie. I had slept over at his house one time, years before. They looked suspicious. "Didn't his family move away?" Mom asked.

"Yeah," Dad said, "and I thought McCoughtrie killed himself. But maybe I'm thinking of Mike McCutcheon."

"No, that was Mike McCoughtrie," Mom said, adding that Mike McCoughtrie had been a great basketball player and should have gone to college for it.

"You always were hung up on that guy," Dad said.

"I just think it's a shame he's dead is all. When someone's so good at something it makes it harder to imagine them dead. It's funny is all."

"Nothing funny about being dead."

I said, "So, um, is it okay if I go?"

They said okay so I hit the road.

I walked the way Carl had driven me home, which was only a mile and had a sidewalk the whole time. It was a pretty nice walk.

In Haislip, all the houses were the same size and had the same little screened-in front porch so it took me a while to locate Demarcus's house. When I did, I circled it, peeping in windows for Demarcus, but he wasn't there. No one was there. So I strolled out to the field where I had found him before, and sure enough he was out there stacking rocks in a pile while the older boys played ball. I told him tonight was the night. He asked if I needed his help.

"No way," I said. "It's too dangerous."

"Then why'd you come tell me?" he asked.

I didn't know what to say to that. By then some older boys had noticed me and were approaching us. I worried that if I ran they'd come after me, so I stood my ground. They were bigger than they looked from a distance and crossed their arms to show their muscles. One, the tallest, who was basically a man, asked me who I was.

"A friend of Demarcus," I said, but Demarcus just looked at the ground.

The boy turned to Demarcus. "He a friend of yours?"

Demarcus didn't say anything.

I thought the boys were going to attack, but they just stood there, arms crossed, staring at me. They seemed to be waiting for something. Finally I just turned around and walked away. I didn't dare look back until I heard them hollering, resuming their game, but by then Demarcus wasn't among them.

Who needs him, I thought. Each man stands alone. But I really didn't want to be alone just then. I wished Ruthanne were with me.

I found my way back to the hole under the fence, but I didn't slip through it right away. I strolled around a bit, trying to look casual. Then, when I was sure the coast was clear, I carefully slid my backpack under the fence and slid through after it, on my back. On the other side of the fence I looked up at Trash Mountain. It was reddish from the sunset, like a wayward outcropping of the mountains of hell. Its shaggy piebald flesh of plastic rippled in the breeze. I walked along the base, looking for a spot that was partially blocked from view, in case anybody crept up on me, and I found a nook between two rusted-out refrigerators. I opened my backpack. It smelled like gasoline even though the bottles were closed, and the inside felt greasy. I took out one of the Molotov cocktails and turned it in my hand, appreciating not only my handiwork but the craftsmanship of the bottle itself, which spoke of a bygone era when kids like me hung around corner stores with bar stools and bartenders who served soda instead of beer, and the kids were always stealing candy but the bartender guys just shook their heads and said, Boys will be boys.

There was a rustling nearby. I ducked into one of the refrigerators to hide, and in a moment I saw Demarcus walk past holding a heavy bucket. "Psst," I whispered, and he turned and saw me in the fridge.

"Ben!" he said. He said he was sorry again and again but that Daryl and Boogie one time beat up this white boy for goofing with Boogie's sister.

"What's goofing?" I asked.

"You know," he said, then made his finger and thumb into a circle and stuck another finger through it.

I said the whole thing was no problem, but Demarcus seemed pretty worked up, so I said I absolved him, which was something I saw a priest on TV say.

"Thanks," Demarcus said. He held up his bucket to show me it was half-filled with water in case I lit myself on fire, and we got started.

I had planned to dig a hole in the side of Trash Mountain so I could ignite my Molotov cocktails beneath it, to cause it to collapse from the inside or possibly explode at the top like a volcano, but the trash was so smelly that I gave up digging after just a few minutes. Demarcus said maybe I should just light one and throw it as high as I could, to see what happened. I agreed. I reached into my pocket for the matchbook I had stolen from the kitchen, and while my hand was in there I felt a piece of paper. I took it out and saw my note to Ruthanne. I almost cried, thinking how the note might have burned up with me, without her knowing what it said and how I felt about her. I handed the note to Demarcus. "If anything happens to me," I said, "give this to my sister."

"What does she look like?"

I wasn't sure how to describe her so I told him my address and said she was the girl living there, not the lady. I also told him to deliver the note under cover of night in case FBI snipers were watching the house.

Then I took out the matchbook, lit a match and held it up to the wick. It caught fire real quick, maybe because of the extra gasoline in my backpack, so I sort of panicked and threw the bottle just ten feet or so up onto a trash bag. It landed with a thump and didn't break. I watched the flame peter out, hoping something in the trash pile would catch fire, but nothing did.

Demarcus said I should aim for a big blue metal thing that looked like the fender of a van. It was about thirty feet up, close enough to hit but far enough to be hard to aim at. I accepted the challenge. I took out the second Molotov cocktail, lit it, grabbed it by the bottleneck, as described on the internet, and flung it with force at the fender. But I flung it with so much force that the wind put out the wick and by the time the bottle smashed against the fender, the fire was long gone.

"Fuck, man," I said.

"Maybe throw it softer," Demarcus said.

"How can I throw it softer? I gotta hit the goddamn fender."

"Wait for the rag to be more on fire, maybe. You threw it pretty quick after it was lit."

Demarcus had a point. But I was nervous. This was my last Molotov cocktail, and I had to make it count. The lucky thing was some gasoline was already on the trash from the second Molotov cocktail, so if I could hit the fender again then the fire might be doubly intense. So I took a few deep breaths and shook out my hand, then I lit the final Molotov cocktail and waited. The waiting was eerie, watching the fire slowly devour the wick. Demarcus was watching too, his eyes glistening with tiny reflected flames. When the fire met the bottle I flung it with not quite as much speed but a higher arc, and Demarcus and I watched for what felt like minutes as the flaming bottle traced a trajectory high in the air. At first I thought I had missed, because the bottle went so high, but sure enough it began to sink, and then, suddenly, it shattered against the fender and bright orange flame spread like spilled juice splashing across the floor. We kept watching, stunned, then something else caught fire beneath the fender and rumbled so loud I could feel it in my chest. A tiny fireball shot up and showered sparks. We ran.

The next part is fuzzy. I remember watching Demarcus basically dive under the fence and scoot through on his belly. I followed him, but by the time I got through he was shrinking in the distance, running for home. I looked over my shoulder and saw smoke. I ran along the fence, stumbling over clods of dirt and falling at least once, scuffing the palms of my hands. When I got to the road to Komer I was still running. It was dark and I was running down the sidewalk, not even thinking about perverted hobos or what my parents would say, just desperate to get home. Once or twice I looked over the fence and saw what looked like a plume of smoke in the purplish night sky.

When I got home I fumbled with the doorknob for what felt like an age, then I ran through the empty house to Ruthanne's bedroom. She was there, thank God, reading her paperback. She looked up at me, startled. I told her to look out her window.

"Ben," she said, "are you okay?"

I went over to the window and pulled back the drapes. "See?" I said, but there was nothing to see. There weren't any flames in the distance. Not even smoke. Just the lumbering dark shape of Trash Mountain. Near the top, a big floppy mattress glittered in the moonlight. Its stuffing was coming out in balls, and for days the puffy white balls had been rolling in slow-motion down the raggedy slope. If only I had caught that stuffing on fire, I thought, but the thought rang hollow. To destroy Trash Mountain would take more than a couple Molotov cocktails, I knew. Much more.

Chapter 2

TURNS OUT GARBAGE piles combust from their own heat pretty much all the time, so the night watchman, who sat in this little tower you could see from the road, didn't even call the fire department that night. He just drove out to Trash Mountain in his golf cart, sprayed the side of it with a hose, then turned around and finished his shift. I learned all this from Demarcus a few months later. He did a school report on the dump and interviewed the night watchman, among others, on what was most exciting about working there. Demarcus said the night watchman was a creep. When Demarcus asked him what was most exciting, the night watchman pointed at a pile of porno magazines and winked.

I decided I needed a blowtorch. The best was the Red Dragon 400,000 BTU Backpack Torch Kit with Squeeze Valve. It cost $284.95 online but came empty, so I'd have to pay to fill it with propane. I needed $300 to be safe.

I asked Ruthanne what kind of job I could get that would pay $300. Ruthanne said most places wouldn't hire you until you were sixteen, but I was only almost fourteen. Ruthanne said she knew from experience.

"What kind of job did you try for?" I asked.

"Waiting tables," she said.

"But you couldn't lift the trays."

"Could too. It's not like I'm crippled."

"Well you don't lift nothing around here."

"Around here I *choose* not to. It's nonviolent protest. What do you want a job for anyway? You don't even like girls."

"Do too."

"Well you don't take 'em out on dates, and that's what costs money."

"It's not like *you* go on dates, so why the hell do you want a job?"

"Not to blow up a trash pile, that's for sure."

"Fuck you," I said, and went to my room. Ruthanne followed me, so I picked up *The Highest Mountain* by Bob Bilger, the only book in the room, and pretended to read it.

Ruthanne flopped down on my bed. "Whatcha reading?" she asked, even though she knew what I was reading. Every kid in Komer had to read *The Highest Mountain*, since Bob Bilger talked at school every year. Most kids thought he was boring but I thought he was okay. He had a big white beard and wore western jackets. He cursed on stage.

I tried to ignore her but Ruthanne persisted. "Which part are you on?" she asked, resting her chin on her fist. "The part where he videos the mountain, or the other part where he videos the mountain? Or, wait, the part where he pays some Sherpas to video the mountain?"

I shut the book and left the house, feeling like a fly whose sister was picking off its wings. The problem was Ruthanne was bored. Even though she was the most talkative person in the family, besides Dad, she was shy around other kids. She didn't play sports because of her back, which wasn't her fault, but she didn't do band or yearbook or anything else either. After school she just slinked home, finished her homework in about fifteen minutes, then read one of her sleazy books or watched TV with Mom. She tormented Mom too. For instance, she might say, "Hey, Mom, *Price is Right* is on. Want me to turn it up full volume?" Mom would say sure, not really listening, and Ruthanne would do it. The TV would be rattling but Ruthanne would just be sitting there, watching, smiling kind of crazy, and when the host announced a new car or whatever, Ruthanne would announce it too, real loud, and do a crazy made-up song about the car until Mom told her to shut up so she could hear *Price is Right*.

Sometimes I thought if Ruthanne and I were combined into a sort of hybrid kid (not a hermaphrodite, though) we would be the most successful person ever to come out of Komer/Haislip, bigger than Bob Bilger even, or the lady who did the website where you could click on clothes TV people wore and buy them for yourself. Ruthanne and I might be the ones talking at schools about our exploits, such as floating down the Congo River in an oil drum or inventing the Kitchen Wizard, a space-age kitchen knife with a laser beam for a blade.

I cruised the city on my bike, brainstorming. I knew from movies that sometimes people put HELP WANTED signs in the windows, but the only signs I saw were for pit bull puppies. Dog breeding was an option, but pit bulls were where the money was, clearly, so I would have to catch a few stray pit bulls and make them have puppies. But the strays were scary, and I didn't relish the idea of encouraging them to copulate.

On the window of the drugstore were flyers for paid drug trials, but you had to be eighteen to do them. There were also flyers offering money for blood plasma, but you had to be eighteen for that too, and anyway I had a notion that blood plasma was something only diseased people had, in place of normal liquid blood. I imagined it to be a sort of blood-colored mucus.

Thwarted, I decided to ask Demarcus for advice. He was a year ahead of me even though we were the same age, so he had started at Pansy Gilchrist, the high school, and had friends who were older.

Demarcus told me the best I could hope for were odd jobs like raking leaves for old people, but there were so few odd jobs in Haislip, he said, that for his own part he gave up long ago. "My Dad told me to start a paper route," he said, "but who reads the newspaper anymore? Nobody in Haislip, that's for sure. Maybe Komer's different."

"Probably not," I said, "what with the internet."

"Nobody in Haislip has the internet and they still don't read that shit. As soon as I turn fifteen I'm gonna get a job bagging groceries. That's good money, plus you get a discount on certain items."

"But I don't turn fifteen for a year."

"Me neither." Demarcus thought for a moment, which wrinkled his eyebrows together in a way that made him look older. "One time Dad let Daryl be a coat-check boy at the Motown Lounge."

"What's a coat-check boy?"

"A boy who holds your coat until you're done drinking. Daryl says Dad didn't let him stay up long enough to give people back their coats, though." Demarcus shook his head. "Probably it would be best to invent something."

"Like what?"

"Something everybody needs, like stronger cement that's got a nice color to it, or tinfoil with self-cleaning nanoparticles. But to make money off it you gotta have a patent, so I'm thinking I might become a patent lawyer."

"Don't you have to go to college for that?"

"College and more."

"What about until then?"

Demarcus thought for a moment. "You tried Bi-Cities?"

"What's Bi-Cities?"

"Bi-Cities Sanitation and Recycling. The dump."

"Hell no," I said, kind of offended. A few months ago we had tried to blow the place up, and now Demarcus thought I should *work* there?

"It's the only place that hires," Demarcus said.

"I ain't working for no dump."

"It's not just a dump, though. There's a recycling center and a toxic waste storage facility."

"No way."

"Look, man, you said you needed work."

The idea of working at the dump turned my stomach, but the more I thought about it, the more it made perverse sense. By working at the dump I'd accomplish two things at once: 1) getting money to torch the place later, and 2) casing the place so I could optimize the torching.

"Maybe you're right," I said, "but what kind of job could I get there?"

"There's internships," he said, "but you'd have to lie about your age. That, or gofer type jobs."

I nodded. The idea of lying appealed to me. "Maybe I'll try the dump after all," I said. "*Know your enemy*, isn't that what they say?"

Demarcus nodded seriously. "Let me know how it goes."

I told Demarcus I would, and we shook hands in the elaborate way he favored.

It went horribly.

Bi-Cities headquarters was a squat gray office building that looked like a jailhouse. The building and its parking lot full of pickup trucks were surrounded by a razor-wire fence. The only entrance had a guard booth with tinted windows. I rode up to it on my bike. I was wearing a collared shirt and the pants from my funeral suit to look presentable. The guard was slouched, reading a magazine. It took him a while to notice me down below. When he did, he chuckled like a dimwit. He said, "Can I help you, little partner?"

The term *little partner* was distasteful to me but I smiled. "I'm interested in inquiring about employment opportunities," I said, which was something I got off the internet at school, along with key phrases like "self-starter" and "team-player" and "I'm familiar with the work you do and consider myself an expert in your field."

He chuckled again. "Any particular job posting you're inquiring about?"

"The internship," I lied.

"What internship?"

I hated this man. He had a stubbly red neck pinched by a starched collar, the sort of neck I would come to associate with thoughtless white men in positions of power.

"See," he said, smiling as he put down his magazine to lift up a clipboard, "to get in you have to be on the list."

"How do I get on the list?"

"You make an appointment."

"I have one. They wanna interview me for the internship."

"If you had one you'd be on the list." He took up his magazine again, which was called *POLICE: The Law Enforcement Magazine* and had crosshairs on the *O*.

"There must be a mistake," I said.

"I don't think so," he said.

"Can I use your phone?"

"Nope."

I was kind of thankful he said no, because who would I have called? I didn't have an interview. The rejection allowed me to take the higher ground, to save face as I rode away indignant.

As a last resort, I decided to talk to Dad. I had to wait until the weekend, though. He had taken a construction job in the city two hours away, where he shared a shitty little apartment with guys from work. He stayed there weeknights and got drunk, Mom said, and when he was home she barely talked to him. Neither did Ruthanne. Dad said we were lucky. He said there were dads from the Chinese countryside who lived in big cities all year, working 24/7, who only got to go home for Chinese New Year and by then they were so tired they just slept the whole time. Plus, he said, they often gave the rest of the family communicable city diseases.

When I approached him he was watching a TV news show. "Look at this goddamn idiot," he said about an anchorman with gray hair like a helmet. "Bet he's naked from the waist down behind that fake desk of his. That's how they do, you know. The sports ones too. And when the cameras stop, they bitch and moan like Mickey Rooney."

I asked Dad what kind of job I could get, and he said the first job he ever had was running errands for Donkey Dan Connors.

"You ran errands for a donkey?" I asked.

"A gangster," Dad said. "A two-bit gangster. Whole family is gangsters, Whitey included."

"Who's Whitey?"

"Whitey Connors. He runs the dump."

That was the first I ever heard about Whitey Connors, but the name stuck with me. I imagined a sort of godfather deep inside the Bi-Cities headquarters building, doing favors and putting out hits on people. I wouldn't mind running errands for a person like that, I decided, but then I remembered he ran the dump so I cursed him in my heart.

I biked around the city looking for errands I could run, and odd jobs of the type Demarcus had described. Most of the downtown stores were closed, so I started at the fast food strip along the highway.

The cashiers seemed confused by my offer. They went to get their managers, and the managers said there wasn't anything outside the store that anybody needed, not even office supplies. Everything was right there in the store. The manager at Burger Brothers said, "Burger Brothers is a completely self-contained replicable pod, which is why it's such a successful—and delicious!—franchise burger establishment."

I shifted my focus to non-burger establishments such as pawn shops and bank branches. People there were confused by me too. A lady at Komer United Credit Union said, "What does a little fella like you need a crummy old job for anyway?" which was a pretty stupid question. Everybody knew it was money that made the world go 'round. I almost said something pathetic like "to eat, Miss," but that would have been lying. We were poor, sure, but there was always cereal in the pantry, and macaroni, and a flaccid loaf of bread I could put peanut butter on. We had special big jars of Mormon peanut butter, which the Mormons made cheap for people in Guatemala or wherever, but also for people like us. It was kind of chalky and not very sweet but otherwise pretty decent peanut butter. I thought being Mormon wouldn't be half bad if you got to work in a peanut butter factory and eat peanut butter all the time.

For inspiration I turned to *The Highest Mountain*. Bob Bilger was a mountaineer, after all; he climbed mountains, and I wanted to *destroy* a mountain. The first chapter was about Bob Bilger's childhood in Haislip. He talked about his "dear sweet mother" and his father, "a monomaniac in the style of Long John Silver, who finetuned on his family the tyranny with which he cowed the simpleminded oafs on his road crew." Then he talked about his boyhood pals, "a gang of true rascals," but he didn't mention anything bad they did. The only bad thing he mentioned, the thing that ended the chapter, actually, was how he lied about his age to an Army guy so he could go fight in Vietnam.

That gave me an idea: a thirteen-year-old, unlike a sixteen-year-old, had no driver's license, which as far as I knew was the only means of identification a person could have, so why not just show up at the grocery store and claim to be fifteen?

That's what I did. I approached the oldest looking checkout lady, hoping teens all looked the same to her, and sure enough she gave me a form to fill out. I lied about my birthday and put in a fake social security number, since I didn't know it anyway. Under work experience I put "homework mostly." Under why I wanted the job I wrote "money," to sound honest, and also "to learn the value of hard work and possibly climb my way up to checkout, management, etc." After I finished the application I gave it back to the checkout lady and asked to make an appointment to meet with the manager. The lady said they wouldn't schedule an interview until they reviewed the application, to which I said that in the event they rejected my application I would cherish the opportunity to meet with them and learn what I could have done better on it. "Alright, alright," she said, but I thought she might be lying so I made sure to read her nametag: NELDA.

Two days later somebody else from the grocery store called the house to tell me my application had been rejected and thanks for my time. Before she hung up I told her Nelda had promised me an interview.

"Nelda has no such authority," she said.

"Please," I said, "I know I'm out of the running for this position, but I sure would like to learn what I could do to strengthen my candidacy."

"Persistent, aren't you?" She told me I was welcome to come by the store and meet with her. She said she would give me some pointers.

The next day at school I had my funeral suit balled up in my backpack to meet with this lady, whose name was Darla Waddell, and I just couldn't wait until three so I left at lunch. Maybe if Darla Waddell met me in person, I thought, she wouldn't be able to resist giving me some kind of job. People told me I was a cute kid, or at least they told me that before my voice started changing. Ruthanne said my voice made me more creepy than cute, like the foulmouthed girl in that exorcism movie.

A checkout guy told me Darla Waddell's office was in back, by the bathrooms, so I walked to the back of the store, which smelled like blood from the nearby meat counter. I knocked on a door marked OFFICE.

The woman who answered the door looked much younger than I expected. Her small face was dominated by heavy glasses, and she had long straight hair the color Mom called dishwater. She gestured to a chair across from her desk, which was cluttered with papers and a big dusty computer monitor. The windowless room was lined with big beige file cabinets covered in photos stuck in place by colorful magnets. The photos showed little kids.

"Cute kids," I said.

"They aren't mine," she said. "Are you really fifteen?"

"Yes," I lied.

She stared at me.

"Thirteen," I said, cursing inwardly for giving it away so quick, "but in six days I'll be fourteen. Swear to God."

"Don't swear to God in front of people."

"Sorry, ma'am."

"Don't call women ma'am."

"Okay."

"That's all the advice I can offer, I'm afraid. You seem like a smart kid, though. Come back when you're fifteen. And bring your social security card so you can write down your actual social security number."

"Hmm, I meant to. I must have got a number wrong."

"Your actual social security number has nine digits, not four. If social security numbers had four digits, that would mean there were fewer than ten thousand people in America."

"How many are there?"

"Three hundred million."

"No shit?"

"Don't say shit."

This lady was smart, I decided. Now I wanted a job there more than ever. "Are you sure there isn't anything," I said, "*anything* I can do? Off the books, maybe?"

"You mean illegally?"

"No, no, just, you know—"

"You can offer to carry people's groceries, but you can't do it in the store; we have people we pay to do that."

"And you'll pay me too?"

"No, but the customers might. It's called tipping."

"But if they don't want their groceries carried inside the store, then why would they want them carried *outside* the store?"

"Exactly. And if we get any complaints, I'll call security. Now, if you don't mind, I have a one o'clock with my mother."

She rose and we shook hands. Her handshake was firm, but she didn't look into my eyes. It was like she felt bad for me or something.

When I left I wasn't sure what to think. It seemed Darla Waddell had left the door open for me, but only a crack. I sat on my bike at the edge of the parking lot and scoped the scene.

Almost everybody carried their own groceries, either by hand or in shopping carts, so nobody needed help except really little old ladies who couldn't get the bags from their carts into their trunks. I didn't see any of the helpers Darla Waddell supposedly paid, so after watching for a while I got up the nerve to approach and old lady who was struggling to heft a bag out of her grocery cart. When I offered to help she seemed startled, but when she looked up and down at my wrinkly black suit she sort of grunted "alright." I hefted the bag out of the cart into the trunk, then I did the other bags too. She said thanks but didn't offer me money, so I stood there awkwardly until she said thanks again and got into her car in such a rush that she left her cart behind the car and backed into it before zigzagging into the street.

For the next few days I biked to the grocery store after school and made study of parking lot dynamics. The thing that gave people the most trouble wasn't carrying their groceries; it was returning their carts. They seemed to hate pushing their carts all the way back to the brick wall where the carts were lined up. Some people just left their carts. Others looked from side to side like they were thinking about maybe leaving their carts, but then they grudgingly pushed them back. These people were my target customer, I decided, and I made a few bucks by popping out during their moments of indecision and offering to return their carts for a small fee. I left the fee vague in case they wanted to give me more than a dollar. Sometimes they gave me a quarter, though. One time a guy in a sleeveless denim vest ignored me, left the cart where it was, and backed into it intentionally. It's surprising what some people do.

At the Salvation Army Family Store I bought a little green vest that almost matched the vests the grocery store people wore. It even had a nametag like theirs did, but the name said Roger Talamantez, so when old people leaned close to get a look at my name I had to

lie and say my name was Roger. And once I lied, I kept lying. That
was something I discovered about myself. After I said my name was
Roger, I might say I lived in a trailer down by the river with my older
brother's widow and their three kids, whom I was helping to raise,
or that I was much older than I looked because of a pituitary gland
disease. I might say I was in training to be a checkout person, the
youngest ever, but had to cut my teeth the old fashioned way, "out
on the blacktop," which was grocery store lingo for the parking lot.

The lying made it fun, and almost made up for the times people
blew me off or didn't pay me or damn near backed over me with their
jacked-up trucks. The worst was when old ladies decided I was "playing dress up" and was "just the cutest little thing." That bothered me
because I *was* playing dress up, kind of, but I didn't like to think of
it that way. For me it was serious. I had started to think that if you
dressed and behaved like a person, you could become that person.

I made about two dollars an hour so in two weeks I had almost
thirty dollars in singles. I kept the singles in a shoebox under my
bed. It didn't occur to me to spend any of it until one day I made
thirteen whole dollars because an old man in a tracksuit gave me a
ten, maybe by accident. On the way home I wondered if I should
treat myself to something. The Red Dragon 400,000 BTU Backpack
Torch Kit with Squeeze Valve still loomed large in my mind, but I'd
have enough for it in a few months either way, and in the meantime I
might keep up my gumption with something smaller.

I thought about stuff I liked but didn't get enough of, in my estimation, and decided milkshakes were near the top of the list. But
the drugstore downtown that used to sell milkshakes was closed,
and the only other place I could think of, Yummy Pizza Taco, had a
weird smell that made the milkshakes taste worse. I decided that candy bars, though a distant second, might make me feel at least some
sense of accomplishment, so I stopped in the Drug Time drugstore
and bought a Twix. I ate one bar on the way home, then at home I sat
on my bed and wondered if I should eat the other Twix bar or save it.

Finally I took the bar to Ruthanne's room and asked if she wanted it. She offered to split it with me, so we sat there on her bed crunching the second Twix bar.

I asked her what book she was reading and she said it was none of my business, but then she felt bad and told me the book was about some gang guys in Oklahoma who got in rumbles but secretly cried all the time and loved each other. I wanted to know more about the rumbles, but she changed the subject. She said, "You know, Ben, if you bought candy like this for a different girl, she might let you touch her boobs."

"Shows what you know," I said. I had a notion from Dad that you had to buy a woman at least twenty dollars worth of food before she'd even kiss you, not that I cared about that stuff. I just wanted Ruthanne to allow that I might know a thing or two for myself and not have to be told everything by a smartass like her. I said, "Don't tease me right now. My nerves are shot. A man coming home from work deserves a little respect."

She threw a pillow at my head. "You just hung around a grocery store parking lot for an hour. You call that work?"

"What would *you* call it?"

She shrugged. "I guess I'd call it work too. You know, Ben, I didn't think you'd land a powerbroker-type job like this, but you sure proved me wrong. Pretty soon you'll be CEO of a Fortune 500 company."

"Probably."

From then on I made a point of buying a candy bar at the end of the week for Ruthanne and me to share. It felt good to go into the Drug Time with money in my pocket. But in November I realized it would be cheaper to buy discounted Halloween candy at the grocery store, as long as I had the discipline not to eat it all at once. So I bought a bag of fun-sized Twix and kept them in my closet, and every Saturday I pulled out two and brought them into Ruthanne's room. When the Twix ran out I bought Hershey's Kisses, which she liked, but eventually the Hershey's Kisses got this white stuff all over them, like mildew. I scraped it off but the inside part was hard and tasted like coffee.

The next time I bought candy, to replace the weird Hershey's Kisses, I was standing in line at the Drug Time with a wad of singles in my pocket, listening to the horrible saxophone music they played in there, when I started wondering where was the adventure in making and spending money, especially if you had to spend it someplace like Drug Time or Yummy Pizza Taco or even Burger Brothers, though they had pretty decent burgers. I bought some fun-sized Payday bars, but the thought stuck with me.

That night, after stuffing the rest of the singles into my shoebox, I took out *The Highest Mountain* again. In the part I was on, Bob Bilger was talking about how the Army made him a man. Before the Army, he said, he had been "steadily transforming into a low-rent flimflam man: picking pockets, prying open payphones with a screwdriver, running errands for men my father detested, men who sat in folding chairs all afternoon circling racehorses in the dailies, circulating cash-filled envelopes among themselves, eating sandwiches of truly disquieting girth." His distaste for running errands made sense to me, but the only reason he could stop, it seemed to me, was because he joined the Army, and I was too young to join the Army. Plus the Army seemed pretty boring, what with cleaning latrines and marching until you puked. I skipped ahead until I saw the word "Vietnam," but there was marching in that part too. So much marching! No wonder Bob Bilger's legs got strong enough to climb a mountain.

I closed the book and turned off the lamp to go to sleep. The view through my bedroom window wasn't as good as Ruthanne's, but lying there in the dark I could see a dim glow from the side of Trash Mountain. The glow was from rotting wood, I had learned, but in my heart I considered the glow to be a sign of Trash Mountain's mystical nonhuman power. The glow made me wonder if money and jobs and even school were just tricks to distract me from my secret hidden purpose, which was to destroy Trash Mountain. And maybe, I thought, destroying Trash Mountain was just the first step in what would become a life of adventure.

I couldn't fall asleep so I snuck out on Ruthanne's bike, which I had begun to pay her for in installments of five dollars a month, since Ruthanne's bike was superior to my own in every respect except its lavender color and lady's crossbar.

I headed downtown, where the streets were mostly empty. The city didn't light the street lamps anymore so the only light was the light of the moon, which was full that night, lucky for me, and free from the haze that sometimes made it look like it was shining behind toilet paper. Downtown looked empty, but sometimes old cars came out of alleys so fast that you almost got hit. Sometimes hobos yelled unseen from the pitch black doorways where they made their homes. None of that stuff happened, though, so to make it more exciting I played a game in my head where the cops were chasing me and I had to pedal as fast as I could and be ready to execute escape maneuvers such as hopping the curb or doing a flying wheelie through a plateglass storefront.

Chapter 3

BY THE TIME high-school started I had $726, mostly in singles, which fit in a shoebox after I flattened the crinkled bills inside my copy of *The Highest Mountain*. It was more than enough to buy the Red Dragon 400,000 BTU Backpack Torch Kit with Squeeze Valve, but for some reason I still hadn't bought it. I guess I had lost some of my terroristic spark, I'm ashamed to admit. I blamed the working life.

I was still working the blacktop at the grocery store most days after school, and on Saturdays I worked as a gofer for a lawyer. Her name was Ms. Mikiska and she wore slacks and a vest like an old-time banker. She had short, black hair parted and oiled in a way that made you wish she had a waxed mustache to finish the look. Ms. Mikiska would stand outside her storefront office all day saying hello to the old ladies who still shopped downtown, where the only other businesses were a florist that specialized in funeral arrangements and a couple junk shops that called themselves antique stores. The junk shops picked over the estates of dead people who didn't have family or who didn't pay their rent and got their stuff put outside when they died, but Ms. Mikiska would tell the old ladies that this or that cherry wood breakfront or Queen Anne dining room set out there on the sidewalk had belonged to a sweet old lady who "hadn't managed her estate, bless her heart, so her family will never inherit those lovely heirlooms." My job was to fetch Ms. Mikiska's lunch and to stand outside when she took calls or went to the bathroom. She told me to say stuff to the old ladies, but I never did.

It was boring as hell and paid real bad, but I was glad for the work. I wanted to be home as little as possible. That's because home wasn't our house anymore; it was an apartment. Dad had moved to the city full-time, so when the county offered to buy our house, Mom sold it. Dad didn't want us to move, but Mom said he didn't have a say anymore. Mom said the house was too close to the dump so we were better off. We might feel healthier, she said, but Ruthanne said that was bullshit. Ruthanne said we could still smell the dump so whatever was in the air was still going in our noses. Mom said it was only a matter of time before the county claimed the property anyway. She said it was called imminent domain because it was gonna happen sooner or later. Sooner, probably.

The new apartment was in a complex on the highway that looked like a motel. The doors were on the outside, so when you came out of the apartment everybody else could see you, and people in cars on the highway could see you too, and people inside the Burger Brothers across the way, and some seedy characters slouched on the hoods of cars and drinking from paper bags in the parking lot of the grocery store that closed. One time a guy shouted something at Ruthanne that made her cry, but she was too embarrassed to tell me what it was.

The apartment was nice on the inside, though. The living room and kitchen were like one big room so you could be sitting on the couch and talking to somebody while they washed dishes or microwaved pizza pockets. There were only two bedrooms, but Mom gave Ruthanne and me the big one so we had plenty of room, in my estimation, and a big closet that was bigger than the two closets we used to have combined. But Ruthanne didn't like it. She said there wasn't any privacy and I took up all the space with my junk and gross body. I told her I would shower more if she and Mom didn't hog the bathroom so much.

Grandpa would show up from time to time with a load of food, mostly canned, but also boxes of cereal and dehydrated milk. He told Mom to put the food in the storm shelter, but we didn't have one anymore. He told us the food was for an emergency. What kind of emergency, he never said, and maybe it was the lack of specifics that caused us to eat the food right away, against his instructions. Sometimes the food had labels like MEAT and CHEESE, and that was the best food, believe it or not. The best food at home, I mean. The best food overall was the food at Pansy Gilchrist High School, hands down. At Pansy Gilchrist there were mini pizzas once a week and a hot dog station so you could eat hot dogs every day.

Though the food was tremendous, the ambience at Pansy Gilchrist was lackluster. The cafeteria was noisy and crowded, and I didn't know anybody in my lunch period except Demarcus, who had given up on lunch to study in the library. In the cafeteria, the black kids and the white kids sat at different tables, except for the football players, and the football players only sat together on Fridays when they wore their jerseys. The Komer blacks sat apart from the Haislip blacks, and the Haislip whites sat apart from everybody. Sometimes they didn't sit at all; they just stood around a table with one leg up on chairs so they could lean in and talk in husky voices like they were hashing a conspiracy. They seemed to take pride in being the poorest guys around and living in the shittiest trailers and having the worst looking cars but with the most powerful engines, with trunks full of guns and warm cases of the worst canned beer imaginable. Naturally I was curious about them.

Ruthanne told me they were secret Nazis who wrote a book about killing women and blacks and Mexicans, but I didn't believe her. First off, they didn't seem like literary types. I knew from Bob Bilger's introduction to *The Highest Mountain* that writing a book was a serious endeavor, a mental exercise akin to the physical exercise required to be in tiptop shape for mountaineering. Second, those boys were too poor to have computers at home. Trailers don't have computers, as a rule, or flat-screen TVs or fancy stereos, which is why nobody breaks into them like they do houses. Our old house got broken into five times before we moved. It got to where Mom said we should move into a trailer just for security.

Besides, what did Ruthanne know? She was a senior and spent so little time at school that she didn't even visit her locker. She had to use a rolling suitcase for her bags, because of her spine, so she figured she'd just leave the books in there and save herself the ridicule of standing around the hallways. I kind of envied her.

Classes were by grade but between classes, walking through the hallways, everybody was mixed. I was short and skinny so sometimes I wore two t-shirts to look thicker. It made me hot but gave me confidence. One time I was crouched in front of my locker, which was on the bottom row, and a guy pushed me into it with his foot. He didn't try to shut me inside or anything, but still it was pretty shitty.

I tried to keep a low profile, especially in class. The trick to not getting called on was to sit up real straight, like I was paying attention, but to stare at the chalkboard instead of the teacher, which is counterintuitive, I know, but if you look into a person's eyes then the person feels like they know you, so it's easy to talk to you. I didn't want to be easy to talk to. I wanted to be hard but polite, sort of like the actor Rick Zorn. In *Sudden Kill* (or maybe it's *Out for a Murder?*) these guys come up to Zorn in an alley and he's like, "May I help you?" and they're like, "Yeah, old man, you can help us to your motherfucking wallet." Zorn raises his hands real cool, but you can tell he thinks these guys are jokers. He reaches for his wallet and you think he's gonna pull out a gun or something but he *does* pull out his wallet. Then, just as he's handing it to a guy, he flicks his wrist and a Chinese star comes out and goes right into the guy's crotch area. The other guys start running, but Zorn gets one of them in the butt with another Chinese star.

When I got bored staring straight at the chalkboard, I did drawings: a man using another for a puppet by reaching through his butt, a cowboy with his penis on a conveyor belt being cut into coins like a sausage, etc. I sat in back so nobody saw the drawings except me, but one day Mrs. Bianculli came up behind me without me knowing and shrieked. I was drawing a fat man being quartered by four cholos on dirt bikes. His guts were stretched out like a cat's cradle. It was a pretty good drawing, but Mrs. Bianculli sent me to the principal's office. The moment of exit was awful. Everybody was staring at me. If my goal was to keep a low profile, this was the opposite.

I hadn't ever been sent to the principal's office at Pansy Gilchrist, but I was familiar with the routine from my many visits to Principal Chalmers's office back at Milford Perkins.

I sat in the waiting room between two older boys and kept my mouth shut. There was a sort of secretary across from us who would peek at us from over a counter, like she was making sure none of us made a break for it. There was a window we could have leapt through in a pinch. There was a framed poster behind her of a big black gorilla face and the word EXCELLENCE. At the bottom it said, "Excellence is not an achievement but a never-ending spirit."

Eventually a girl came out of the Principal's office with her head hanging, and the boy next to me went in grumbling. He wore big droopy jeans and had tattoos on his arms. He was a grown man, pretty much. So when he came out minutes later looking like he was coming out of church, I got nervous. It was my turn.

The principal, Principal Winthrope, wasn't anything like Principal Chalmers. First off, she was a black lady. Second, she was young. Her hair was real shiny and draped on her shoulders in stiff-looking curls, sort of like a sculpture of hair. She was wearing a gray suit that had a skirt instead of pants. She said, "Benjamin Shippers. To what do I owe the pleasure?"

"I did a bad drawing," I said. "I'm very sorry for it."

"I believe I know your sister," Principal Winthrope said. She didn't seem to care about the drawing. She said, "Ruthanne Shippers is one of our finest students."

"Really?"

She laughed. "Don't act so surprised. I'm helping Ruthanne apply to college."

It was the first I ever heard about college. I said, "Thank you. That's very nice of you. Which college is she gonna go to?"

Principal Winthrope laughed again. I guess I was a comedian to her. She said, "Ruthanne hasn't applied yet, Ben. Do you mind if I call you Ben?"

"No."

"Tell me, Ben, do you care about your sister?"

"Yes."

"Will you help me?"

"I guess."

"Your sister has a bright future. I want you to encourage her."

"To go to college?"

"That's up to her. But I want you to let her know she can do anything she wants to do, and that goes for you too." The last part sounded like an afterthought.

"Okay," I said. "Should I go back to class now?"

"That would be fine," she said. "It was a pleasure to meet you."

I left with mixed feelings. On one hand, I was glad to get off easy without a big lecture, but on the other I was confused about Ruthanne. I had only a vague understanding of college but knew it involved leaving home most times. I had a notion that most college graduates were bankers, because that's what Grandpa called everybody who wore a suit to work, and the ones who weren't bankers were teachers. Even gym teachers had to go to college. But Ruthanne was too shy to be a teacher.

It wasn't long before kids asked to see the drawing that earned a shriek from Mrs. Bianculli, plus got me sent to the principal's office, and I showed it to them gladly. Mostly kids said "gross!" or "you're sick!" but sometimes they liked it. One time this guy Pete Gomez said, "Dang, you're a good drawer," which wasn't something I had thought about myself. I just drew because I was bored.

Pete Gomez seemed like a pretty nice guy, so when he waved to me in the parking lot a few days later, I waved back. Then I noticed who he was standing with: the Haislip white boys. I was curious about those boys, but also wary. In addition to what Ruthanne said about them being secret Nazis, there was the fact that girls avoided them, which was a bad sign in my experience, not because I was interested in girls but because girls had more sense about danger. But now that the boys were looking at me, I didn't have a choice but to head towards them. I was nervous. I hooked my thumbs through the shoulder-straps of my backpack so I wouldn't fidget my hands.

The boys were gathered around an open trunk. They showed me what was inside it: a little rifle and a warm twelve-pack of beer. They asked me, what did I think about that? I said it looked good to me, and they laughed like hell.

"Listen to this white trash motherfucker," Pete said, and the others laughed some more. The only one who didn't laugh was a boy named Ronnie Mlezcko, who I knew by reputation. Ronnie Mlezcko had looked real big and old in middle school, but now he was kind of small, like me, and just plain old. His hair was black and greasy, and he didn't wear any of the cowboy stuff his friends wore. He wore dirty black jeans and boxy button-down shirts with pit-stains, like something a jailbird would wear.

Pete asked if I knew how to shoot but before I could answer, Ronnie said, "Of course he doesn't. He's just a kid. A pussy, too, by the smell of him."

"You're right," I said cautiously, "I don't know how to shoot."

Ronnie seemed confused by my approach. He said, "Damn right you don't."

"Yep," I said.

A handsome boy in a cammo cap said, "Don't be a dick, Ronnie. Let's go," and they all piled into the car. I didn't know if I was supposed to go with them. I didn't want to, frankly, so I was thankful when Pete gave me a low five and said, "See ya, dog."

That night I couldn't sleep, thinking about those boys. I wondered what it would be like to be part of a group like that. I wondered what they saw in me. I expected they knew I was trouble, like them.

Pete Gomez kept waving me over to the parking lot during lunch and after school, where they'd be standing around the same car, which turned out to belong to a silent boy called Red Dog who had big sideburns and reddish stubble. Sometimes they'd show me a gun they had, or some more beer, or a bottle of whiskey, or some porno magazines, which I didn't understand the use of until I remembered they didn't have internet at home in their trailers, and probably not much privacy either.

By the end of the week I was just standing there nodding while they talked about stuff, wondering what exactly my purpose was but not daring to speak unless spoken to. Their conversations were mostly about shooting and drinking and this or that girl who had "big old titties" or "juicy black thighs," or this or that guy who gave one of them a dirty look and was "gonna get his soon enough." Their speech was peppered with old-timey words and phrases like "reckon" and "hell-bent for leather," whatever that meant. One time Ronnie said as soon as he turned eighteen he was gonna "light out for the territories," which I took to mean someplace like Utah with lots of canyons and whatnot for hiding out.

The group dynamics were odd. Pete Gomez remained the friendliest of them, and he had to be since they razzed him so hard for being Mexican. Pete had a wispy mustache and wore his black hair in a ragged fade he did himself, using dog clippers. "I ain't nothing but a dog," he said with pride. The handsome boy in the cammo cap was named Kyle James, and he seemed to fancy himself a romantic figure. He said that with a name like Kyle James how could he avoid a life of crime? I guess he meant like Jesse James, but really he was the prudest of the bunch. He went to church with his parents, Pete said, and he didn't actually live in a trailer, just a regular house. Kyle James even had a girlfriend, off and on, and when it was off he would act real surly and complain about her, then the other guys would ask him what it was like to "bang" her and he would tell them she was "the worst piece of pussy" he ever had. I was surprised they said all that stuff in front of me. It made me uncomfortable, frankly, but the moment it got too serious Pete would pop the trunk and show me, say, an unmarked bottle of clear whiskey made by Red Dog's people and ask me what did I think about that? Like always, I told him it looked alright to me, and they laughed like hell. The only one who didn't laugh was Ronnie. He seemed suspicious, like he didn't want to say too much in front of me for fear of having his darkest true thoughts used against him, later. I respected him for that. He seemed like a person with a secret inner life, whatever it was.

One day Pete waved me over and things seemed a bit different. Nobody was laughing and everybody was looking at me instead of ignoring me. There was a sort of solemnity over the group. Pete said, "We got something important to show you."

I thought it was some kind of prank until Ronnie said, "Don't show this kid shit, you Mexican idiot."

"Be cool," Pete said, but Ronnie stormed off to the other side of the car, where he sat on the hood with his back to us.

"You don't have to tell me about it," I said, and not just to placate Ronnie; I had a sense that something bad was about to happen, like they were gonna open the trunk and show me a dead body.

"You're goddamn right we don't have to," Kyle James said, "but we're going to." He looked at Red Dog, who popped the trunk.

Inside the trunk was a greasy looking towel wrapped around something about the size and shape of a phone book. Pete reached in and peeled back the towel to reveal a tan metal box with a combination lock on it, like a briefcase. Kyle put his hand on my shoulder, maybe to keep me from grabbing the box and making a break for it, and Pete spun the box so I couldn't see the lock while he fooled with the combination, hunched over and squinting, his tongue sticking out from concentration. The box popped open. There were papers inside it, and notebooks. The top paper said SATANS MANIFESTO in big block letters.

I was intrigued, remembering what Ruthanne told me about their secret Nazi book. I was flattered, too, that they trusted me enough to show me their work. They were the first people besides Bob Bilger I ever met who did a book. Anyway, Kyle gingerly raised the top corner of the title page between his thumb and pointer finger and turned it over to reveal a page of type-written text, like a paper for school.

"The notebooks are first drafts," Kyle said, "and we've got lots of them, enough for ten books probably. Now we go through them and pick the best stuff and sort of fix it up, then Red Dog types it."

Red Dog nodded.

"What we need," Kyle said, "is illustrations."

I was stunned. I was happy too, because this gave my presence some meaning. They had seen my dirty drawings and wanted my help. They respected my abilities.

Pete raised the lockbox towards me and I was about to read the first typewritten page when Ronnie came quickly around the car hollering about how they couldn't trust me yet. He snatched the box out of Pete's hands and slammed it closed.

"This is important work," Ronnie said.

"We know that," Kyle said. "That's why we want illustrations, to make it better."

"More engaging," Pete said. "We *talked* about this, dog."

Ronnie said, "Yeah, well, that was before I found out this kid's such a pussy."

I didn't take the comment personally. To Ronnie, everybody was a pussy, or had a pussy, or didn't care about anything except pussy. He said to Pete, "We can't trust him yet, you pussy."

"Yet?" Pete asked.

"He has to prove himself. The stakes are high. We could go to jail for this shit."

I expected the others to tell Ronnie he was being ridiculous, but they seemed to agree with him. I wondered what kind of book could get a person put in jail. At Milford Perkins, there'd been a story about a kid who sold drugs and got put in jail for life when they found a bloody gun in his locker. The judge wanted to hang him, but the governor said no, he was just a kid. As a compromise they put him in a man's jail with grown men, and people said you could see him at his window at night with his hands together praying for a quick and painless death.

"You have to earn our trust," Ronnie told me. It might have been the first time he spoke to me directly without looking at somebody else. His eyes were bright and fierce, but the skin around them was purplish, like he was tired. His face made me think of the prickly, sore-eyed feeling I got when I woke up too early, and I imagined that was how Ronnie felt every second of every day.

"How can I earn it?" I asked.

"Go to the dump," he said.

I nodded, thinking I had this in the bag. I knew all about the dump. But I had to play dumb. I said, "But it's got a big fence around it."

"Break in," Ronnie said. "There's things there I want you to find for me."

"I'll try," I said.

"You'll *do*," he said, "if you want us to trust you. Find me a used crack-pipe."

Kyle shook his head. "Come on, Ronnie—"

Ronnie spun on Kyle. "Don't you get it? It has to be incriminating. It's this or we make him commit an honest-to-God crime like stealing liquor, but he's too much of a pussy for that. Now shut up until I'm finished. A used crack pipe," he continued, "and a dirty needle. And a used condom!"

"What's incriminating about a used condom?" Kyle asked.

"Nothing, but it's risky. He might get AIDS. That'll show his commitment."

"I don't know—"

"Make that *five* used condoms."

I looked at Pete, who shrugged, and that was that. I had no choice. These boys were better than nothing, friend-wise, and I really was curious about that book. So I headed to the dump in search of a crack pipe, a dirty needle, and five used condoms. I didn't even know what a crack pipe looked like.

I rode to the dump on Ruthanne's bike, which I owned outright by then. The first thing I did after I finished the six-month installment plan was paint it black, but I accidentally bought paint with matte finish so it looked weird. I used a paintbrush to add badass flames but the enamel paint was expensive so I only had one color, and the color turned out to look more red than orange so the flames looked like I was bleeding all over my bike or had rode through a slaughterhouse, which was pretty badass too, I guess.

The closest part of the dump was where our house used to be, but I didn't want to go there. I wasn't as upset about moving as Ruthanne was, but I didn't want to see another kid staring out my window at Trash Mountain. I might feel like I was missing out. So I rode to the Haislip side.

Trash Mountain still loomed, taller than ever, but the perimeter of the dump was changing. In some spots the fence was reinforced by plywood, and holes like the one I climbed through with Demarcus were plugged up with blobs of tangled barbed wire, half buried so there was no way to push them aside. I figured it was the dump workers, cracking down, but there were rumors of hobos who tried to seal up the dump for a lair. There were rumors too of a coven of witches and wizards who conjured spells using cat's blood and precious ingredients they gathered from Trash Mountain. One time a gray-haired coot who caught me snooping behind my old house told me space aliens crash landed there, years before, and the trash was to hide them, but now the government wanted to study them and had to make the site impregnable. Who knows. All I knew was I had to get in there.

Since the fence was stronger than ever, and topped by gleaming coils of brand-new razor wire, I started inspecting the junctures between the fence and various outbuildings. Nearby was a giant tin structure like an airplane hangar, for the trucks and loaders, and sure enough the fence post was fastened to the side of the building with nothing but plastic zip ties. I tried tugging one of the ties apart, then biting it, but it was tougher than it looked, like the handcuffs plainclothes cops use in movies.

There was a dumpster behind the tin hangar, and I thought that from the lip of the dumpster I might be able to jump up and grab the edge of the hangar, climb onto the hangar roof, then scramble overtop of it and lower myself into the dump. But the lip of the dumpster was slippery with trash juice so it was hard to get a good jump, and when I did, I couldn't get a good grip on the hangar roof. I scraped my hands on the edge of the roof and fell to the ground. It didn't hurt too bad, but the whole thing was embarrassing and made an awful clamor, so I crouched down behind the dumpster to hide for a while.

I was hiding there, plotting my next move, when somebody said, "Hey, little buddy."

I looked around, startled, but I didn't see anybody.

"Over here, buddy." It was a man's voice, sort of nasal and wet sounding.

I thought about running but decided a grown man could probably outrun me, and if I took the time to mount my bike he'd have me for sure. So I mustered a tough, deep voice and said, "Who is it?"

"Boss," he said.

"The boss of what?" I asked.

"Boss of nothing," he said. "They call me Boss is all."

I wondered if the man was a hobo. Hobos had nicknames, I knew. Grandpa told stories about a childhood hobo named Charlie Nickels who trained a pigeon to filch cigarettes. I prepared in my mind for a vicious thieving hobo to slit my throat from ear to ear.

"You looking for somebody?" he asked.

"No," I said. "I'm sorry. I'll leave right now."

"Easy, buddy. Come around here so we can talk."

The man didn't sound like a murderer, I had to admit, so I opened my eyes, which had been closed from fear, and looked around. Nobody was there. I looked up at the edge of the hangar roof, but nobody was there either. I peeked inside the dumpster. Nobody.

"Where are you?" I asked, preparing in my mind to mount my bike and escape.

"On the other side of the fence. I saw you jumping and came to tell you to be careful. If they catch you they'll send you away."

"Send me away where?"

"They'll load you into a van and take you to a place outside of town and leave you there in the middle of the night with nothing but the shirt on your back, like a goddamned raccoon."

That didn't sound like a logical punishment to me, but the man, Boss, seemed pretty worked up so I didn't comment.

"Like a grown man can't find his way back to a place he been before," he was muttering. "What're you doing here anyway?"

"I'm supposed to get some stuff for some guys."

"Sounds secret."

"Pretty much."

"Tell me what you need and I can help, maybe."

I didn't want to tell him, from embarrassment, so I asked if there was a secret way to get inside. "Not that I don't appreciate your offer," I said. "It's just, you know—"

"It's secret, I hear you. Unfortunately there ain't no way to sneak in here like there used to be."

"Then how'd *you* get in?"

He paused. "I work here."

I was relieved. If he worked there as a garbage man or whatever, then he wasn't a hobo; I could trust him. I said, "Okay, here it goes: I need a crack pipe, a dirty needle, and five used condoms."

"That's disgusting."

"I know. I'm real sorry. You don't have to get it."

"No, no, I can get it."

"For real? You got that stuff?"

"Oh yeah, we got it. If you can name it, it's in here. This place, it's like a second world where everything's mushed together within easy reach."

The term *second world* intrigued me. I thought about the netherworld occupied by ghosts and wizards, and possibly Jesus and God.

The man told me about some bio-waste bags from the hospital that were supposed to go to a special bio-waste site, but the hospital cheaped out and put them in the dump, which meant plenty of dirty needles. And condoms were pretty much everywhere, the man said, but highly concentrated in a spot where they put what got filtered out of the sewer water, since people were always flushing condoms down the toilets. "As for the crack pipe," he said, "I'm not too sure. Most of that stuff gets tossed on the floor and crunched up underfoot. The one-hitters, I mean. People don't just throw away nicer pipes. But I'll see what I can do." He asked if I could meet him there the next day, and I said I would.

I wasn't sure what to make of the man's kindness. I wondered if he worked for the dump and didn't have enough to do, or if he liked little boys. I had never met a sex offender but knew they existed. I also knew that sometimes adults without kids, like Ms. Mikiska, took a special interest in kids and liked to do nice things for them then give long-winded advice afterward.

The next day at school I avoided Ronnie and them because I didn't have the stuff yet, and I didn't want to seem like a failure in case they expected me to procure it within twenty-four hours. That meant I had to sneak out before last period, which I didn't mind. That, in turn, meant I showed up at the hangar building an hour early. There was water dribbling through the fence, and when I got close I could hear men talking. I thought my contact might be among them, but I didn't hear his weird nasal voice.

The men were hosing something off, and I pressed my eye to the gap between the fence and the hangar and saw a brand new frontloader, red and shining. One man was blasting it with a hose while another gesticulated beside him. Both wore gray coveralls like garbage men. The old yellow frontloader I used to watch from Ruthanne's window was idling in the distance, waiting its turn. Beyond the frontloaders was an honest-to-God excavator. It was like a construction site in there, like they were building Trash Mountain on purpose. The idea bothered me, but I had to admit it would be pretty cool to ride those machines when nobody was around, even just to sit in the driver's seat and pretend.

I hid behind the dumpster like before and kept quiet until the voices stopped. I waited until I smelled cigarette smoke, at which point I poked my head out and saw the back of a tall man leaning into the narrow gap between the fence pole and the side of the hangar. He wore black rubber waders caked in mud. Above the collar of his dirty flannel shirt was a sunburned neck and some greasy tentacular hair.

I didn't know what to say in case the man *wasn't* my contact so I mounted my bike preemptively, to be ready for a getaway. "Boss," I whispered.

The man turned his head to look over his shoulder. His big white face was like a cinderblock, with blonde stubble and a sort of gash going up from the top lip to a thick crooked nose. Maybe whatever broke his nose had broken the lip part too.

He held up a brown plastic grocery bag. "I got good news and bad news," he said. "Good news is the needles and prophylactics was easy. Bad news is the crack pipe, but check it out." He lowered the grocery bag and opened it so I could see. There was a thick syringe with red-dish liquid crystallized inside, and some condoms that were caked in mud but obviously hard used. There was also a glass tube of some sort. The man picked up the tube between his thumb and forefinger and held it close to the gap for me to see. There was some dark stuff inside one half of the tube, and the glass looked smoky.

"Is that a real crack pipe?" I asked, kind of bewildered. The idea of crack was mysterious and frightening to me.

"Nope," he said. "It's just a glass thing I got from the bio-waste pile. What I did was stick some mud in it then light it on fire. Looks pretty convincing, huh?"

"Definitely," I said, though I wouldn't have known a crack pipe from a corncob.

He tried to push the bag through the gap but couldn't get his big hand through. "Reach in here and grab it," he said.

In a flash I pictured him grabbing my wrist and holding me until some other men captured me from behind. I had to remind myself he wasn't a sex-offending hobo. This man had done right by me, and I owed it to him to show my trust. Plus I wanted the stuff he got me. So I reached through the gap and grabbed the bag, and when he let go I pulled it through.

"Thank you," I said. "Can I pay you or something? I have some money at home."

"On the house," he said. "Favors always come back around."

I thanked him again, caught off guard by his friendliness. I wasn't used to people doing nice things for me, let alone garbage men, who tended to be stoic or surly, maybe on account of having to wake up so early. Or maybe this man *wasn't* a garbage man, it occurred to me. He wasn't wearing coveralls, and he kept glancing over his shoulder. Come to think of it, he had been speaking in a loud whisper ever since we started talking. But if he wasn't a garbage man, what was he? And what was he doing in the dump?

Asking those questions might scare the man off, I decided, so I waved in the direction of the new frontloader and said real casual, "You ever get to ride that rig?"

The man laughed. "I wish," he said. "It would make my life easier, let me tell you. Better picking than ever in here."

"I bet," I said, though I had no idea what he was talking about. "What kind of picking they got, nowadays?"

"Oh, all sorts of stuff. You could live five lifetimes on the stuff they skip over."

"Valuable stuff?"

"Hell yes. That's why they did up the fence like they did."

"Who's they?"

"Bi-Cities."

"But don't *you* work for Bi-Cities?"

The man eyed me suspiciously. He was onto me, I could tell, but I couldn't stop talking. I said, "You don't work here, do you?"

"Not in an official capacity."

"So you work here off the books?"

The man said nothing.

"In secret?"

The man glanced over his shoulder.

"You're there in *secret*?" I repeated, unable to contain my excitement. "Shit, man, you gotta tell me how you get in there."

"I gotta go," the man said, and before I could ask another question he was striding away from me across the landscape of trash. He moved quick for such a big fellow. I watched him disappear over a distant ragged hill, and I cursed myself for scaring him off like that, for blowing the opportunity to learn more about the inner workings of the dump. I had to get in there to sabotage it, and a contact on the inside could have helped, but would I ever see the man again? Grandpa once said if you shot at a puma and missed, you wouldn't see the puma again until the night it crept up and killed you.

Chapter 4

THE NEXT DAY after school I went out to the parking lot where the boys were gathered and handed the grocery bag to Pete. He looked inside and pretended to gag. The other boys looked with disgust at the contents and said they couldn't believe it. Only Ronnie seemed unimpressed. He asked me how I got into the dump, and I told him about the gap between the fence and the outbuilding. He nodded, but he seemed suspicious.

Red Dog had the syringe and was pretending to inject Kyle James. Ronnie told them to quit horsing around. He said, "Bring out the Manifesto," and they went through the same ceremony of opening the trunk, taking out the lockbox, unlocking it, and lifting the cluttered manuscript towards me.

I reached for the manuscript, but Ronnie swatted my hand. "We'll turn the pages," he said. Somebody groaned, but Ronnie ignored it.

The contents of Satans Manifesto are hard to describe. The part I started reading had been "done up," as Ronnie said, but it was still pretty jumbled. There were rants about girls and blacks and Mexicans, some discussion of a possible race war, and an extended sex scene between Principal Winthrope and a zombie-type creature of unknown origin. The scene was written in bedroom language ("the creature tongued the dark circles of her pert nipples," etc.) straight out of Ruthanne's sleazy novels. The zombie-type creature was called a Sleeper. Satans Manifesto was full of Sleepers. They lurked in abandoned buildings. They hid behind the seats of cars and bit off the backs of people's heads while they drove. They stole babies and melted them to fuel a laser cannon to incinerate the White House, and while everybody ran screaming from the Oval Office and secret champagne rooms, this one Sleeper jammed his penis in the President's ear until the President "talked like a penis." The Sleepers were a strange crew, for sure. Original too, which was why it bothered me I couldn't picture them.

"These Sleepers," I said, "what do they look like?"

"Like humans," Pete said, "but with melted faces and shit, and their guts hanging out."

"So they're zombies?"

"Yeah," Pete said.

"A sleeper is *nothing* like a zombie," Ronnie said. "A zombie just goes around eating up everything, but a Sleeper is discerning. He doesn't just eat the flesh of a man; he eats his knowledge, his memories, all the stuff that's in the grayish slime of his brain. It's symbolic."

The others nodded.

I kept reading. It turned out Sleepers were unlike zombies in another important respect: they came from outer space. "Millennia ago," according to the document, and they'd been laying underground since then, biding their time; hence the name Sleepers. They had skeletons on the outside of their guts, just under their skin, which made them impervious to bullets. The skin itself was moist and flaky, absorbing water from the damp ground. Now the Sleepers were waking up "to set things right."

Over the next few days I read Satans Manifesto while the boys joked and bullshitted, and Ronnie kept one eye on me in case I ran off with it, or maybe to gauge my reaction. I have to admit I got to enjoying it. Care had been taken with it (by Ronnie, most likely), especially on the Sleeper parts. Some of the sex and murder parts were okay too. They were kind of funny, the way shitty horror movies are funny. But as I got deeper into the Manifesto, I started seeing the names of popular girls in school, popular black kids too, and this Mexican kid named Rudy Tovar. Rudy seemed kind of gay, I guess, but he was Vice President of the student council and everybody liked him. In the Manifesto, he got his head bit off and his brains sucked out while a Sleeper "with a spiny penis like a fish penis" sodomized him until he "wore out dead."

The Rudy part made me want to stop reading, so I skimmed the next couple pages until I got to the end of the section and had an excuse to stop. "Pretty crazy, y'all," I said, trying to smile.

"Pretty crazy?" Ronnie said. "That's all you got?"

"There's some interesting ideas in it."

"That's nothing. Wait 'til you start the next section."

"My eyes are kind of tired."

"You mean your pussy is tired."

"What?"

Kyle said, "Come on, Ronnie, we been standing here an hour. It's almost dark. I told Jen I would meet her at—"

"Jen can eat my pussy. We gotta get this kid straight about the facts."

Jen was Kyle's off-and-on girlfriend, so I wasn't sure how he would take this comment from Ronnie, but he ignored it. He seemed tired. He said, "Kid, Ben, whatever your name is, we want you to do drawings for the Manifesto."

Having read Satans Manifesto, I no longer relished the idea of doing drawings for it, but I did like the attention. And I liked the way it felt to have some people to meet in the parking lot after school instead of wandering off by myself. So I told them I would do it.

"Hell yeah, homes," Pete said and bumped my fist.

That night I tried to draw a Sleeper, but I couldn't do it right. Everything I drew was just a dumb zombie, with none of the menace contained by Ronnie's Sleeper concept. So the next day, when they asked for a drawing, I told them I was waiting for inspiration. "And after it strikes," I said, "it'll take me a while to get the drawing just right. I'm a perfectionist, is what I'm saying." It was the most words I had ever strung together in front of those boys, and they seemed kind of surprised by it, or put off. I added the excuse of the Sleeper concept being complicated, hoping it would flatter Ronnie and keep him off my back.

"Then don't start with Sleepers," Ronnie said. "Start with a murder or something. How about the spree killing at the Drug Time, in the third part?"

"I haven't read that part yet."

"Read it. Red Dog, get the Manifesto."

"Um," Red Dog said.

"What is it?" Ronnie demanded.

"I guess I left it at home."

Ronnie shook his head like Red Dog, and all the rest of us, were bad hired help.

I dodged a bullet that afternoon, but they kept pestering me, so to satisfy them I tore old drawings out of my notebook and pretended they were new. Some of them fit the Manifesto pretty well, since it contained just about every atrocity imaginable, and if it didn't I would say maybe they should add something like that. Even Ronnie had to admit when he had overlooked something choice, like a motorcycle with razor wheels that cut people in half.

Sometimes I came out to the parking lot and it was just Ronnie and Red Dog, and sometimes it was just Ronnie. When it was just Ronnie he didn't act as mean. The other guys seemed to annoy him just as much as I did.

One time I gave Ronnie a drawing of Hitler giving a donkey a blowjob and Ronnie made a sort of grunting noise that for him was laughing. I asked him where were the other guys, and he said they were busy eating Kyle's pussy. He went on a long rant about Kyle. It turned out Ronnie thought Kyle was "chickenhearted" and that the other guys only liked him out of weakness, because it flattered their egos to hang out with a good-looking guy who, in a different life, could have been popular. Ronnie said guys like Pete secretly just wanted to be popular. "Not like you and me," he said.

I didn't quite know what to make of that, but I nodded.

"I knew it wasn't a crack-pipe," Ronnie said.

"Pardon?"

"That thing you brought us, from the dump—I knew it wasn't real, but I didn't say nothing."

"Thanks," I said, but I was kind of annoyed. Ronnie was talking like he had done me some big favor by not mentioning it to the others, but the others wouldn't have cared, and I suspected he knew that.

"I was impressed regardless," Ronnie said. "Doing it up like that took creativity."

"Thanks," I said, feeling guilty. I didn't tell him it was Boss who did it, not me.

"Breaking in, too," Ronnie said, "that took balls. I can tell you got big fat balls. It's cuz you got nothing to lose, am I right?"

"I guess not."

"It's because you don't fear death."

"Sure," I said, though I certainly did fear death. I didn't want to give Ronnie any ideas about using me as a suicide bomber, if that was his line.

Ronnie sighed and pitched a rock as far as he could. It hit the hubcap on a shiny red pickup and he grunted, satisfied. He said, "Sometimes I think about that dump like a big old throbbing tumor in the middle of this place. Somebody oughta bust it up from the inside."

I almost told him how I tried to, but telling Ronnie would have cheapened the memory, I decided, coarsened it somehow, so I just stood there nodding while he talked about the dump and how shitty and stupid it was. In retrospect, I wish I had opened up to him. Ronnie and I might have had more in common than I thought.

Ronnie started talking about how I needed to draw more girls. He had noticed my drawings were always of guys. He said if it was a problem of anatomy he could get me a magazine. "Red Dog has a dozen in his trunk," Ronnie said, "and fifty more at home. You ain't afraid to draw girls or nothing, right?"

"No," I said.

"Would it bother you to draw them?"

"I don't know," I said, and I didn't. I hadn't ever tried drawing girls before. I guess it wasn't as funny to me seeing girls get dismembered and whatnot.

"Well it shouldn't bother you," Ronnie said. "Girls are just as shitty as guys. When the war comes they'll get theirs too."

I almost asked if he meant the race war or the war against rogue machines, but it was time for me to go to the grocery store, and both wars were subjects on which Ronnie had many lengthy rants. I told Ronnie I had to go, and he grunted without looking at me. I left him there alone.

When I got home that night I tried to draw some girls, out of curiosity more than anything, a sort of personal challenge, but I struggled. It wasn't the violence that made it hard; it was the embarrassment I felt when I started to draw boobs or even buttcheeks, and a pair of buttcheeks might just as easily have belonged to a man I was drawing getting disemboweled, not a woman. Honestly, though, the main reason I didn't want to draw girls was because of Ruthanne. It made me think of how the girls in Satans Manifesto could have been her.

Thinking about the girls in the Manifesto made me want to check on Ruthanne, to talk to her and know she was safe. It was like when I was a kid. Back then, whenever I had a bad dream and got afraid, I would sneak into Ruthanne's room and wake her up. Or if I was feeling more generous I might just creep into bed next to her and lay there quietly for a while. Later, I had to make it into a prank. I would poke my head into her room and say something to get a rise out of her, then she'd say "What is it, you dumbass?" and I'd say something stupid like "Just got a good fart out, is all" and she'd throw a book at my head, or the stapler, and that'd be the end of it. I'd be satisfied. This feeling was different, though. It wasn't enough just to see her. I had to hear her voice and know she was happy.

I didn't have to creep into her bedroom anymore since we shared the same room. I had been drawing in the bathroom, for privacy. When I went to the bedroom I knocked on the door, to be polite.

Ruthanne was reading a book in bed, as usual, and looked up at me surprised. "Yeah?" she said.

"Can I come in?" I asked.

"It's your own goddamned bedroom."

"I just want you to know you can have some privacy if you want."

"How thoughtful."

Instead of going to my own sloppy looking bed I went to hers and sat down on the foot of it, hunched and staring at the floor.

Ruthanne kept reading, ignoring me. She sighed a few times like it was real annoying for her to have me in her bed like that, like if it wasn't for me she would have done jumping jacks. I thought about how in her old bedroom I would have been able to see Trash Mountain from where I sat. I thought about the marks on the windowsill, to record its height. I wondered how high the marks would have been if we had kept marking them.

"Mind if we talk a bit?" I asked.

"In a minute," Ruthanne said. "I'm at a good part."

"You mean a sex part?"

She slapped the book down beside her and glared at me. "Feeling lonely, huh? Maybe you should call Ronnie Mlezcko."

"Shut up," I said.

"Don't tell me to shut up in my own bedroom."

"Then don't say stupid stuff."

"Stupid? I'll tell you what's stupid, Ben. Hanging out with a degenerate like Ronnie Mlezcko, that's stupid."

"It isn't your business who I hang out with."

"It is when it's a buncha future school shooters."

"They aren't like that."

"Oh, I'm sorry, I meant future meth-heads. Future sexual sadist serial murderers. Ronnie Melzcko is a twenty-five-year-old retard who can't get out of tenth grade."

"He isn't retarded." I had no idea why I was defending Ronnie Mlezcko, a boy who pretty much tormented me each afternoon. "Sorry everybody isn't as smart as you, Ruthanne. Sorry everybody can't go to college!"

She eyed me. "I ain't going to college. You think we have money for college?"

"College is free if you're smart enough."

"Who told you that?"

"Everybody knows that."

"Who told you?"

I told Ruthanne about what Principal Winthrope had said, how I got dragged in there for doing a bad drawing and all she wanted to talk about was my sister. "Ruthanne this, Ruthanne that," I said. "Tell your sister she can do anything she wants to do."

"Barf!"

"What's the matter?"

"I wish that bitch would get out of my face."

"She said she was helping you."

"Helping me? Don't I have enough to worry about without worrying about college?"

"I don't know. What do you worry about?"

"Don't be a smartass."

"I'm serious. It's just school, right? You like school. Maybe you can be a banker."

"I don't want to be a banker."

"What do you wanna be?"

"A pearl diver."

"What?"

"A cosmonaut. A wind-turbine repairman."

"Seriously?"

"You know the guy who wraps burned houses in blue tarps so the furniture doesn't get wet? That's what I wanna be."

I could tell she was shitting me so I got up and went to my own bed. I didn't know why she was being such a jerk about college. I would have been happy if Principal Winthrope took an interest in me. It was flattering. And plenty of people went to college. Bob Bilger went to college on the GI bill after Vietnam, and the actor Rick Zorn went someplace called Colby College, which must have been a pretty good college.

I couldn't sleep that night, I was so steamed at Ruthanne, and in my anger and exhaustion I got a vision in the dark. It was of a tall, hollow-eyed man with skin so pale it was almost green. The moldy looking skin came off in flakes whenever he touched anything with his bony white hand. His hair barely stuck to his head, the skin there was so soft, so he was bald except for a sickly thin frizz. His eyes alone had a sharpness the rest of him didn't. It was as though the eyes were artificial, or inorganic, like dark polished stones from the depths of the earth. His teeth, too, although yellow and rotten, were strong as elephant bones and sharp as little shovels.

Inspired, I pulled the bed sheet over my head and drew in a frenzy. Before I fell asleep I had drawn two guys getting their skulls cracked open by the lusty rotten teeth of this creature, the Sleeper, and another where a big strong Sleeper had ripped a man's arms off and the man was staggering around with blood shooting out of the sockets. Last I drew a drawing where a man got his brain sucked out by a long stiff Sleeper tongue like the nozzle of a gas pump. The tongue was my own addition—no mention of a nozzle tongue in the Manifesto.

The boys were impressed. After Ronnie studied all three drawings, he stroked his chin as though in deep consideration of the vision of the Sleepers that my drawings put forth. It was true to his own vision but also a slight departure, an elaboration. Finally he said, "These are good."

"Thank you," I said.

"They show vision."

"Thanks. That means a lot."

"That other stuff, it was more jokey, but this—these—we should think about what they show us. The Sleepers, when they come, they'll come fierce. I wonder if even guys like us will be able to fend 'em off. We know our way around guns, sure, but what does it matter? The best we can hope for is to scrounge out a living at the expense of lesser humans until the Sleepers take total control. By then we may have proved our worth to them."

"Hmm," I said. It hadn't occurred to me that Ronnie thought Sleepers were coming for real. I glanced quickly around the group, to gauge how seriously they took the Sleeper threat. Their expressions were cryptic. Red Dog spat on the ground.

"Maybe we should take this kid shooting," Pete said, "to practice."

Ronnie nodded.

We piled into Red Dog's car. I was in the middle of the backseat, feeling nervous. It was the first time I had driven anywhere with them. Actually, it was the first time I had driven anywhere with someone I would call a kid, except for Carl, the guy who used to drive Ruthanne and me to school. But back then Carl had seemed like an adult to me.

Kyle was in front fiddling with the radio while Red Dog drove. He found a station playing a goofy old country song and left it.

Beside me Pete said, "Turn off that cracker shit," so Kyle turned up the volume.

I was surprised Ronnie didn't say anything. He hated country music, preferring metal and horrorcore, but he seemed to have his mind on something else. He was staring out the window at the billboards and gas stations. We were going pretty far, it seemed to me, but if we were gonna shoot off guns I guess it was good to be far

away. I hadn't ever shot a gun before. Demarcus had shot a rifle at
a Christian camp and told me it was easy if you did it real fast and
didn't think too hard about it, but he'd kept closing his eyes when
he pulled the trigger, he said, which the counselor said was bad for
aiming. I made a note not to close my eyes. I knew these boys would
be watching me, so I had to seem like I shot guns all the time and
so practicing was a minor, though agreeable, imposition. I thought
about how Rick Zorn shot guns in movies, from the hip, sliding over
the hoods of cars.

We passed a big yellow billboard that said JESUS in block letters.
The back of the billboard said COMING SOON!

We turned off the highway onto a road I hadn't ever been on before. We passed a store called XXX Videos, then some trailers, but
mostly it was trees. The trees were unkempt and covered in vines.
Red Dog turned off the road onto a gravel path and we drove on that
until we came to a bright green clearing. The clearing was so nice that
it should have had straw-bales, but instead it had a row of rusty cars.
It was like the start of a new junkyard. Red Dog parked at the end of
the row of cars and we got out. Red Dog's car didn't look much different than the junk cars, honestly, and I got a weird flash in my mind
that the other cars had belonged to kids like us who accidentally shot
themselves then trudged off into the woods to die.

The boys began ceremoniously to open the trunk, inspect the
rifle, fill it with ammunition, and crack open beers. Pete, smiling,
handed me a sweaty golden can of Miller High Life. The can was
body temperature.

I never had a beer before so I sipped it carefully, expecting the
worst. It wasn't too bad, though. The warmth made it go down easy.

"What do you think about that?" Pete asked.

"Not bad," I said. "Kind of sweet, huh?"

"High Life has a sweet finish," Red Dog offered. He was cleaning
the barrel of the rifle with something that smelled like gasoline. Pete
and I watched him. I expected him to elaborate on the sweetness of

High Life, and whether or not this was a desirable quality, but he didn't.

"Fuck yeah," Pete said, which gave some closure to the subject.

I wondered what we were going to shoot at until I noticed the billboard. I guess we were closer to the highway than I thought. The billboard showed the face of a man and some stars and stripes and the words, WHITEY CONNORS FOR COMPTROLLER. The name sounded familiar. The man, Whitey Connors, had a big smile on his face and floppy dark blond hair that was sort of twisted across his forehead in a stylish way. Stylish for kids, I mean. The hair was unbecoming on a man, and his whole face had a sort of fake quality. The eyes were too bright.

While Red Dog took aim I asked Pete who Whitey Connors was. I wondered why the name sounded familiar to me.

Pete, who was sitting on the hood of Red Dog's car, twisted to holler, "Yo! Who's Whitey Connors?"

Pete had hollered in the direction of Kyle, but it was Ronnie who answered. "He owns Bi-Cities."

"What's Bi-Cities?" Pete asked.

"The dump, dumbass."

"I ain't no dumbass."

"He's in the Manifesto!"

"I thought the city owned Bi-Cities," I said, "or the county or something."

"They used to, but now it's private," Ronnie said.

That sounded weird to me, but I would look it up a few days later and learn it was true. Bi-Cities Sanitation & Recycling was privately owned. Whitey Connors was CEO and Chairman of the Board. I also learned that the "Bi-Cities" were Komer and Haislip, which hadn't occurred to me. Nobody called them that. Haislip wasn't even a city anymore, technically, since the population had dipped under ten thousand. I wondered if Whitey Connors had coined the name himself, to sound bigtime.

Red Dog shot Whitey Connors right in the earlobe and everybody congratulated him on piercing the man's ear. On his next shot he missed the face but hit the white part of the sign right next to it. The others razzed him, and he reluctantly handed the rifle to Pete, who made a show of taking aim real careful then missed entirely.

"Blam!" Pete said. "Got him good."

"Got nothin'," Red Dog said.

"I was aiming for his heart, homes, *below* that shit." He slid his finger across his own throat. "Kill shot."

Pete handed the rifle to me and stood next to me while I took aim. The rifle was heavier than I expected, and wobbled in my hands.

"Use the sight," Pete said. "I go for the forehead, but you can aim wherever. It's just for fun."

I got the sight to where the shiny pupil of Whitey Connors's left eye was looking back at me between the crosshairs. The eye was creepy. The sight magnified it so I could see that the white was too pure, without any of the veiny stuff real eyes have. It was like a cyborg's eye. The trigger on the rifle was harder to squeeze than I expected, and I could hear Red Dog sniggering, and Kyle saying "he ain't gonna shoot," but I did shoot. The rifle boomed and jerked so hard I closed my eyes. When I opened my eyes again, to look through the sight, I was staring at a telephone pole fifty yards from the billboard. Got knows what I hit—not any part of Whitey Connors or his billboard.

"Not bad," Pete said. He gave me a low five. "I think I saw it go in that tree next to his head. Closer than mine, anyway."

"That was horrible," Kyle said. He took the rifle from me. Kyle was the best shot, everybody agreed, and Pete and Red Dog cheered him on as he took aim. He shot Whitey Connors in the eyeball, quickly reloaded, then aimed at the dot over the *i* in "Whitey" and narrowly missed. He laughed, and everybody teased him. Everybody except Ronnie, that is. Ronnie hadn't even watched. He was sitting on the trunk of a rusty car, staring into the distance. The rest of us looked at him. It was his turn.

Ronnie rose from the trunk and came towards us. He gruffly took the rifle from Kyle, but instead of aiming it at the billboard, he aimed it right at Kyle's chest.

"Come on, Ronnie," Kyle said. "Quit kidding around."

"Who's kidding," Ronnie said. "If you're willing to kill and go to prison for it, it doesn't matter how good a shot you are, because you do it up close."

Ronnie didn't shoot, though. He lowered the rifle and handed it by the butt to Red Dog.

Chapter 5

BY THE TIME tenth grade came around, I didn't have much use for school anymore. I was sixteen and feeling pretty old. Me and those boys usually knocked off school at lunch to go shooting or hang around a big empty strip mall where the Randy's used to be. Randy's was a defunct sporting goods store where there were still big dusty boxes in the back full of flat tennis balls and camp-stove fuel and these plastic toy bow-and-arrows we used for a game called manhunter. Manhunter was like hide-and-seek except everybody was hiding and seeking at the same time, and everybody had a plastic bow-and-arrow to shoot everybody else. If you got shot, you were out. It was scary because the Randy's was dark and all the shelves were still there, like a maze, and also because the plastic bow-and-arrows hurt pretty bad even though they were toys. The boxes they came in said for ages twelve and up and never to shoot at other people with them. Ronnie made it even scarier by hiding in the shelves, curled into a ball, so when you passed by he could shoot you point-blank in the side of the head. One time he painted his face black to hide better, but the other guys made fun of him so he didn't do it again. Another time I won by fashioning a makeshift atlatl from a yardstick. An atlatl is what Indians used before the bow-and-arrow. It's like a stick that makes your arm longer so you can throw the arrow real far. An archeologist guy came to school and showed us how to do stuff the ancient Indian way, like grinding up little corncobs with a rock, which was pretty useless, but also the thing with the atlatl. I listened close and when it was my turn I threw the arrow a couple hundred yards at least. The archeologist guy said I was a natural, and did I have some Ocmoolga blood? I told him I did, but who knows. Maybe I could have been an Indian if it wasn't for Trash Mountain. Anyway, I stood on top of a shelf with my atlatl and picked off the other boys one by one before they knew what hit them. Afterward Red Dog said atlatls weren't legal, but Ronnie told him to stop being a pussy.

I loved playing manhunter, but the other guys mostly wanted to sit around drinking beer or Red Dog's clear whiskey. I'd nurse one beer the whole time, and if they razzed me it was Ronnie who defended me. He said I was smart not to get "all drunk and stupid" like them. "We gotta be ready," he said. He was always talking about being ready. The beer was okay, but I only pretended to sip the whiskey, and if they brought out a joint I didn't smoke it, which suited them fine because weed was precious. It was Pete who usually got it, from his sister's boyfriend, a guy called Milk Dog who sold it "Mexican style," Pete said, "like that cartel shit." Pete said Milk Dog once stabbed a guy who didn't pay him. We asked who was the guy he stabbed, since we probably knew him, or *of* him, but Pete said the guy fled the country. "Milk Dog comes hard," Pete said. "The guy probably be hiding out or some shit, like a monk."

Hanging around those boys was a big change in my life, for better and for worse, but an even bigger change was coming.

Ruthanne had graduated high school in the spring and applied to college, but she didn't apply in time to be admitted for the fall. I knew she did it late on purpose but she told Mom it was an accident and Mom believed her. Mom was kind of an idiot about college. One night Principal Winthrope called our apartment to speak directly to Ruthanne. Ruthanne paced around rolling her eyes while they talked.

Principal Winthope told Ruthanne that if she got good grades at a community college she could enroll at a four-year college the next semester.

"There ain't no community college in Komer," Ruthanne said. Whenever she talked about college, she used bad grammar on purpose. It was pretty stupid.

Principal Winthrope told Ruthanne there was a community college an hour away.

Ruthanne said she couldn't get there because she couldn't drive, on account of her spine, even though her spine hardly bothered her anymore. Her doctor said the muscles had built up around it so it might not bother her again until she was old and gray. I knew what he said because I was there. Ruthanne could have gone to the DMV and gotten a driver's license, but she didn't want to. She wanted to sit at home. That was the whole problem. I wanted to go into Principal Winthrope's office and tell her what a lazy bum Ruthanne was being, but I wasn't at school enough to do it. Plus I was in hot water with most of my teachers so I might have gotten a lecture for my trouble.

"And it's not like I have a goddamned car anyway," Ruthanne told Principal Winthrope. "Who's gonna drive me? You?"

At that point Principal Winthrope said something to Ruthanne that caused Ruthanne to hang up. I figured Principal Winthrope had snapped at her—Ruthanne had it coming—but it turned out to be something else. It came out over dinner that night. We were splitting a pot of macaroni with frozen peas in it. Mom and I were quiet because Ruthanne was still steaming and there wasn't any talking to her in that condition.

"That Principal Winthrope has such a nerve," Ruthanne said.

"Oh Ruthie," Mom said, "she just wants what's best for you."

"What's worst is more like it. You'll never believe what she said. Of all the nerve."

Neither of us asked what Principal Winthrope said. We wanted Ruthanne to calm down.

Ruthanne slapped her macaroni with the back of her spoon—
splat, splat, splat—until she said, "Principal Winthrope said there
was a better community college in the city. She said she knows that's
where Dad lives, and maybe I could live there with him. Can you
believe that shit?"

"She meant well," Mom said. "She doesn't know your daddy."

"Or his stupid girlfriend," Ruthanne said.

Dad had a new girlfriend. This, more than anything, made the
situation repellent to Ruthanne. Before, Ruthanne had got on with
Dad better than any of us. They were similarly inclined to complain
and make fun of things. I didn't know why Ruthanne hated the girlfriend so much. Her name was Geraldine, and we hadn't ever met her
because we never visited Dad in the city (he always came to us), but
Ruthanne was sure she was a bimbo. That her name was Geraldine
made me wonder, though. It sounded like an old librarian's name.

Mom didn't say anything. Maybe she didn't understand the value of college, not having gone there herself, or maybe she just didn't
like the idea of Ruthanne leaving home. I didn't like it either, but I
knew how the world worked, or at least I was starting to think I did.
I was starting to think of myself as having the ability to make tough,
no-nonsense decisions. So I bypassed Mom and called Dad myself.

It was the first time I ever called him (he called us, we didn't call
him) so he was surprised to hear from me. The first thing he did was
tell me how this shitty HR lady screwed up his HSA cafeteria plan
pre-tax deposits. When he was through I told him about Ruthanne.

"Hmm," he said. "I wasn't aware college was an option."

"It won't cost much," I said. "Principal Winthrope said Ruthanne
could go for free except for books and fees and whatnot."

"Fees, huh? Sounds like tuition in disguise."

"Maybe," I said.

"I'll have to think on it. I'll have to speak to Geraldine."

"Okay."

We hung up, and I felt hopeful. Dad wanted at least to *seem* fatherly, I knew. His own dad had left him, his mother, brother, and three sisters without a word goodbye. Dad never missed an opportunity to do a rant about how if his brother Ricky hadn't got the job at the meatpacking plant then the whole family would have starved to death. Dad said they ate parts of a cow I never heard of, parts which were illegal even in Cambodia, which was the country where his favorite uncle Dermot had lost his life on a secret war mission nobody was allowed to talk about (the subject of a separate rant). Dad said he looked forward to the day he would run into his father on accident—"by the side of the road maybe, me dressed for church and him slouching along drunk without a tooth in his head"—so he could tell him how he, Dad, was a real man who took care of his fatherly responsibilities and mostly held down a job.

Geraldine must have told Dad she didn't mind Ruthanne living with them, because Dad started pestering Ruthanne as much as Principal Winthrope did, and by Christmas Ruthanne had decided to move to the city. Dad came down to get her on New Years. It was a tearful goodbye. Ruthanne told me to be nice to Mom and to stay out of trouble.

"It's no business of mine who your friends are," she said, and I must have rolled my eyes because she scowled and grabbed my chin, "but please don't get into trouble. I mean *serious* trouble. Hear me?"

I told her I wouldn't, though to me "serious trouble" meant the jailhouse whereas to her it might have meant something less onerous.

Ruthanne kept hugging me, and I hugged her back. I cried a little but hid it because I didn't want to encourage her; she was crying like crazy. Mom was too. After Ruthanne left, Mom was too far gone to speak, let alone be consoled. She locked herself in her bedroom and I barely saw her for two days.

The apartment felt creepy, like we were mourning a death, so I avoided the place. After school I hung out with the boys and spent extra time in the grocery store parking lot even though working there had gotten harder with age. I wasn't cute enough anymore to accost people. One time a mom with a baby pulled out pepper spray. The day I turned sixteen I had tried to see Darla Waddell about official part-time employment, but a checkout lady told me Darla quit a long time ago. The checkout lady told me the new guy was a jerk with a mustache and if I asked he might tell me I couldn't even hang around the parking lot, let alone work there on the books.

That Saturday I spent all day at Ms. Mikiska's office. I asked her if I could come in Sunday, too. She closed the office on Sundays to make the right impression on her clientele, but I knew she was there working in secret, drawing up wills and whatnot. I was sure I could help do a will if she gave me a chance. But when I asked about Sunday, Ms. Mikiska sighed. I felt embarrassed.

Ms. Mikiska said she had some bad news. I was sure she was going to fire me for asking about Sunday (what an idiot I was!) but instead she told me she was getting married. I was confused. Wasn't getting married *good* news? She explained how she and her girlfriend had to take a trip to New York City to get married, since both of them were ladies, and they weren't coming back. I asked if they were gonna live in New York City and she said they were moving to an island I never heard of. I guess her girlfriend had some money. She was pretty old.

"We're darn excited," Ms. Mikiska said, but she said it kind of sad. "I meant to tell you sooner, but I kept putting it off. It was like if I didn't say anything it wouldn't happen."

"It's cool. Islands seem pretty cool."

"You bet they are. I love surfing—it's great for your core—and the heat's good for Barbara's rheumatism. But I'll miss this place." She gestured vaguely at the office around us then dragged her hand along the shiny wooden surface of her big clean desk, sort of puckering her lips like she could taste the desk through her palm. She looked out the window at the antique store across the street. Tables and chairs were stacked outside it.

"Tell me," Ms. Mikiska said, "what's your dream job?"

I hadn't ever been asked that before. There was a time I would have said terrorist, no question, but with age I had become aware that terrorism wasn't considered an acceptable career in most circles. "I don't know," I said, "the grocery store, I guess?"

Ms. Mikiska seemed disappointed but quickly gathered herself. She was a positive person. She said, "Well, what you've got to do is prove yourself indispensible. Go out and grab it by the balls and twist."

"Grab the job's balls?"

"That's right."

I almost told her I had been trying for years to be indispensable, with no luck, but I didn't want her to feel guilty for leaving.

A moment later she opened a desk drawer, withdrew a crisp fifty-dollar bill, and held it aloft between two fingers. "Severance pay," she declared.

I didn't know what severance was so I was confused until she held the fifty towards me. I took it before she could change her mind. "Thank you," I said.

"No," she said, "thank *you*."

She smiled and told me I'd go far in life. Then she took out her yellow notepad, scribbled something, tore off the sheet, and handed it to me. "My new address," she said. "Feel free to list me as a reference on your résumé. And I hope it goes without saying that I'd be willing to write a letter on your behalf, with proper notice."

"Thank you," I said, but I wondered what kind of letter she meant. People on death row got letters written to the governor about them, but that seemed pretty dire.

Before I left I asked if she knew anybody who was hiring.

"Besides the dump?" she asked, laughing.

I mustered a laugh.

"Actually," she said, "I know a guy there. You're sixteen now so you might be eligible for their internship program. I'll put in a word."

"Thank you," I said, hiding my disgust.

The next day, Sunday, in the shadow of my dashed hope of spending the day with Ms. Mikiska, I was even more bored than usual. Ruthanne wasn't around and Mom was still in her bedroom. She had dragged the TV in there so I couldn't watch it unless I climbed into bed with her, and her bedroom smelled like dirty tissues. I tried riding around on my bike, but it didn't bring the same pleasure it used to. I was sixteen. I couldn't escape the feeling that I should have been driving instead of riding around on a lady's bike. I almost called Pete Gomez, but I hadn't ever spent a Saturday or Sunday with those boys and I got the sense, from the stories they told on Mondays, that the weekends were when they really got into trouble. Maybe *serious* trouble, like Ruthanne said.

Monday wasn't much better. I didn't have the gumption to go to the grocery store, since I barely made any tips anymore, and at home I felt restless. There was schoolwork, sure, but the books they made us read were pretty boring. The only good one I ever read besides *The Highest Mountain* was about a lady in Florida whose husband caught rabies so she shot him. I would have read that one again, but we were done talking about it.

I decided I needed a part-time job. A *real* part-time job with fixed hours, on the books. I didn't care if I had to miss school for it. I considered myself a bit of an idea man, but a man whose ideas belonged in the real world, not a schoolhouse. I was sure that wherever I landed I could work my way up in no time. Working would give me purpose, I thought, and also money for food. Grandpa hadn't come around in a while with a MEAT and CHEESE delivery. I was a little worried about the old codger, but that could wait.

The next day during lunch I went to the library and found Demarcus sitting at a table with two girls. They had school books open in front of them. When I sat down he said hello, but the girls didn't look up. I wondered if I had a reputation now. The idea kind of pleased me.

I asked Demarcus what he was up to, and he nodded at the book. "The teacher said if I work ahead I maybe could skip into calculus next year."

"And that's a good thing?"

"One less class to pay for at college."

On the subject of college, I told Demarcus about Ruthanne.

Demarcus approved. "Anybody with a brain in their head does as much as they can at a community college before transferring to a four-year college," he said. "It's cheaper, and the diploma looks the same either way."

The girls nodded. They seemed to think highly of Demarcus. I recognized one from my year, but she wasn't in any of my classes, unsurprisingly. The other looked older. She was skinny and black and had nice braided hair with little beads at the end.

"You come here to study?" Demarcus asked.

"I came for advice," I said. "I need a job."

"Me too." He laughed softly. The girl with braids laughed too. Then she shook her head and returned to her book. Probably she thought I was a dummy, but I didn't care. I didn't have time for all this studying like they did. I was an idea man, like I said, plus a man of action.

"I came to you because you got all the angles," I said, "so do you got ideas for part-time jobs or don't you?"

"You'd be better off waiting 'til the summer and doing an internship," Demarcus said.

I remembered what Ms. Mikiska said about the internship at the dump. "What's the difference between an internship and a regular job?" I asked.

"An internship is like a practice job, for a career."

"What kind of career?"

"Any kind that's good has an internship."

"Huh." I wasn't entirely clear on the word *career*, like what made it different than a job. "What kind of career do you wanna do?"

"Corporate lawyer, because all you gotta do is make good grades. It's supposed to be real boring, but I'm good at reading boring stuff without falling asleep. Plus I like to sit down. What about you?"

"You mean, like, what kind of career?" I had been thinking about that question since Ms. Mikiska asked about my dream job, but I hadn't come up with anything. The problem was I couldn't picture myself in the future, as a terrorist or otherwise. The future was like a big blank to me. I wanted to ask Demarcus if he ever felt that way about the future, if he ever worried about it, but I didn't want to say that stuff in front of the girls so I said, "Who makes the most money?"

"Entrepreneurs and Wall Street bankers."

"One of them."

"For that kind of job you need an internship for sure."

"Then I guess I'll be an intern. How much money do they make?"

"Interns work for free."

I was confused.

"The internship is to learn the ropes," Demarcus explained, "then maybe they'll hire you after college."

"Who said anything about college?"

"Look, man, I'm just telling you how it is."

"Are you gonna do an internship?"

"Not yet. Maybe in college. But I been thinking about how to do an internship and make some money too. You could do the internship and sell something while you're there, like those guys who sell candy outside the baseball games. Before and after work you set up shop in the parking lot and sell, like, hot coffee or bagels. Rich people are always eating bagels."

I admired the way Demarcus had worked it all out in his head, and maybe he was right about internships, I decided. I had money already, and I wasn't doing anything with it. What I was after was more than money, maybe better than money, but I just couldn't quite articulate what it was. I told Demarcus what Ms. Mikiska said about the internship at the dump.

Demarcus nodded. He seemed to like the idea of me working there. He said, "Sometimes it's easier to affect change from the inside, playing by the other man's rules."

"Infiltration," the girl with braids said, without looking up from her work.

Demarcus smiled. "That's one way to put it."

The word *infiltration* rattled around in my head. The idea of getting into the dump and changing it around from the inside appealed to me, for its deviousness.

Demarcus said he would help me with my résumé, and we got on a library computer to look online at the internship program. The Bi-Cities people wanted "self-starting high school graduates currently enrolled for credit at a college or university." Demarcus asked if I was willing to lie on my résumé, and I said for sure.

Demarcus did the résumé so I graduated from high school already and had relevant experience as a "sales intern" with Ms. Mikiska. Under "skills" he listed recycling, MS Word and Excel, typing 100 words per minute, conversational Spanish, and driving. I told him I didn't have a license, but he said I could cross that bridge when I came to it. Under education I wanted to put someplace prestigious like Notre Dame or Colby College, but Demarcus said I should put the community college to make it more believable. Plus, he said, the community college kept bad records so the Bi-Cities HR people might not bother calling to verify my enrollment.

In the cover letter Demarcus said we should emphasize how poor I was and how wretched my life had become, living fatherless in a dingy apartment and whatnot. Demarcus wrote a short paragraph introducing me, a long paragraph about why sanitation and recycling were "particular passions of mine, having grown up in the shadows of the majestic compound that is Bi-Cities Sanitation and Recycling," then another short paragraph signing off with lots of flattery about how I, "as a Komer native and patriot," understood the importance of the work they did.

We read over the letter and résumé a couple times then emailed them to the email address listed on the website.

"Now, we wait," Demarcus said.

That night I called Ruthanne to tell her I had listed her phone number for a reference, and that she had to pretend to be a counselor at a leadership conference for gifted young people.

"You little liar," she said, "what are you up to?"

I explained how I was applying for an internship at Bi-Cities.

"They got internships for high school sophomores?"

"For gifted ones."

"Hmm," she said. "Internships don't pay money. You know that, right?"

"I'm investing in my future."

Ruthanne seemed doubtful, and I felt doubtful too, honestly, but then I got an email asking me to come to Bi-Cities HQ for an interview. I told Demarcus, who told me I had to wear a suit. My funeral suit had gotten to where it bunched up in the armpits and crotch area, and I didn't want to look like a monkey, so I went to the Salvation Army Family Store.

The Salvation Army Family Store was the biggest clothing store in town and had lots of suits, but mostly for fatties. I gathered the smallest suits I could find and took them to the dressing room. A couple jackets looked decent but the pants were a problem. The waists were too big so I had to cinch them with a belt, which made me look like a vagrant losing weight from his seedy lifestyle, or a grave-robbing hobo dressed up in a dead man's suit. There was a cream-colored suit that fit pretty well, but Dad said light-colored suits were for preachers and con artists. Plus it had a big purple wine stain on one lapel, and I didn't want to look like a wino. I expanded my search to jackets and found a black one that fit just right. It was made of stretchy material like the shorts gym coaches wear and had nice piping on the shoulders and back with points like a cowboy shirt. To match it I found a pair of dark jeans, hoping with a necktie to pull off a sort of western businessman look. The whole ensemble cost ten bucks, including a VHS copy of *Blood Bank*. That's the one where Rick Zorn breaks into a bank just to show them how bad their security is so they'll hire him as a security expert, only he's secretly an undercover agent with Interpol and it's a trick to catch the bankers doing cover-ups.

When I got to the guard booth at the dump, the security guard was the same fat jerk who had sassed me last time because I wasn't on his stupid clipboard. I wished he would say something like "Back for more?" so I could say "Big time, motherfucker, so you best come strapped," but I was on the clipboard so he treated me cordially. He gave careful instructions on which door to go in, and a badge on a string to wear around my neck. It was like I was visiting the White House.

I stuck my bike behind an ashtray garbage can and went through a set of double doors into a waiting room, where a receptionist lady took a look at my nametag and got on the phone to tell somebody I was there. It felt good to have somebody expecting me, like I was a dignitary of some sort, or at least a salesman from the city.

The receptionist told me to have a seat, and it was then that I noticed the other kids. There were six or seven, all of them in suits and dresses. I tried to sit apart from them so they wouldn't see my face, in case they'd gone to Pansy Gilchrist and might recognize me for being a freshman when they were seniors.

I grabbed a copy of *POLICE: The Law Enforcement Magazine* and hunched over it, pretending to read about advancements in body armor technology but really thinking about how nice the other boys looked in their suits. Those suits were wool, probably, nothing like the polyester cheapo I was wearing, which I couldn't take off because it was so hot that my armpits had already sweat through my shirt.

I waited, pretending to read, while each of the other kids got called on by the receptionist and led away. They'd be gone for ten minutes then come back looking dazed. I wondered if they had been interrogated. Probably Whitey Connors had instructed his HR person to make sure everybody's story checked out. Maybe there was a heat lamp and *two* HR people, one good, one bad, and the bad one yelled about how you lied on your résumé and could go to jail for it while the good one offered you soda and whatnot. By the time all the other kids had gone, I was prepared for the worst.

A tall girl in a nice long dress came unsteadily from around the reception desk and left without a word. The receptionist shuffled some papers and said, "Benjamin Shippers?"

"That's me," I said.

The receptionist led me down a hallway to an office where a mustachioed man in a short-sleeved dress shirt was sitting behind a pristine desk. His necktie was pinned to the front of his shirt. The receptionist handed the man some papers and he put on reading glasses to examine them.

"Shippers," he said. "Is that Dutch?"

"Partly," I said, though I had no idea.

"Sit down for Pete's sake."

I sat down in a chair across the desk from the mustachioed man. Behind him was a window with crooked venetian blinds. The sun was peeking through, about to set.

"Local boy, huh?"

"That's right, sir."

He glanced at me over his reading glasses. "You look a bit like you're from out west."

I didn't want this man to think I was a hayseed so I wracked my brain for a lie. "This jacket was my father's," I said, "and used to be part of a very fine suit. The pants were lost in a tragic house fire."

The man wrote something on a notepad. He put down my résumé and started reading my cover letter, which emphasized poverty and fatherlessness. Demarcus told me that was my angle. I thought about the boys and girls who went before me, in their nice clothes, and decided to play up the difference between us.

"Excuse me, sir," I said. "I want our relationship to get off on the right foot so I'm going to tell you the truth. This jacket wasn't my father's. My father never wore a jacket a day in his life. He does brake boxes at a factory in the city. I bought this jacket at the Salvation Army because I like it. I suppose I consider myself a westerner in spirit. The wide open spaces fire my imagination." I couldn't believe the bullshit that was coming out of my mouth. I was trying to tell the truth, but I couldn't stop lying!

The man leaned back in his chair and examined me. "The clothes don't make the man," he said, "but careful grooming sometimes does."

The word *grooming* made me think of dogs.

"Pared fingernails," the man continued, "a cleanly shaved face. Take your haircut, for example."

I prepared for the worst. Mom used to cut my hair with shaving clippers but she hadn't cut it in a long time so I tried it myself the day before, but I screwed up and had to shave the whole thing down to a quarter inch. My ears stuck out like mug handles.

"Most of these boys have mops on their heads," the man continued, "but your tidy haircut tells me you don't have time to stand around styling yourself in front of a mirror."

"Thank you, sir," I said. "I cut it myself."

"Why, you don't even have time to go to the barbershop!"

"That's right."

"A self-starter," the man said, rolling the words around in his mouth, "a self-starter by God." He seemed to really like self-starters. He picked up my résumé again. "Hmm," he said. "Why do you want to work at Bi-Cities Sanitation?"

Demarcus had prepared me for just that question. I said, "I want to be part of a thriving and well-run business such as Bi-Cities Sanitation."

"But why do you, Benjamin Shippers, want to join the Bi-Cities team?"

"Well, I guess I want—I just want"—the word *infiltration* kept trying to come out of my mouth, but I held it back—"I want to make a difference."

"Glad to hear it," the man said flatly. He eyed my résumé. "What's your major?"

Shit, I thought. I didn't remember which major we put. "Um," I said, searching for a lie, "sanitation science?"

"Says here it's undeclared."

"Well, I been thinking pretty hard about sanitation science."

"Hmm. You ever had an internship before?"

"Yes, sir, with Toni Mikiska."

"I didn't know Toni hired interns. How is she, by the way?"

"Good. She moved to an island with her wife."

The man eyed me. "If I called Toni right now, what would she say about you?"

"She'd say I worked hard but was kind of shy, maybe. She wanted me to talk to the old ladies, but I didn't. Honestly old people kind of scare me, except my grandpa. He lives outside the city. He used to work in the kaolin mine. You know kaolin, china clay?"

The man nodded and I kept talking about Grandpa, then a bunch of other things. I couldn't shut up!

"You don't seem shy to me," the man said.

"I guess I'm nervous," I said.

"Because this résumé is embellished?"

I said nothing. I was caught. I had a vision of being thrown in some kind of basement detention facility until the cops came for me.

"Look," the man said, "you're a self-starter—that much is plain to see—but this internship is for high-achieving college students. Not that any high-achieving college students are applying," the man added, muttering. "Tell you what, I'll pass this along."

"My résumé? But I thought you said—"

"Don't look a gift horse in the mouth."

I nodded, confused. Was the man the horse or the gift?

"No promises," he said, "but who knows, maybe it'll stick some-where." The man stood up, so I did too, and we shook hands.

"Thank you, sir," I said, but I didn't have high hopes. I didn't know what it took for a résumé to stick somewhere, but I was pretty sure mine didn't have it.

When I left the man's office it was after five o'clock, and the place was real quiet. I walked down the hallway to where the waiting room was, and the waiting room was empty. Even the receptionist was gone. So I turned around and kept walking down the hallway. I passed closed door after closed door, some with little windows so I could peek in and see darkened conference rooms and offices full of desks and computers and all kinds of big machines. I'd never been inside an office building before, and the unfamiliar surroundings were kind of scary to me, but I had to put my fear aside in order to infiltrate, I decided. I might not get another chance. For courage I thought about *Blood Bank*. At the end, Rick Zorn is running around a skyscraper with guys shooting at him until he finds the main bad guy banker standing in front of a plate-glass window, holding a gre-nade with the pin pulled. The banker guy laughs real crazy and says, "I guess you think you caught me, huh?" and Zorn says, "Red handed," then shoots the guy's hand off. The grenade flies bloody through the plate-glass window, shattering it, and explodes in the distance near a helicopter with some other bad bankers inside who catch fire and fall screaming to their deaths.

Nobody was going to shoot at me or pull out a grenade, of course, but still I stayed on my toes. The first open door I saw led to a sort of break room with a stinky microwave and a couple couches. I fought the urge to go in there and poke around for snacks, in case I got caught by a janitor or the guy who just interviewed me, which would have been a pretty good way to make sure my résumé *didn't* stick.

The hallway ended in a metal door with a porthole window. I looked through the window and saw sinuous hills of garbage. Be-

yond the hills, bluish in the dwindling sunlight, was the hulking
shape of Trash Mountain.

I didn't see any garbage men or office people, so I tried the door.
The door was unlocked.

Chapter 6

TRASH MOUNTAIN LOOKED different. There weren't as many oversized items as there used to be, no busted fridges or soiled loveseats or floppy mattresses with their stuffing hanging out. Maybe there was a separate area filled with those items, a wasteland of home furnishings. Trash Mountain itself was more uniform, almost featureless. It looked taller. Wider, too. And there was a sort of mini-mountain to the side of the main peak, like Lhotse, the 27,940-foot mountain connected to Everest by the South Col. Anywhere else, Lhotse would have been the biggest thing around. It was only Everest that made it seem small.

In front of me, between the foothills, was a long straight clearing like an unpaved road. I walked along the slippery mixture of flattened garbage and red clay, listening for workers, preparing in my mind what I'd say by way of excuse, but I didn't see a soul. There were tread marks where garbage trucks or loaders had been. Some of the foothills were girded by chicken-wire, the kind you see along the highway to keep rocks from tumbling into the road. Here and there, narrower trails like footpaths meandered away from the main road and disappeared between hills of trash.

When I got to the base of Trash Mountain, I looked up. Two black vultures circled high overhead, which made me wonder if there were animal carcasses tucked in shallow graves of garbage: either vermin or pets people were too lazy to bury, or maybe human bodies missing fingers and teeth so the cops couldn't solve the murders.

At the base of Trash Mountain, the wide road veered right, towards the center of the dump, but a footpath went left towards Komer. I took the footpath. A couple times I came to forks in the path, and each time I went left, hoping to be able to retrace my steps in case I got lost or had to make an escape. In a pinch I figured I could dive into the trash and bury myself until the threat, human or vehicular, passed me by.

It wasn't too long before I heard a noise, like scraping. Because I hadn't seen any people I assumed it to be a vulture scraping meat off a bone, but it might have been a puma so I stood still and made no sound. That's when I heard voices. Someone said "Gimme that" and another person grunted.

I crept along the path, expecting to see garbage men doing maintenance on Trash Mountain, but the only evidence I saw of human activity was an overturned wheelbarrow by the side of the path. The voices were louder now. One was a man's voice. He said, "Don't touch that." A second voice said, "Fuck off." The second voice was deep and crabby, but I knew it was a woman's voice. Ms. Mikiska told me how women speak in five tones but men in only three. That's basic voice science.

I was listening, wondering what these people were up to and if it was secret, when I felt a big hand on my shoulder. I turned, frightened, and saw the tar-black belly of a set of rubber waders. Above me was a big stubbly face staring down.

It was Boss, the man who had gathered my used condoms and improvised crack pipe.

"Hey there," he said with a wet click, as friendly as if he had run into me on the street, not trespassing at his place of work.

"Hey," I said.

"Whatcha doing here?"

"Just checking out the scene."

"A nice evening for it." He looked over top of the nearest trash pile at the lowering sun, then sniffed the air. When he spoke again it was in a serious whisper: "It isn't safe for you here."

"Why's that?" I asked.

"Leo and Candy will be mad if they see you."

"Who are Leo and Candy?"

Boss winced a little, like he knew he shouldn't have said those names and was wondering what to do now that he said them. I wondered if they were his crew. Maybe the crew scavenged copper. I knew about copper scavenging because Grandpa said forest hobos did it to abandoned houses. If Grandpa stayed indoors a few days in a row, during one of his spells, the hobos would start scavenging *his* house. Just because Boss wasn't a hobo didn't mean he wasn't scavenging copper. There was good money in it.

"I won't tell anybody," I said. "I got my own thing going, so silence would be mutually beneficial, know what I mean?"

"I don't," Boss said. "What kind of thing you got going?"

"I was just, well—" I found it hard to describe the sequence of events that had led me inside the dump. "I was looking for a job, but I know they won't give it to me, so I snuck in."

"To raise hell?" Boss asked.

"To know my enemy, is more like it."

Boss nodded. "I can see why you think this place is your enemy. It smells bad and looks worse and, well, I guess it's pretty much horrible to have something like this next to where you live. Leo thinks about it different, though. He says it's like the ocean and we're like fisherman. We harvest what's inside it and have to take good care of it. He calls what we do *husbandry*."

"Like with a wife?"

Boss squinted, thinking. "Maybe, but I was thinking more like animals. Animal husbandry."

"What's that?"

"Milking animals and delivering their babies and such."

I nodded. Leo sounded like a very wise person to me. I hoped to meet him.

"Clarence!" came the gruff lady's voice. "Who you talking to?"

"Shit," Boss mouthed.

I should have run to save my hide, and maybe Boss's too, since he was the low man on the totem pole, clearly, but my curiosity got the best of me. Candy sounded tough, sure, but what could she do? Worst case she'd put out a cigarette on my forearm, like that gypsy pimp in the Rick Zorn movie where he rescues orphans by making them a Kung Fu team, but a cigarette burn would be worth it to know what these people were up to.

A round black lady with a red bandana on her head came out from between two trash hills and saw us. "Goddamn, Clarence," she muttered. "Who's this?"

"Just a kid," Boss said.

"I see that. You know him?"

"Oh, yeah. For sure."

"What's he doing here?"

I wanted to speak on my own behalf, but I couldn't get a word out before this Candy lady said "I ain't talking to you" in such an un-maternal way that I shut up immediately.

"He know our business?" she asked Boss.

"He won't say nothing," Boss said. "He's a good boy."

Candy sighed. "We better take him to Leo."

Now I was worried. Leo sounded wise, sure, but true wise men were unsentimental, and what if he did me in to cover his tracks?

Candy turned around and headed back where she came from, and Boss nodded for me to follow her. I did, with Boss close behind.

We came to a small clearing surrounded on all sides by hills of trash, like a little valley. In the middle of the clearing was a kitchen table with a linoleum top and rusty metal legs. There were a couple school chairs around the table, and in one chair a man sat hunched in a bulky green terrycloth bathrobe. He had a bushy black beard and thick glasses perched on the tip of his long nose. In front of him on the table was a pile of circuit boards, one of which was suspended by a vice. The man was using an exacto razor to scrape something off the circuit board into a small ceramic bowl. He didn't seem to notice us.

Candy said, "Leo, baby, sorry to interrupt."

The man, Leo, dropped his exacto, muttering, and turned to face us. He pushed his glasses up his nose with a dirty finger. Behind the heavy glasses, his eyes were huge. The big dark irises looked like giant pupils, like a cartoon character's eyes, and they lit right on me.

"Who's this?" Leo asked. His voice was raspy and high-pitched.

"My nephew," Boss lied.

Candy said, "Goddamn, Clarence, for real?"

"No," Boss said, wrinkling up his face like he was thinking. I expected him to come up with another lie but he didn't. I had to speak for myself.

"I'm just a kid," I said. "I snuck in to check the place out. I was curious. I'm only twelve."

"A spy," Leo said. "You work for Bi-Cities, don't you?"

Candy said, "He's twelve, Leo."

Leo eyed me. "He's lying. I can hear the jingle of coins in his puerile voice, so he's old enough to want money."

Unnerved, I said, "I swear, mister—"

"This is how they operate," Leo said, ignoring me. "They have spies at the schools now, men who look like children. Baby-faced midgets. Always listening. In school, that's where it starts. There, and in the Mexican encampments. It's the Mexicans they're worried about nowadays. In my day it was the blacks and ethnics." Leo talked about undercover agents whose origin and purpose got murkier as he talked until eventually I started to tune him out and survey the scene. In addition to the circuit boards on the table, there were piles of copper, as I suspected, and plastics piled by color on the wet ground.

When the talking stopped I saw, to my horror, that Leo was holding a chef's knife. The knife looked old and dirty, but the blade-edge gleamed, which meant it was sharp.

"Tell me, you midget spy," Leo said, "why shouldn't I cut your throat right now?"

I was stunned. I got a vision of them killing me and burying me under a pile of trash, never to be found. The only clue would be the circling vultures. I didn't know what to say. What did Leo want to hear?

Boss put his hand on the back of my neck. It was probably for my protection, so he could throw me out of the way if need be, but in that moment I was sure he was holding me steady so Leo could slash my throat.

"I came here to look for work," I said. My voice was cracking. "People said Bi-Cities was hiring and—"

"So that's what you're after," Leo said. "A piece of the action. If you leave right now and never show your face again, I'll spare your life."

A normal person would have run away at this point, but words kept coming out of my mouth: "What kind of action do you mean?"

Leo stood up and raised the chef's knife high over his head, blade downward. Had he been closer I might have made a break for it, but he was on the other side of the small clearing. His bulky robe flapped open to reveal a yellowing v-neck undershirt and droopy trousers cinched by a belt. He twirled the knife in the air so it caught the light of the setting sun. The gesture was pretty flamboyant, which made me think it might be for show. He began a slow and menacing creep in my direction, knife held aloft at a jaunty angle. Boss inched forward so he was a little closer to Leo than I was.

"So you want a piece of the action, do you?" Leo asked.

"That's right," I said, "and I can help you."

"How?"

"I'll be your intern."

"Ridiculous."

"What's the harm? Interns don't get paid." I pictured Demarcus shaking his head and telling me I got the intern idea all wrong. This work did *not* have career potential. But I perceived in these scavengers a closeness to Trash Mountain that I wanted for myself. My childhood memories—my whole life—was wrapped up in that place. "I'll gather whatever you want," I said, "so you can spend more time scraping it or whatever, or supervising."

Leo shuffled sideways to get between me and his work table, blocking my view of the circuit boards. "What have you seen me scrape?" he asked.

"Nothing. I don't care what it is. I'll just gather it, I swear."

"I have Clarence for that."

"Two is better than one. Plus I'm smaller. Clarence, Boss, can tell me where to go, and I can sort of root around in there and get the small stuff, like a truffle pig."

Leo lowered the knife and looked at Boss. "*Boss*, huh? That's cute."

Boss said, "Honest, Leo, I could use the help. You're always telling me I don't get the stuff fast enough."

"Fine. Use him. Pay him if you want. *Boss* him around a little, if that's what you're after." Leo winked. "Do what you like with him, just don't show him our ways."

"Can I show him how to get in?" Boss asked.

"Absolutely not."

"But—"

"How'd he get in this time?"

I said, "The back door of the building."

Leo laughed like a big crazy bird. "Good luck with *that,* kiddo. I might not be seeing you after all." He shook his head and went back to his table, still laughing.

Boss ushered me out of the clearing and onto the path where we had met. "Leo can be a real dick," he said.

"He seems pretty mean."

"Yeah. He never stabbed anybody, though. He mostly yells. He don't ever leave that table so you don't have to see him if you don't want to." Boss stared at the dirt, thinking. "I could use the help, like I said, but I can't pay you."

"No worries," I said. I didn't need money. I had $1,567 in two shoeboxes, and I would have had more if I didn't buy groceries for Mom and me sometimes. I liked buying groceries because I got to buy what I liked: marshmallow cereal, frozen tater tots, and Country Home baked beans with maple-smoked bacon flavor.

"If you need money," Boss said, "I can show you where there's good stuff to sell."

"But what about you?"

"We make our money gathering recyclables, mostly."

"What kind of recyclables?"

"Oh, you know, glass, tin, plastics one, two and five, some other stuff."

"What other stuff?"

"I'm not supposed to talk about it. Please don't ask again. I talk too much." Boss shook his head like he was sick of himself.

"Don't sweat it," I said, "I'm not in it for the money."

Boss looked down at me quizzically. "Then what are you in it for?"

I didn't want to say infiltration, in case that sounded nefarious, so I just thanked Boss and told him I'd come by the next day after school. He told me the best picking was early in the morning, right after the fleet left. I didn't relish the idea of waking up before dawn, but I told him I'd try.

By the time I got home it was late enough that the yahoos had gathered in the strip mall parking lot across from the apartment. When I passed on my bike, they threw bottles into the street and called me faggot.

At the apartment complex, I went straight to the basement laundry room, where I stripped off my clothes and stuffed them into the washer, hoping to get the stink of the dump off my new jacket and jeans. The stink of Leo, too. Not that Leo smelled bad (I didn't get close enough to smell him), but the way he looked made me feel dirty. Those grimy cinched trousers.

I changed back into my school clothes and went upstairs, where Mom was talking on the phone to Ruthanne. I wanted to talk to Ruthanne when Mom was through. To get the phone I had to go into Mom's room, where she was lying in bed under the covers. All over the bedspread were used tissues. The mucusy smell was overpowering, and made worse by a flowery perfume she spritzed to mask it.

The phone smelled like the perfume so I wiped it on my shirt. When I got it to my ear Ruthanne was saying, "Took you long enough. I was about to hang up."

"Would have served me right," I said, which seemed to confuse her. I was still feeling dirty and guilty from my day at the dump. I wanted to tell her about it but didn't know where to start. I remembered what she said about serious trouble. Did trespassing count?

Ruthanne started up her usual rigmarole about Geraldine. "Mom might be fat," Ruthanne said, "but this bitch is ugly. And did I mention she's a bitch?"

I tried to laugh, but my mind was elsewhere. It didn't matter to Ruthanne, though. She kept going about how the community college classes were for dummies and there was an old guy who kept talking to her. "I swear to God, Ben, he must be thirty at least. He's got a metal leg so I guess he was in the Army. He's got a Mexican name, but he speaks English regular."

"Sounds like you like him," I said.

"Shows what you know," she said.

I wanted to ask Ruthanne if it was crazy to work part-time in the dump, off the books, but I was embarrassed. Ruthanne was in college. College was the opposite of a dump! Our lives were headed in different directions.

"How's Dad?" I asked.

"Annoying," she said. "I come home from class and he's stretched out on the couch yelling at the TV. Geraldine does all the shopping and cooking, and from what I can tell she works longer hours than Dad does. He's worried the Chinese are spying on him. He says there's gonna be a war between us and the Chinese."

"Probably so," I said.

"He says you and Mom will be safe because you live in a low priority target area."

"I'll say."

"But he says if the war starts we'll have to move to a bunker, maybe Grandpa's. I told him fat chance. Grandpa thinks Dad's lazy and can't pull his weight around a farmhouse, which is true, but it's not like I can either. I can barely even cook. Goddamn, Ben, I better get a good job out of this college deal. Geraldine says even to be a librarian you have to have a master's nowadays. Listen, Ben, I gotta go. But what you been up to?"

"Oh, you know, school and whatnot." I wasn't really listening. I was looking out the window at the people across the street in the parking lot. A familiar figure was strolling towards them with his hands thrust in the pockets of a black hooded sweatshirt.

"Well, remember what I told you," Ruthanne was saying.

"About what?"

"Serious trouble. Stay out of it."

"Yeah, yeah," I said, and hung up.

The figure, a small man, nodded to a group of drunks standing in a circle, then walked up to a Pontiac Firebird and bent over the driver's side window. Words were exchanged, and something else. When the figure turned to walk away, I could see his face: Ronnie Mlezcko.

I came out the front door waving my arms. Ronnie looked up, but I guess he couldn't see me in the dark. Our cheapskate landlord only kept one lamp lit in the parking lot, just outside the office, which was also the superintendent's apartment.

I hollered "Ronnie!" but he didn't stop. I came down the stairs and saw him walking down the road away from me. "Ronnie!" I yelled.

The drunks in the parking lot took up a chorus: "Ronnie! Ronnie! Ooh, Ronnie!"

I felt like an idiot, but it was too late to run back. Ronnie had noticed me. I expected him to be pissed, and honestly I had no idea what I was doing. I guess I just liked the idea of running into a friend from school, which never happened to me. The people across the street in the parking lot kept cat-calling me and parroting Ronnie's name and laughing, and I felt like crawling into the gutter. But I was afraid to go back inside because they'd see where I went and maybe tag our door. Somebody wrote GO BACK TO MEXICO on a door downstairs. I felt like I was stranded, like in this dream I used to have where instead of Bob Bilger it was me on the wooden stage back at Milford Perkins, only I was naked and Mr. B, the computer teacher, was sitting in the front row covering his eyes with both hands.

But it turned out I didn't have to worry. Ronnie had turned back to the people in the parking lot. He didn't say anything, just looked at them. They looked back at him, still shouting "Ronnie!" and kind of laughing, but then the shouting stopped, and the laughing did too. I knew the face they were seeing, the face he had turned on Kyle James when he pointed the rifle at him. Ronnie was the kind of person you could imagine bursting into a buffet restaurant with an automatic weapon. I didn't have that kind of face, but it would have been nice to, sometimes. There was power in it. Terrifying power. Because there wasn't anything you could do to stop a truly hard-hearted crazy person. Not that Ronnie was like that. He just *looked* like that.

Ronnie turned away from the crowd and came towards me, slowly, hands thrust in his pockets. His face was still hard from the confrontation. He raised his chin at me, unsmiling. "Walk with me," he said.

We walked to the back of the apartment building, out of sight of the parking lot people. I didn't ask Ronnie about those people or what he was doing there, but I could tell they were still on his mind. He was shaking his head and sneering so his crooked front teeth showed like weird fangs.

"Assholes," he said. His face looked thinner than I thought it was, older too. Maybe Ronnie was different outside of school, I thought. Maybe I didn't really know him. It was stupid to have come out to talk to him.

"You live around here?" he asked.

I pointed upstairs to the apartment, but there weren't any windows in the back of the building so it looked like a warehouse.

"What a dump," he said.

"Don't I know it," I said. Then I told him how we used to have a house right next to Trash Mountain.

"Trash Mountain?" he repeated. "You mean that big old trash pile?"

"Yeah, that's what I call it. My sister does too."

"Ruthanne, right? How's she doing?"

I was surprised Ronnie knew Ruthanne's name. This had quickly become the most civil conversation we ever had. "She's good," I said, and told him how she moved away for community college.

Ronnie didn't seem to be listening, just staring at something far beyond me. "Trash Mountain," he murmured. "I like that." His expression changed. "Fucking garbage. Fucking Bi-Cities Sanitation. Motherfucking Whitey Connors." He spat on the pavement, disgusted. He told me if he had a nickel for every fucked-up thing Whitey Connors did, he'd stuff the nickels up Whitey Connors's asshole and throw him in the Ocmoolga to drown. I must have looked confused because Ronnie felt the need to clarify: "He'd drown from the weight of them nickels in his stomach. Only problem with drowning a man is you can't hear him scream."

"Hmm," I said.

"I got a new tattoo. Check it out."

He lifted his hoodie and t-shirt, and there were little doodles on his pale white flanks and some writing on his hairy stomach. But those tattoos were old, he said. The one he wanted to show me was on his back. It was Jesus Christ on the cross, only instead of Jesus's bearded face in bliss or agony it was a flaming skull.

"Pretty tight, huh?" he said.

"Yeah, tight," I said, but honestly I was kind of disturbed—not by the content so much as the sheer size of the tattoo. It covered his whole damn back. The flaming skull Jesus was the size of a real-life toddler.

I was careful not to ask Ronnie too much about his life, but he offered some things. He said his mom was a real dick. He said his brother Bill was on the run and was "a goddamn idiot who didn't know how to handle his business." He said he spent many hours wandering at night, which gave him time to reflect.

"On what?" I asked, curious about Ronnie's inner life.

"On what's coming," he said ominously.

"What's coming?"

"A race war," he said, "the apocalypse."

"Sure," I said, kind of disappointed. I'd heard Ronnie speak many times on both those subjects.

"What?" Ronnie said. "You don't believe me?"

"I don't know. I mean, the race war *and* the apocalypse?"

"One leads to the other, obviously. It's already happening. In the old days Komer and Haislip were mixed, but now the races have separated. The lines are being drawn. And it's happening everywhere in America, especially in prisons. In prison you have to choose sides already."

Ronnie had two uncles in prison and, despite his tendency for drama, basically knew what he was talking about on that front.

To change the subject I said, "So, you mostly on foot then?"

Ronnie said he didn't have a car so he was always on foot. He said bikes were for kids. He said he wasn't in a rush to get anywhere anyway, so who gave a fuck. Then he raised his hand for me to clasp, and I clasped it. He pulled me in for half a hug and patted me one time hard on the back. "Take care of yourself," he said, then he flipped up his hood and sauntered off into the darkness. He had his shoulders up and his hands stuck deep in his pockets, sort of swaying from side to side like thugs on TV. It wasn't the way he walked at school. I wondered if it was because he knew I was watching him, or because *somebody* might be watching him, and he had to make the right impression.

Chapter 7

THE NEXT MORNING, I crept out of bed before sunrise and biked to the dump. It was still dark when I got to an overgrown field across the street from the gate where the garbage trucks came and went. I laid down my bike and got behind some bushes to watch, and pretty soon a few sets of headlights came on. The trucks were mustering. A man with a clipboard wheeled open the gate, and the garbage trucks came out one by one like tanks in a convoy. Each truck had two fellows in the cab. Probably one would be hanging off the back later on.

Sometimes the man with a clipboard would wave his hand for them to stop so he could write something on the clipboard, maybe how a door was dinged or a tire looked flat. This man was the last one standing after all the trucks left. He looked out at the wide street with his arms crossed and his chest puffed out like he had just sent a brood of kids off to school.

Eventually the man took a deep breath of morning air then went inside. I tucked my bike up under the bushes and ran through the scraggly trees until I was a couple hundred yards down the road, where I emerged, crossed the road, then slinked along the fence towards the gate. It was still open, so I crept around the corner of the open gate and dashed behind a big tin wall where they blasted the trucks with a fire-hose to clean them.

The space between the tin wall and the fence was long and narrow. The smell was awful. Slime and scraps of trash had accumulated ankle-high. My shoes and socks and the legs of my jeans were wet with foul-smelling water, but I kept going. I trudged through the narrow passage, trying not to breathe through my nose and to ignore the squishing of the slimy garbage.

By the time I got to the other side, the cleaning guys had emerged. Some spoke English, some Spanish. Then the water came on, and the sound of water blasting the tin wall right beside me was so loud it rattled my skull. As I waited, covering my ears with both hands, the sky began to brighten in the narrow space above me. By the time the water stopped and the voices dwindled, the morning sun had emerged to my left, on the Komer side, and put a soft pink color on the rolling hills of trash.

I found my way to the central lane, behind the HQ building, and followed the same route I had with Boss. Pretty soon I heard Leo and Candy talking. I didn't want to see them, in case Leo tried to cut my throat again, so I waited behind a smelly pile of white kitchen trashbags until Boss came around with his wheelbarrow.

"Morning!" he said. "Just a sec."

He wheeled the wheelbarrow over the hill to where Leo and Candy were, then a few minutes later came back with the wheelbarrow empty. He asked if I had any gloves. I didn't, so he led me to a spot where he kept some extra clothes inside a shiny blue suitcase: shirts and socks, a second set of waders, and a tattered pair of garden gloves with white rubber grip pads. He handed the gloves to me. They were big as gauntlets so I had to hold my hands up or ball them into fists to keep the gloves from falling off, but I was thankful. I didn't relish the idea of touching trash barehanded.

Right away Boss started showing me the ropes. We didn't have much time to lose, he said, because they were dumping that day, which meant some trucks would be arriving with big loads from construction sites.

"Where's there any construction around here?" I asked.

"Not around here," Boss said. "Up the highway, near the city."

"Then why don't they put the trash someplace in the city?"

Boss shrugged.

The reason Boss wore waders, I soon learned, was he trudged in and out of trash piles all day looking for cans, bottles, greasy pieces of cardboard, and so much other stuff I couldn't keep track. There were inspections twice a year, he explained, to make sure the dump wasn't trashing recyclables, and it was cheaper for Bi-Cities to let people like him go through the trash looking for recyclables than to pay their own people to do it. I asked him why there were so many recyclables in the trash since we all had county-issue recycling containers.

"Nobody knows what goes in which," Boss said, and that was true in my experience. At home the only things we put in the recycling container were beer and soda cans. Boss said even if you recycled right you ran out of room because the containers were way too small and didn't have wheels so lazy people never used them.

If Boss ever found pipe, he collected that too. The same went for hardware like faucets and doorknobs, and for electronics, though most of the new looking stuff was cheaply made and busted beyond repair. Appliances were another favorite. Boss said Leo could fix almost any appliance. One time Boss came down the north slope of Trash Mountain holding a busted microwave in his arms like a baby calf. He told me Leo would be thrilled. The microwave was good as new except the front glass was cracked, which broke the seal and made it so it wouldn't work, so people wouldn't accidentally radioactivate themselves, Boss explained, but it would work if Leo bypassed a meddlesome built-in safety feature.

The items that made Boss most excited, though, were remote controls and cell phones. I was surprised he found so many cell phones. Weren't cell phones expensive? When I asked, Boss said people were always buying new phones and didn't know what to do with the old ones so they threw them away. He said that was stupid, because you could get good money for a used phone.

"So y'all sell them?" I asked.

"Sometimes," Boss said, "but mostly they're too far gone."

"So what do you do with them?"

Boss shrugged, which was unusual for him. Usually he has lots to say. And when I asked him why anybody would want a remote control without the TV it went to, Boss thought for a long time before he said, "People sometimes lose them. Ain't you ever lost a remote?"

"I guess," I said, but I wondered if he wasn't telling me the whole story. Some of the remotes he collected looked pretty crappy. It was hard to imagine them working on any TV at all.

For the first couple weeks, I just followed Boss around and stood beside him trying to find stuff but getting beat by Boss every time. He had laser eyes. When the wheelbarrow was full we'd go back to HQ, as he called it, and I'd wait in the path while Boss pushed the wheelbarrow over the hill to Candy and Leo. Eventually it got to where I followed Boss into HQ, to speed up the sorting and piling of recyclables. We gave Leo and Candy a wide berth, but sometimes I caught Leo peering at me over his glasses. I stayed ready for a fight. I wasn't very strong, but I was young and light on my feet. As long as it was only Leo, I could get in one punch to stun him then run for it. That was my plan, at least. But pretty soon Leo seemed to forget I was there.

One day Boss and I came over the hill to find Leo operating an unusual contraption: a sort of wand hooked up to a metal box. Leo passed the wand slowly back and forth over the little circuit boards of phones and remote controls until it made a noise like *whoo, whoo!* The wand was intriguing to me, like something from an old sci-fi movie with radioactive monsters roaming the Earth in the wake of an A-bomb attack.

Candy caught me staring and said, "If you got so much time on your hands, how 'bout refilling the cooler?"

She meant the big orange cooler they had. It weighed about a thousand pounds when it was full, and the spigot was at the base of an outbuilding way over where the garbage trucks were parked, but I did as I was told.

I took my time, continuing my study of the various paths and features of the garbage landscape, and when I got to the spigot there was a garbage man filling a bucket. By the time I noticed him I was too close to run without looking like a criminal. Boss had told me not to worry about garbage men—they had an understanding, he said—but I was nervous. I wondered what to say when he turned around and saw me ("Morning"? "What's up"? dignified nod?), but when he did, he didn't even acknowledge me. It was like I was invisible.

For the first couple weeks, I left the dump right at 8:15 to get to school by 8:30, for first period, but eventually I started running late. Usually it was because I was in the middle of a barrow-load at 8:15, and I couldn't well leave it there unsorted. After I got to school late a few times I decided I might as well skip first period entirely, so I started leaving the dump at 9:05 to get to school by 9:20. It seemed to me a tenable situation.

Principal Winthrope didn't agree. She saw me in the halls one day and asked me to her office. Kids were staring. Probably they wondered what was wrong with me. I went through the school day tired and embarrassed, thinking I smelled like trash. *Knowing* I smelled like trash but unable to smell it anymore, which was a blessing and a curse.

Principal Winthrope was pretty and smelled good so I felt extra self-conscious, like I was contaminating her nice office. While she talked I stared at her desk, where there was a statue of Jesus helping two kids play football.

Right away she was asking about Ruthanne. Did I hear from her? How was college? How was she faring in the city? "We're all very proud of her," Principal Winthrope said. "I'm sure she's doing great."

"Oh, yeah, college is great alright," I said, "except for this old Mexican vet who's trying to get in her pants."

"Pardon?"

I was too embarrassed to clarify.

"Ben, is something on your mind?"

"No."

"Things must be different at home, with Ruthanne gone."

"Same song, different verse."

"What do you mean by that?"

I didn't know what I meant. I said, "I guess you wonder why I smell this way, huh? Is that why you brought me in here?"

"Smell what way? Ben, I—"

"A man's gotta work."

"Everybody's got to work—eventually. Now isn't the time for you to be working. School will be out soon, and I can help you find a job for the summer."

"Ain't no jobs in this town."

"You're being very surly."

I shrugged.

"It seems you want to cut to the chase, so I will. You've been late six days in a row. That's not acceptable."

"Since when? I used to knock off at lunch half the time."

"I'm sorry to hear that." She stood up and circled in front of her desk, closer to me. In a softer voice she said, "I notice you have some new friends. Friends are good, Ben. We all need friends. But if your friends pressure you to do things you're uncomfortable with, you have to be able to tell them you're uncomfortable. If they ignore your concerns or make fun of you, then they aren't true friends."

I sat there listening while she went on about friends. I wanted to tell her that my so-called friends weren't the problem. I was working at the dump! But there was something pleasurable about not telling her the whole story. It allowed me to see myself as a hard case, an iceberg. I had a secret life as an infiltrator, after all. Anyway, it was better to say nothing and act nice than to keep talking and be a jerk. I was surly. She was right. I needed more sleep, probably, and not to skip breakfast in my rush to get to the dump and school.

At the end of our meeting I said I was sorry for acting surly and promised to try to get to school on time. The word *try* made it so I wasn't lying.

On my way back to class I found Pete sitting under the stairs with his legs flopped out in front of him and his head hanging down. He was asleep. He had dark circles around his eyes and his shirt was buttoned wrong. I hadn't been seeing him or the other boys as much as I used to, because by the end of school I was tired and just wanted to go home. I kicked Pete's foot.

Pete looked up with surprise. "Shit, dog," he said, looking around. Had he forgotten he was at school?

I wanted to ask if everything was okay, but I was afraid to in case he said something serious, like his sister's boyfriend Milk Dog was in jail. I wouldn't know what to say about something like that. So instead I said, "Check this out," and took out my notebook to show him a drawing. It was an old drawing, but I never showed it before because it was gross. It was pretty good, though. I knew Pete would like it.

The drawing showed a big old Sleeper jamming his veiny boner through the windshield of a car with a family inside. The mom was screaming and the dad was trying to cover the kid's eyes. The kid was screaming too. The windshield was all cracked around the boner. The cracks were the best part. They looked just like how a real windshield cracks, like a spider web.

Pete laughed like hell. "Goddamn, dog," he said, "this is the best one yet! You gotta show Ronnie and them."

"Sure," I said, and after school that day I went to the parking lot to show the drawing to Kyle James and Red Dog and a guy named Shawn Jermyn who had big wispy sideburns. Ronnie wasn't around.

The day was warm and the leaves were coming out in bright green buds on the tree branches above the crumbling asphalt, where we stood among the cars. People were all around us talking and laughing, smoking and dipping, flirting in the grab-assy way they did.

Kyle and Red Dog laughed at the drawing, and Red Dog made Shawn Jermyn look away while he unlocked the secret lockbox and added the drawing to Satans Manifesto. That made me feel good, but it wasn't the same without Ronnie. I wanted to ask where he was, but I guess I kind of knew. Whatever good feelings I had about the drawing, the other boys, and the sunny afternoon were colored by a deeper, darker feeling. Maybe I had a premonition of what was to come.

A week later Red Dog got pulled over for driving drunk, and his rifle happened to be in the backseat. That gave the policemen probable cause to search the whole car, whereupon they discovered three bottles of moonshine and Satans Manifesto. At first the Manifesto was of no interest to them. Just some school papers, they thought. Then they saw the name Ronnie Mlezcko on it, and they happened to be working a case against somebody named Bill "Junk" Mlezcko (Ronnie's brother, though they didn't know it at the time), so they went through the Manifesto for clues. They were understandably disgusted. The police were just regular folks, I guess, not used to reading about mutant zombie psychopaths perpetrating acts of terror. They couldn't press charges, but they called up Principal Winthrope to ask what the hell kind of operation she was running over there at the Pansy Gilchrist. She was embarrassed. And pissed.

Ronnie got expelled. Pete and Kyle James got suspended. I don't know what happened to Red Dog, but he was eighteen so he might have gone to jail. As for me, I got lucky. My drawings hadn't yet been integrated in the manuscript. Pete had wanted to do it immediately, but Ronnie told him how in real books there were words and pictures on the same page, so they'd have to shrink the drawings with a photocopier and "do them up" on a computer. Everyone had agreed Ronnie knew best, and that saved my skin. Here's the thing, though:

those drawings were on torn-out sheets of notebook paper right in
the box with the book proper. Principal Winthrope saw all the papers
in that box, and she had seen at least one of those drawings before,
with her own eyes, the drawing that got me called to her office, which
meant that she chose not to punish me, but why? Maybe, I thought,
she saw through my iceberg routine to my secret inner life, and she
approved of it. Maybe that was why she didn't ask about my grimy
clothes. And maybe she didn't ask about college because she knew I
was on a different path. A harder and longer path, more righteous
too. Principal Winthrope was a smart lady. I didn't know whether to
thank her or avoid her. I chose avoidance, but I did start coming to
school on time, for a while at least.

Pete came back after five weeks and kept a low profile. He showed
up right on time, hid out in the parking lot during lunch, and left
right after school. He told me he was worried about retribution. I
told him nobody except Principal Winthrope and the police knew
what was inside the book, just that it was bad.

"If I was the police," he said, "I'd let it leak which people got mentioned and let those people do my work for me, know what I'm saying?"

"What work?" I asked.

He drew a finger across his throat.

Pete said he wished he was expelled like Ronnie. I asked if he
knew why Ronnie was expelled and the rest of us weren't. We both
knew Ronnie was the mastermind, though we wouldn't have said as
much, but the police had no way of knowing that.

"Teachers like me okay," Pete said, "and they feel bad for me because of my family situation. Because of my dad or whatever."

I asked him what he meant, and he told me his dad got a DUI
and was repatriated to Mexico. I had no idea. I felt sorry, but I didn't
know what to say.

Pete changed the subject to Kyle James. Kyle was back at school
after only one week, Pete said, but Kyle's parents told him he couldn't
hang out with us anymore because we were a bad influence. "He al-

ways was a mama's boy," Pete said, then spat in the dirt. "Motherfucker thinks he's better than us."

I nodded and spat next to where Pete spat, but deep down I wondered if Kyle *was* better than us, not in a snotty way or in the "too
cool" way commonly understood, but in a more fundamental way.
Kyle had a nice family who expected things of him. He took some
care with his appearance. He had a girlfriend. No wonder Ronnie
hated him. Pete said Ronnie and Kyle had been friends since they
were little kids. The whole thing made me feel even worse for Ronnie. I wondered what he was doing with all his free time, but I guess
I kind of knew. I tried to stay up late enough to see him across the
street from my apartment, but the action there didn't get started until nine or ten at night, and by then I was asleep or drifting in and
out on the couch. The problem was I woke up so damn early to get
to the dump, but the idea of sleeping in, of skipping the dump, never
crossed my mind.

Chapter 8

PRETTY SOON BOSS said I was doing almost as good as he was. He rigged me up my own wheelbarrow out of a peach crate with a Big Wheel underneath, and he drew up a little map of the paths in and around Trash Mountain and divided them between us. I pushed my wheelbarrow with some pride, I'm not ashamed to admit, even though I spent almost as much time repairing the makeshift wheelbarrow as gathering recyclables.

I was pretty much on my own except I ran into Boss more often than made sense. It made me wonder if he watched me from afar to make sure I was doing right. When I noticed him he'd say "Atta boy!" or "We'll make a digger outta you yet!" Boss was the only one who used the term *digger*. When I asked him about it he said he was trying to make it catch on. He said his dad had been an iron pig so at first he had tried to coin *trash pig*, but Candy said it was demeaning.

"What's an iron pig?" I asked, picturing a pig man with an iron breastplate. I wondered if a pig man could father a pureblood human such as Boss.

"A miner," Boss said.

I told him Grandpa used to be a miner, and Boss seemed interested.

"It was a kaolin mine," I said. "You know, china clay?"

"Sure," Boss said. "You can eat it to keep from feeling hungry."

"Huh. Well, the stuff Grandpa mined was for paper and industrial ceramics. Lots of people got dust in their lungs and died."

"I can believe it," Boss said.

The kaolin dust made me think of the trash particles in the air, and for some reason I told Boss about Ruthanne and her weird spine.

Boss said he could believe that too, and he pulled up his sleeve to show me his forearm. It was covered with crispy looking spots like fish-scales.

"Did the trash do that?" I asked, kind of horrified. For my own part I was wearing a t-shirt. My bare arms were covered in grime.

"That," Boss said, "or psoriasis."

My legs weren't exposed like my arms, but my jeans were soaked with trash water, and I could feel the cold dampness creeping down through my socks into my sneakers. I asked Boss if I should be wearing waders like he did. Boss said yeah, probably, but they were expensive. He said he found his in the trash, which was why they were so tight that the straps barely went over his shoulders. I asked him about his backup set, in the suitcase, and he said those had a big rip in the front, which made me picture a fisherman getting gored to death by a swordfish.

The talk with Boss made me think I should shower after leaving the dump, before school, so I started biking home, showering, then hustling to get to school by 7:30. That meant less time at the dump, so I started waking up even earlier. To get inside the dump before the trucks left I used wire clippers to cut a few links in a weak part of the fence near the back, by the shitty woods. The garbage men never went back there, and the cut links were barely noticeable if I used a plastic tie to keep them closed.

I made it to school on time, but usually I nodded off in class. Sometimes I even nodded off on my bike, on the way home from school. My head would sort of tip downward then snap up, and I'd be swerving. One day in May it was so hot and sunny that I just couldn't make it home. I laid down my bike in a little strip of grass next to the railroad tracks, hooked my arm through the frame so it wouldn't get stolen, and slept right there in the sun. When I woke up, it was dark. Frogs were croaking in the trees and a breeze was skittering along the grass. I wondered if that was what it was like to be a hobo, to sleep out there like that. If so, it wasn't too bad.

That got me thinking it might be better to go home right after school and sleep, then to wake up in the middle of the night and be somewhat alert by the time I got to the dump. The only problem was Mom was asleep by the time I woke up, and she had moved the TV into her bedroom after Ruthanne left, which meant I couldn't watch it. Without the TV there wasn't much to do in the apartment so I mostly cruised around on my bike. Cruising was way better at night because there weren't any cars, and barely any people except for a few drunks outside Frizell's downtown and some others outside a bar on the outskirts called Zitio's. It was interesting to watch them. I liked the feeling of watching other people without them knowing.

Mostly I stuck to Komer since it was closer, and since there weren't as many street lamps in Haislip, which made it harder to avoid potholes and the broken glass and chunks of asphalt in the roads. When I did go to Haislip I made sure to cruise down a street called Grande Esplanade, where there were big old houses with fancy ironwork and shutters and pointy roofs. One house had a round part in front like the tower of a castle. Most of the houses had been converted to apartments or rooming houses, and some were empty. The empty ones had broken windows and peeling paint and looked haunted. I liked them.

Sometimes I cruised all the way out to the Motown Lounge, the bar Demarcus's dad owned. It was more of a pool hall than a bar, which meant people could smoke inside, so there weren't any people outside unless they were coming or going or using the payphone. It was pretty boring to watch somebody use a payphone, but at closing time I could watch Demarcus's dad sweep the sidewalk. I wondered if he would recognize me. I wanted to say hello, but I didn't want him to ask why I was out so late. I had a fantasy where somebody would drink and drive into a lamppost or have a heart attack out on the sidewalk and I'd run in hollering "Mister Caruthers, call 911!" and he'd do it and say it was lucky I was out there, not just because I saved the man's life but because it gave us a chance to renew our acquaintance. He'd say he always thought I was an interesting fellow.

Because of the dark, quiet nighttime, I started thinking about different stuff than I used to think about. Darkness and cold were the real things, I decided, what was left when the sun went away. And quiet was what was left when people went away. I suspected that one day all the people would be gone from Komer and Haislip. They were half gone already, and going fast enough that even someone young as me had noticed. Take Ms. Mikiska, for example. The windows of her old storefront downtown were already broken, and who knows what happened to the house she lived in, or the house her old lady wife lived in before they got married and moved to their island. Maybe the county bought up the houses for trash. Buildings and things only stayed un-trash as long as people used them, was the way I saw it. When people left, their stuff started turning to trash immediately. Trash for the dump. For Trash Mountain. And it wasn't just buildings and things; it was people too. If nobody saw you, what was to stop you from turning to trash? That's just an example of the stuff I thought about. Nighttime thoughts.

One night when I came home after a couple hours of cruising and thinking, it was two or three in the morning, but Mom was still awake, watching TV. She had the covers pulled to her chin and a half-empty bowl of marshmallow cereal next to her.

I asked her why she was awake and she said she couldn't sleep. She held out her hand for me to squeeze, and it felt kind of weak, even for her.

On TV was a news show where a handsome gray-haired man was talking about a new law that made it so you could bring your gun into churches and bars. The man said it was good because we needed protection from all the crazy shooters, but then another man came on and said the opposite. This other man was fat and had a sweaty face. The first man, the host, laid into the second man about how a real man protects his family.

Mom asked me to fetch her the phone and the grocery catalogue, which was for a delivery service offered by the superstore outside of town. Most people ordered online, but there was also a phone option, for elderly people and Mom. Mom called the number before she even opened the catalogue, so the whole time she was browsing there was a person on the phone who she could ask about this or that item, like if the store-brand stuffing tasted like the stuffing she usually bought. Sometimes she just asked what was good, like which fruits were ripe, even though we never bought fruit except for apples, and the apples we got from the delivery service were always mealy. I never ate them. I told Mom the person on the phone gave her bad advice, and she said she knew it. She said the man on the phone was in the Philippines, but she liked to talk to him anyway.

I went back to my room and I must have fallen asleep, I guess, because the alarm went off at 4:30 and I was startled by it. The TV was still on in Mom's room, so I thought she was awake. I went in there to get the cereal box, and what I saw shocked me: Mom was half out of bed, with her face smushed down on the carpet and her arms flopped out in front of her. Since her legs were still in the bed, her torso was kind of stretched out and her shirt had come up to show her big white belly. At first I thought she was drunk, though it had been a long time since I saw her drunk, and back when she drank she just passed out on the couch or in the bathtub. Then something about the way her legs were still in bed, sort of crooked, made me think she might be dead. My heart started racing.

"Mom," I said, just standing there like a dummy. "Mom. Mom! Eileen!" Eileen was her name. I thought she might respond to it because it was deeper in her brain, from childhood. "Eileen Shippers! Eileen Durnin!" Durnin was her maiden name.

I knew I was supposed to feel her neck for a pulse, but I was afraid. I didn't want to know she was dead. I almost called Ruthanne but heading for the phone got me moving towards Mom and from there I got the courage to touch her neck. The neck was warm. It took a while to find the pulse because her neck had gotten pretty fat, and when I did, the pulse was real slow, just a beat every couple seconds, and the beats were real weak, but maybe that was because the fat muffled them? I put her reading glasses up to her mouth to test for breath, which was something else I had a notion I was supposed to do, and the reading glasses fogged up. She was breathing. I shook her to wake her up but she didn't wake up. I called 911.

The lady at 911 asked if Mom took any medications so I went through the vials and bottles in the drawer of her bedside table and read the names: Avandia, Precose, Glumetza, GlucoTrol XL, Tofranil, Tofranil PM, Novolog, Lantus, and a Levemir FlexPen.

"So she has diabetes?" the lady asked.

"Yeah," I said.

"And depression?"

"I guess."

The lady asked if there were any insulin needles in the house, but I couldn't find any. The lady said not to move Mom and that the ambulance would be there soon. She asked if I wanted her to stay on the phone with me, but I said no.

While I waited for the ambulance I got pissed. It was just like Mom to let her needles run out, she was so lazy. All she had to do was tell me and I could have picked them up, but she was embarrassed about taking so many drugs and kept them in a drawer to pretend she didn't. I tried not to look at her. I knew if I looked at her I would get sad instead of mad.

The ambulance made an awful racket and lots of people came to the windows and doors of their apartments. It was five in the morning. The EMT guys pounded on the door, and when I opened it they came through like a SWAT team. They talked in loud voices while they felt Mom's pulse and stuck her with a needle. One guy talked into a walkie-talkie while another swept her medicine bottles and vials into a bag and asked me if there was any more in the bathroom. I said I didn't know so he went in there and crashed around searching. I wanted to help, but he was moving so fast it seemed dangerous to be near him, like a bucking bronco almost. They lifted Mom onto a stretcher and strapped her down. A lady EMT asked if I wanted to ride in the ambulance with them, and I said did I ever.

In the ambulance I asked the lady EMT how Mom was doing, and she said okay. Her vitals were good, she said, and that made me feel relieved enough that I could look out the back windows while we drove. I had never gone so fast in a car before. It was crazy. Even crazier because of the backward view. The cars had parted for us and everybody was staring. One time a car didn't get over fast enough and the ambulance had to swerve, and the car that came into the view, the perpetrator, was a big blue Cadillac with an old man in front wearing glasses and a detective hat. The old sucker raised his hands from the steering wheel and had his mouth hanging open, and I thought for sure we scared him into a heart attack and would have to pick him up later.

The big hospital was way down the highway, and by the time we got there the lady EMT had told me Mom's pulse was stronger. The ambulance swung into the emergency zone so fast it felt like it was going to tip over from speed. When it stopped, everybody filed out like a SWAT team again, pushing Mom on her stretcher while I followed, running, until we were in a sad yellow hallway full of wheelchairs. A big guy in pink scrubs told me I should wait in the waiting area.

The waiting area was like a brightly lit bus station. Men and women in various states of pain and discomfort waited patiently, and sometimes not so patiently. A few kids either slept or played hide-and-seek under the chairs. From time to time the sliding doors crashed open and a stretcher wheeled past surrounded by EMTs or people in pastel scrubs (pink, yellow, baby blue). I tried to look at the people around me without them noticing and to guess what was wrong with them. Some might have been friends and family, like me, but some must have been injured or sick. A somber Latino couple sat in one corner holding hands. Was one of them dying? Nearby, a pale-faced boy not much older than me was dozing with his arms crossed and his hood up. Was he a junkie? Had his girlfriend over-dosed? Directly across from me, a haggard looking man was using one hand to hold the other by the wrist. The held hand was limp and gray. Had it been severed? Was this fact concealed by the sleeve of his corduroy jacket? The man looked bashful, maybe homeless and afraid to demand attention. The possibility that he was a hobo made him less sympathetic to me.

A cop in uniform walked past us every few minutes. At first he walked slow, like he was on a beat, but then he started walking faster and stopping here and there to mutter something into his shoulder radio, which crackled. The cop was the most interesting feature of the waiting room by far, so everybody watched him. It got to where everybody stiffened when he walked by, and why not? He might have been searching for a violent madman. I pictured a madman crouch-ing in a dark stairwell, his hairy butt hanging out the back of a hos-pital gown while he pulled at his madman's beard, quietly plotting his escape.

There was a big black family where everybody was asleep except one little girl who was hiding under the chairs and crawling through them like a tunnel. At some point she started grabbing people's an-kles, to scare them. When she grabbed the ankle of the man with the severed hand, the man kicked his leg. The girl, who was too young to be afraid, got mad and started yelling. In one fluid motion her father rose, scanned the room, located the child, and headed towards her like a terminator cyborg. A brief chase ensued.

My magazine options were *Popular Mechanics*, *National Geo-graphic*, and *POLICE: The Law Enforcement Magazine*. The cover of *POLICE* showed a fat, expressionless cop staring down the length of a single-barrel shotgun, with the cover story "10 Essential Skills to Win a Gunfight."

I was reading about the second skill ("A solid grip on your pistol is a must . . .") when a thin man in a necktie and a lab coat came out to ask if I was Ben Shippers. I said I was. He said his name was Dr. Chakrabarti. I thought he was a black guy with his hair straightened like a TV preacher, but maybe he was foreign.

Dr. Chakrabarti asked me about my home life, who cooked and stuff like that. He was being a little too polite, it seemed to me, so for a while I thought he was building up the courage to say "she's gone" or "we lost her," like they do on TV, but he ended up saying Mom was okay. He gave me a little plastic deal with letters for the days of the week and a list of which pills to put in there on which days. It was a long list. He said he was taking her off a couple pills and adding a few more. I said okay. He gave me a speech about helping her take her medicine on time and making sure her pills didn't run out, like I was supposed to sneak into her bedroom while she was sleeping and count the pills in her pill bottles. I wanted to tell him the pill factory should just send her the goddamned pills when she needed them, since she was supposed to take one per day so it didn't take a genius to figure out when she'd need more. But I didn't say any of that. I just nodded, trying to look friendly, and at the end of his speech Dr. Chakrabarti seemed pleased to have held my attention for so long. He offered his hand and we shook. The hand was soft as a fat little baby's hand.

A few minutes later Mom came out in a wheelchair being pushed by the big guy in pink scrubs. She looked good, all things considered, but she was smiling so big I could tell it was for show. The guy in pink scrubs knelt down next to her to ask if she needed anything and she said no, and he took off before I could ask him how the hell we were supposed to get home. The ambulance that drove us was nowhere to be found, and we didn't have a dollar to our names for a cab. I ended up pushing Mom in her wheelchair along the highway. For a while she talked but before long she started nodding off. The walk took two hours and both of us were sunburned afterward.

Grandpa came over that afternoon. He was going through a good spell and had been coming over most Sundays to deliver MEAT and CHEESE and sweet potatoes from his garden, where the only thing he grew anymore were sweet potatoes. The man loved sweet potatoes. He showed me how to bake them, mash them, and fry them in the oven like french fries, then dip them in mayonnaise instead of ketchup. He said mayonnaise was better for sweet potatoes.

Usually Mom fussed over him and made him a bourbon and soda, but that day she stayed in her bedroom, for obvious reasons. He went in there and talked to her for a few minutes, and when he came out he seemed agitated. He stood in the kitchen biting his fingernails while I boiled water and washed two fat O'Henry sweet potatoes. The O'Henry is a North Carolina sweet potato famous for its smooth white flesh.

Grandpa was a small man with a wide, flat body and white hair that was thin all over, like the memory of hair still clinging to his head in the shape it had been in his youth. He kept a close white beard. His pants were cinched because he was shrinking, and his short-sleeved plaid shirt puffed out like a Hawaiian.

"How's her diabetes?" he asked.

"Pretty good," I said. I summarized what Dr. Chakrabarti told me and showed Grandpa the days-of-the-week pill thing.

"She looks fat," he said.

"Fatter than usual?"

"Don't joke like that about your momma."

"I wasn't joking."

"Don't talk back."

I held my tongue. He was sore, I could tell.

"How's Ruthanne?" he asked.

"Pretty good," I said. "She calls most nights and talks to Mom."

Grandpa shook his head. "Your momma lives through that girl. It isn't healthy. What happens when she gets married? She won't have time to talk every night, I'll tell you that much, not unless her husband don't like his meals home cooked."

I nodded. I almost told him about the one-legged Mexican veteran, who loomed large in my mind, but it wasn't as fun to see Grandpa rant and rave as it used to be. He was pretty old.

I started chopping a sweet potato for sweet potato french fries while Grandpa watched. It made him nervous to see me with a kitchen knife, like I was still a little kid. I could tell he wanted to take it from me and do it himself—and he would have done it much faster, he was an ace with a knife—but he refrained. He said, "You two ought to come out to the farm."

"To visit? Sure, but you'll have to drive us. Dad's got the car."

"To live."

He mentioned this every time he came over, so I didn't put much stake in the offer, but this time he seemed more serious. Probably because of the hospital. Mom was his daughter, and the idea of outliving her might have been scary to him. Grandma had died of lung cancer when I was a little kid. I barely remembered her. Mom said that when she got diagnosed, Grandpa had quit smoking right away, but Grandma couldn't do it and smoked until she died. Grandpa thought Grandma was weak, Mom said, and in secret he looked down on her. But Mom said it wasn't a matter of weakness or strength, just addiction, and addiction was stronger in some people than in others.

The idea of living with Grandpa appealed. I hadn't been to the farm in years, but I had fond memories of tramping around the property foraging mushrooms and whatnot. The property was full of tall pecan trees and one time I picked up the pecans and put them in a special sack while Grandpa led the way with his shotgun over his shoulder, in case of hobos. He said it was important to evacuate hobos before they got squatter's rights.

When Mom smelled the sweet potato fries in the oven she came out and joined us, and we ate and talked. Grandpa didn't mention the farm again. After we ate, he left.

Ruthanne came home that night and fussed over Mom nonstop. She yelled at me about how the apartment was a pigsty, but she yelled it in a whisper so Mom couldn't hear from her bedroom, where she lay in bed watching TV and looked up angelically whenever Ruthanne came into the room with a glass of lemonade or a big bowl of mac and cheese.

Ruthanne wanted to move back permanently, but Mom said no. Ruthanne had already enrolled in summer classes in order to "get the whole thing over with as quickly as possible," meaning college, and it was too late to get her money back. Mom said wasting money like that was plain stupid. To her credit, Mom may have suspected that if Ruthanne moved back in with us she might never graduate. It had taken a miracle to get her out of Komer in the first place.

Ruthanne's next big idea was for Mom and me to come live with her in the city. We could get our own apartment, she said, and "leave Dad and goddamned Geraldine to wallow in their den of iniquity."

Mom told Ruthanne to hush up about Geraldine, who had taken her in, after all. But Mom liked the idea of moving to the city, I could tell. It wasn't like she had a job to hold down, and Ruthanne said apartments in the city were much nicer than apartments in Komer, especially ours, which was pretty much the worst anybody could imagine.

I played along, saying how good it would be for them to be together again but leaving myself out of the picture they were painting, which didn't seem to bother them too much. But the night before Ruthanne left because summer classes were about to start, she started talking to me about when we were going to make the move. She had July in mind. That would give her time to find a decent place and to see about borrowing a truck from this guy she knew.

"Maybe I can find a three bedroom," she said.

"You'll only need two," I said.

"We're too old to share a room."

"I'm staying."

"What?"

"I'm a Komer man."

"You aren't a man at all, jackass. You're a kid. And who gives a shit about Komer?"

"I do. It's where I live. My friends are here. I have a job now." I told her about my work at Bi-Cities, trying to cast it in a positive light, which was difficult. I emphasized the hands-on skills I was learning, the upward mobility. I may have used the word "internship."

Ruthanne wasn't having any of it. "Scrounging around the *dump?*" she said. "That's halfway to pushing a shopping cart and sleeping in the streets." Her eyes brimmed with tears, maybe thinking about me out on the streets like that. It made me feel bad, but also happy because it meant she still loved me even though she was far away.

"It's not like that," I said, and I told her about Boss and Leo and Candy. I tried to communicate Leo's idea of trash husbandry but by then it was third-hand so it came out pretty confusing.

"Those people are hobos!" Ruthanne said.

"No, they're not!" I was shocked Ruthanne would say such a thing. She knew how I felt about hobos. Boss and them were shabby, sure, but they weren't crooks or discernibly drunk. They didn't lurk in the woods or steal babies. They didn't have names like Boxcar Johnny or Charlie Peepers. Candy was a woman, for gosh sakes.

"Do they live in a shantytown?" Ruthanne asked.

"Of course not."

"Then where do they live?"

"How should I know? I'm not gonna live with them." Anyway it didn't matter. Living with Boss and them wasn't my plan. My plan, my *true* plan, was only beginning to crystallize. Here was the first step: "I'm gonna live with Grandpa."

"What in God's name?"

"He said he wanted me to come out there."

"To visit, you dummy. He doesn't want you living with him."

"He does, though. He likes me."

"What about his spells?"

She meant his good spells and bad spells, as Mom called them, but the way I saw it his spells weren't any worse than Mom's, and Mom had been in a bad spell since the day Ruthanne left. I told Ruthanne Mom didn't do anything but lay in bed watching TV.

"She sounds fine on the phone," Ruthanne said.

"That's because it's you! The moment you hang up she sleeps for twelve hours."

Ruthanne didn't believe me. She was pretty worked up, maybe from guilt. She said we had to talk to Mom about it, since I was only sixteen (almost seventeen, I interjected), and Ruthanne was mad we had to bring it up to Mom because it might upset her. I knew it wouldn't, though. I guess I knew Mom better than Ruthanne did. I was more like Mom than Ruthanne was. What made Mom happy were the things inside her.

We went into Mom's room and the two of us sat on the bed with her and rehashed our conversation from before. Mom nodded. When the part about me staying behind came up she muted the TV. The silver-haired anchorman was talking, but no words came out. Without words, his face lacked urgency. He was going through the motions.

"It'll be cheaper with just the two of you," I said. "You can get a shitty little apartment, and I'll visit sometimes. I'll be fine."

"You're sixteen years old," Mom said.

"Almost seventeen," I said.

"A boy belongs with his family."

"I'm not leaving." I was surprised to hear myself say that, and Mom was too, it seemed. It was a while before she said, "Well, what about school?"

Ruthanne was shocked. "You can't seriously be entertaining this."

"He's been as good as on his own since you left," Mom said. "Fact is, both of you kids been on your own for a long time now. That was why I knew you'd be fine up there in the city, Ruthie. I knew you could take care of yourself, and Ben can too."

"But he's just a kid!"

"Kid nothing," I said.

"Don't be a stinkpot," Mom said. "Now what about school?"

"Grandpa's place is in the county, same school."

"I know that. But will you go to it? It's a long way off and you don't have a car, nor much interest in getting there on time, seems to me."

"I'll get Grandpa to drive me. He doesn't do anything all day except water his sweet potatoes and check puma traps."

"What if he's having a spell?"

"Then I'll drive his truck. If he's having a spell he won't need it."

"You don't have a license."

"I'll get one."

Ruthanne scoffed. "You gotta take a class, dummy. They don't just hand out driver's licenses."

"Summer's coming," I said. "I got months to take a class and pass a test or whatever."

"Not if you spend all day in the dump gathering trash," Ruthanne said.

Mom closed her eyes. We hadn't ever talked about why I woke up so early and wore such raggedy clothes all the time, but she knew, I could tell. She just wanted to pretend I was still a little kid who was happy riding his bike around all day, so she wouldn't have to worry I'd get in trouble. And I *wasn't* in trouble. Not yet, at least. It seemed to me I deserved a pat on the back for the stick-to-itiveness with which I pursued my goals. So what if the goals were infiltration and a yet-to-be-determined act of terror?

"Nobody's going anywhere," Mom said. "Ruthie, you should come live with us right here. It's the summer."

Ruthanne nodded. She didn't remind Mom of what Mom said before, about not wasting the deposit for summer school. Maybe Ruthanne felt sorry for Mom. Maybe she didn't want to upset her. It made me think Ruthanne was growing up, which was a weird thing for a little brother to think about an older sister, but it was true. I could tell from the disappointed look on Ruthanne's face that she wasn't coming home. I was sad at first, because it would have been nice to see her more often, but I ended up glad. Having her around would have been tough. I kept such weird hours. Ruthanne would have been on my case for sure.

Chapter 9

LIVING WITH GRANDPA was great and it was terrible. There were days in the sun and nights in the cold spooky darkness. There were suppers of sugary beans with bacon, and breakfasts of corn flakes with water because Grandpa forgot to buy milk. There were grilled cheese sandwiches and mustard sandwiches. Sweet potato stew and tomato soup made from ketchup. The screens had holes so there were mosquitoes in the house, but Grandpa didn't care. His leathery skin had lost its food-like aspect. Mine had not. I tried to sleep under the covers but got so hot at night that if I did manage to sleep I would kick off the covers and wake up with mosquito bites on my face and neck. There wasn't central AC, and the only room with a window unit was Grandpa's bedroom, but he never used it. He said part of getting old was feeling cold all the time, no matter how warm it was. It was closeness to death, he said. He had come to terms with the fact that he would never feel warm again.

I slept upstairs in Dinwiddie's bedroom. Dinwiddie was my mother's brother. He died when he was a kid so I never knew him. It was something with his heart. Anyway, his bedroom was tiny. Drafty too. As a kid I used to fuss about it because Ruthanne got to sleep across the hall in Mom and Aunt Sheila's old bedroom. There were two beds in that bedroom so I could have slept there too, was the way I saw it, but Mom got mad when I complained. She said Grandma wanted me in Dinwiddie's room. It was before Grandma died of lung cancer, but she was already on her way so everybody was extra nice to her all the time.

Between the heat and the mosquitoes and the possible ghost of Dinwiddie, it was hard to get a decent night's sleep. Add the creaking noises the big old wooden house made as it cooled at night, plus the weights inside the old windows that knocked against the sills like insane clocks keeping random time, plus Grandpa, who could be heard snoring in the distance, or pacing on the squeaky floorboards, or opening and closing drawers, and it was damn near impossible to sleep for more than ten minutes at a time.

The lack of sleep might have been tolerable if Grandpa hadn't been trying to work me to death. First, we dug postholes for a new fence. We dug twenty-seven postholes in one day and would have dug thirty-two if one of the wood handles on the posthole digger hadn't broke. I was used to laboring in the heat from my work at the dump, but this was a whole different level. To keep my strength up, Grandpa fed me huge helpings of pinto beans from big pots he made every Sunday, with onions and garlic and a bay leaf for flavor. Those beans were damn good after a day in the sun. We used white bread to sop what was left in our bowls.

Second, we tended Grandpa's sweet potatoes. The sweet potatoes were planted in ragged tires full of dirt. The oldest plants had big dark triangular leaves and little white and purple flowers. The foliage was dense, and my job was to reach under the leaves and pull up all the mushrooms that grew on the damp soil beneath. I also pulled up weeds and Bermuda grass and seedlings that kept creeping through. Pecan seedlings were the worst. Sometimes the little pecans that hatched them were a foot deep and clung for dear life.

On the porch was a shelf where Grandpa kept his sweet potato slips. Slips were little plants that came off the sweet potatoes. Back in March, Grandpa had sliced in half a nice oblong specimen of each sweet potato variety and suspended each half, via toothpicks, in a mason jar. Over time, when the little eyes started to sprout, the sprouts in the water turned into roots and the sprouts in the air turned into slips. When the slips were finger-length and had a few nice green and purple leaves, Grandpa would twist them off the sweet potato and stick them in their own little mason jar until they grew long white roots with little hairy parts. The hairy parts meant the slips were ready for planting, and we would roll out another tire from Grandpa's pyramid of stacked tires. He got the tires for free because tire shops had to pay to recycle them. The best tires for sweet potatoes were high-performance tires, Grandpa said, because the hub-cabs on sports cars were almost as big as the tires themselves, which left lots of room for soil. He had a couple Bridgestone Potenzas he prized in particular.

We filled the tires with dirt, topped the dirt with compost, then dug little holes for the slips. The key was to spread out the slip roots and lay them sideways so the sweet potatoes could grow downward along the surface of the soil. By the time I moved in there were two dozen tires already, and within weeks we added a dozen more. There were three varieties of sweet potato: Jewel, Georgia Jet, and the less commonplace O'Henry of North Carolina.

Third, we roamed the property to check the puma traps, hunt for hobo beds, and forage mushrooms. Grandpa had a little book he sometimes checked to make sure we didn't eat anything poisonous. One time we got a puffball big as the top of a skull. Grandpa fried it in slices.

The mushrooms were the reason we roamed, clearly, but always it was under the pretense of checking for pumas and hobos. As a kid I never questioned the routine, but now, seeing it with fresh eyes, something didn't add up. The puma traps were rusted open like they never clamped shut, and they looked pretty small to me, like coyote traps, and who in his right mind would trap a puma anyway? What would you do with a puma if you trapped it? The hobo beds were another matter. For all Grandpa's talk about hobos, we never saw a single bed.

I didn't say anything about it for a while. Grandpa had his reasons, I figured. But a few days later we started setting posts in Quikrete for the new fence. Setting posts was hard work. I had to stand still for a long time, holding each post, and the lye in the Quikrete burned the skin on my hands, which was abraded from the sand. I had never questioned the fence before, just assumed it was to keep out pumas and hobos, but now I was grumpy.

"Grandpa," I said, "why are we building this fence?"

"For the goats," he said.

Goddamn, I thought. First hobos, then pumas, now goats?

"What goats?" I asked.

Grandpa explained that to get an Ag exemption for a reduction in his property tax he had to raise something for profit. He was working on growing his sweet potato operation but until then he had to stick to goats.

I was confused. "Um, Grandpa, there aren't any goats."

"There were." He said this portentously, as though something terrible had happened, possibly involving pumas or vicious thieving hobos. I let the subject drop, annoyed, but I decided Grandpa might be a little crazy, and why not? All we did was work, eat, and sleep. We never left the house except to buy groceries and pick up Grandpa's books from the library. I started to worry I might go a little crazy too, if I didn't get out and do my own thing. Plus I was starting to feel guilty. I had explained the situation to Boss before I moved, and he seemed to understand, but weeks had passed. I worried I was letting him down.

I decided to tell Grandpa about my work at the dump. I had to spin the job as more official than it was so he wouldn't worry I was breaking-and-entering just to be there. To set the stage I told him about losing my jobs at the grocery store and Ms. Mikiska's and how a boy like me ("a good worker, as you know") just couldn't find decent work anymore. "So I got a job off the books," I said.

Grandpa eyed me. "Dealing dope?"

"What? No. Of course not."

Grandpa had extreme notions about the corrupting influence of cities, even little ones like Komer. But the extremity of dope-dealing worked in my favor, since scavenging the dump was minor by comparison.

"I never touch the stuff," I said, "and I don't approve of those who do. The job I mean is scavenging. There's lots of recyclables people miss that are worth good money. One week I made fifty bucks." That was a lie, but I could show Grandpa some cash and pretend it was from the dump. I wasn't ready to admit I worked for free almost, since admitting that might lead to an awkward conversation about my infiltration and yet-to-be-determined act of terror. Grandpa seemed confused so I laid it on thick: "I work with a crew of old-timers, not unlike yourself."

"Do I know 'em?"

"Probably not." I had to throw him a bone, to be convincing. "Um, there's this one named Leo who's pretty old, maybe fifty." Or a hundred, I was thinking. Leo looked like shit.

"Leo what?"

"I don't know his last name. I think it's Italian."

"Never trust an Italian."

"Sure, of course. But he's got skills. He fixes toasters and stuff, and scrapes stuff off cell phones."

"Rare earth metals?"

"I guess." I had no idea what Leo scraped out of those cell phones, but if rare earth metals, whatever they were, made it sound good to Grandpa, that was fine by me.

Grandpa went on a rant about how the Chinese had cornered the rare earth market and price-gouged Americans and also manipulated their currency, or something. It was pretty confusing. When he was done with the rant he said, "So, where does all this happen? A recycling facility? I have great respect for recycling and recyclers. I grow my sweet potatoes in recycled tires, as you know."

"That's right," I said. This was going quite well, in my estimation. "It happens at the dump."

Grandpa didn't say anything. He seemed confused.

"Komer doesn't have a recycling center," I explained. "We sort through the garbage at the dump and pull out the recyclables."

Still Grandpa didn't say anything. His expression was inscrutable.

"Yep," I said. "It's lifting those recyclables that gives me the strength to dig postholes, and the fortitude to work with you all day in the sun."

"The dump, you say?"

"Yeah, Bi-Cities," I said with perverse pride. Maybe people's admiration for the place, as the only growing business in town, had begun to rub off on me.

Grandpa spat in the dirt. "That goddamned Whitey Connors is trying to raise property taxes. He favors poor folks who don't own property, folks whose oversized broods filling up the schools is why we have to pay property tax in the first place. I hate that man. He's as crooked as his father."

"Donkey Dan?"

Grandpa nodded. I wanted to ask him about Donkey Dan and Whitey and how crooked they were, to fortify my resolve against Trash Mountain, but he had started in on a rant about the dump: how it was a haven for hobos, a cesspool, a den of iniquity, a charnel house. Half the things he said I couldn't understand. I wanted to tell him I spent lots of time there and never once saw a hobo, just my colleagues and the occasional unfeeling garbage man, but he was pretty worked up. I let it drop.

I decided I should probably avoid the subject of my work at the dump, so what I did was tell Grandpa I wanted to ride my bike to town and see some friends. He offered to drive me, but I told him I needed the exercise. He seemed suspicious.

"A man who has energy for exercise," he said, "isn't working hard enough."

"Sure," I said, "but I enjoy the scenery, the country roads and whatnot."

Grandpa nodded. He seemed to appreciate the sentiment.

The next morning I woke up before dawn and sat in the kitchen looking through the window until the sun peeked over the tops of the pecan trees beyond the clearing of Grandpa's big back yard. Then I got on my bike and headed for town. It took an hour almost, and when I got to the spot I had cut in the fence, it was gone. The fence was different. The whole shape of the dump seemed kind of different, like maybe it expanded. I biked around to the garbage truck gate. By the time I got there the trucks were long gone, but the fence was still open so I snuck inside like I used to and found my way to the clearing where Leo, Candy, and Boss had their operation.

The clearing was empty. The table and chairs were gone, the recyclables too. It was just flattened trash.

While I was standing there, confused, I heard some people speaking Spanish so I crouched down and hid. The Spanish speakers passed by, laughing. Bi-Cities people, no doubt. I wondered if their number had grown to the point that there wasn't any room for Leo and them to hide. If so, where had they gone to?

I lay on my back until the laughter dwindled. Beyond the low trash hills that encircled me loomed Trash Mountain, hazy in the distance. A black vulture was standing near the top, the shoulders of its wings hiked up to its burrowed head. Another vulture circled then came down beside it.

I climbed back onto the path and walked deeper into the dump, trying to maintain a mental map in case I had to run for cover again. There seemed to be more paths than before. I was way off to the left, on the Komer side, when I decided there was something different. It was like I was in a whole new part, familiar but strange, like a dream. The trash itself had a different quality: brighter and newer, the hills less settled. The fence was like that too. It was the same type of fence as before, but the mesh was darker and the tips of the razor wire were brighter in the sunlight.

"Psst!"

At the sound of the human voice I searched for a place to dive and bury myself in trash, but before I could make my next move I saw Boss. He was a ways up the path, crouched like he was hiding. He waved me towards him.

When I got close he raised his finger to his lips. He turned and walked, still crouching, and I followed him away from the path, over some well-worn trash, to a spot where his wheelbarrow was leaning against the fence.

"Welcome back!" Boss smiled and made conversation like nothing was different. When I asked what happened to Leo and Candy, he said they had a new hideout. He had worked on it for two whole weeks while Candy gathered trash for Leo, who had set up shop in a new spot each day. "We could have used ya," he said, and I felt bad.

"Sorry it's been so long," I said. "My Grandpa lives real far away."

"Why don't you stake out your own place?"

"Maybe I will," I said, though I wasn't sure what he meant by that.

Boss said he was on his way to the hideout, if I wanted to join him, then he righted his wheelbarrow and we set off along the fence. I knew without asking that he had cleared the path himself, to keep out of sight. I wondered why all the secrecy. Didn't Boss and the garbage men have an understanding?

I asked Boss why the fence looked different, and he said they had expanded the dump again. The part we were standing on was brand new. He described with amazement how one day they just dug up the fence and moved it. "All that was here before was a crumbly street, some tree stumps and a couple concrete slab foundations," he said, "so I guess there were houses here, years ago. But mostly it was just weeds."

I was disturbed. My old house had a concrete slab foundation. I pressed my face to the fence to see where we were, in terms of Komer, but the weave in the mesh was too tight. All I could see were tiny pinpricks of light. "Right here where we're standing?" I asked.

"Yep," he said. "They covered it in trash pretty quick. The trash is brand new so it's high-yield picking, is the good news. Bad news is there's way more people around."

We entered an older part of the dump, near the shitty woods, and came to a long flat hill of ancient looking trash. Beside the fence were stacks of different recyclables—cardboard, cans, bottles, the usual—and Boss started pulling stuff out of his wheelbarrow. I helped.

"This is the new spot?" I asked, kind of disappointed.

Boss laughed. "Out in the open like this? Hell no. In the new spot there isn't room for this cheap stuff, so I leave it out here."

When the only stuff left in the wheelbarrow was cell phones, remote controls and the like, Boss pushed the wheelbarrow about a hundred yards further along the fence, where he rested it. Then he got down on his knees and started pushing through trash like he was looking for something. What he was looking for, it turned out, was a roughhewn wooden hatch like the door to a cellar. He opened it just wide enough for me to creep through, which I did with some trepidation. The space it led to was dark and cold. Boss came down after me and wedged his wheelbarrow halfway in the door to keep it propped.

The propped door let in enough light that I could see we were in a tiny room reinforced by wood and sheet metal. Leo and Candy were sitting across from us, tinkering. A dim camping lantern hung between them. Boss started pulling stuff out of the wheelbarrow and piling it at Leo and Candy's feet. The ceiling was so low he had to sit down, but he could reach from the door to the table without moving, like he planned it that way.

"Hey there, sugar," Candy said without looking. "Like our new digs?"

"Seems pretty secret," I said.

"That's the idea."

Leo didn't look at me or say anything. But later, when I was help-ing Boss unload the wheelbarrow, I caught him giving me a dirty glance.

Back on the surface, making our rounds, Boss apologized for Leo. He said Leo was even more paranoid than before on account of being arrested.

"Leo got arrested?"

"For trespassing. Spent the night in jail." Boss said the unspoken agreement they used to have about collecting recyclables, to beat the inspectors, didn't seem to hold anymore. He didn't know why. "Thing is," he said, "I never see those Bi-Cities boys scavenging for bottles and such, but there'd be plenty to go round even if they did. This new trash is filthy with it." He pointed with his shoe at six brown beer bottles in a cardboard case, neat and tidy. "See what I mean?"

"Maybe they're after the rare earth," I said, testing Grandpa's theory.

"Maybe so," Boss said. "Leo tells me to keep the phones in my pockets in case I run into trouble, but my waders don't have pock-ets so I still put them in the wheelbarrow." Boss laughed. "Old Leo probably thought you was a spy sent by Whitey Connors to infiltrate our operation."

I laughed, to be congenial, but the name Whitey Connors was starting to make my blood boil. These were hard working people, the way I saw it, and Whitey Connors was stabbing them in the back. I wondered if I should tell Boss I was turning it around on Whitey Connors—that *I* was going to infiltrate *him*—but I decided to keep it secret.

Boss gathered electronics while I gathered the more obvious re-cyclables. Boss said he had my makeshift wheelbarrow in a secret place but that I shouldn't use it until I got a feel for how things had changed, since we had to be extra careful.

The wheelbarrow was almost full when Boss whispered "Shh!" and got low. He knocked the cheap recyclables off the wheelbarrow with a sweep of one long arm and started stuffing the cell-phones down the front of his waders. "Take cover," he whispered, and we scrambled over the nearest pile of trash. He started digging into the pile until he had made a sort of hollow for himself. I dug too, but my hollow was so close to his that by the time we slid into our respective hollows and started covering ourselves with trash, to hide, we were right next to each other. The smell of the trash wouldn't have been so bad—I was used to it by then—if it weren't for the reek of Boss's steamy breath. His breath was tinged with the sweet smell of decay, like the trash all around us had somehow contaminated his body.

Some men strolled past, speaking Spanish. One made a joke, I guess, because the others laughed like hell. I was afraid. I should have listened to Grandpa, I thought. I should have listened to Ruthanne. This was *serious trouble*. What we were doing was illegal now, if it hadn't been before. Leo had spent the night in jail for it. My heart was racing. I tried to control my breathing like Rick Zorn in *Detroit Ninja*, where some ninjas show him how they slow their heart-rates until they're legally dead, but I just couldn't do it. I wasn't a ninja, and I wasn't Rick Zorn. By the time those garbage men were out of earshot I was ready to burst. I clawed my way out of the trash Boss had piled on top of us and hunched over with my hands on my knees. I was almost crying. Boss leaned over me and said he was sorry. I said I was too. I said I had to go home.

I would have gone straight home, to Grandpa's, if I could have found my bike. I had left it in my old hiding place behind some bushes next to the gravel parking lot across the street from the dump, but it was gone. At first I was confused. I thought I must have left it somewhere else, by mistake. I looked behind all the bushes and all the trees until it dawned on me that my bike had been stolen. I couldn't believe it. It was a kid's bike! Sure I was sixteen, seventeen almost, but nobody would have known that by looking at the bike. What was the world coming to?

I considered calling Grandpa to explain and get a ride home, but I didn't have any money for a payphone and I didn't feel like going anywhere to ask to use a regular phone. I was angry. I was also hungry. I would have bought a sandwich except I didn't have any money, like I said. What an idiot I was.

The walk to Grandpa's took much longer than I expected, and was pretty awful. I was hungry from the start, and the two-lane highway was so narrow I had to jump out of it a couple times to avoid oncoming cars. By the time I got to Grandpa's it was well past nightfall.

Grandpa had the front light on and was waiting for me in the kitchen, which surprised me. I wasn't used to having anybody wait up for me. When I came through the door, he set down his book and lowered his reading glasses. He looked pissed.

"I called Bi-Cities," he said, "and no one named Leo is on the payroll."

"Huh," I said.

"Don't play dumb. There isn't any recycling program either."

"But I've been recycling. I swear."

"These people you work with, where do they sleep?"

"How should I know?"

"Don't talk back. Where do they sleep?"

I thought of the shelter Boss had dug. "I really don't know," I said. "Trailers, maybe?"

"How do they smell? Are their clothes clean?"

I wanted to say Boss smelled great and dressed like a banker, but I couldn't. I was tired of lying. I was upset, too, because I knew what Grandpa was getting at. I said, "Don't hobos, like, ride the rails and stuff?"

"Sometimes," Grandpa said, "but sometimes they stay put in one place for quite a while. The important part is they live by stealing. This so-called scavenging business is just stealing by another name."

"Leo had a deal with Whitey Connors."

"If he's dealing with Whitey Connors, then he got what he deserved. My God, boy, do you realize the danger you're in?"

"I'm not in danger."

"Not in danger, huh? Hobos use sodomy as initiation!"

"They aren't hobos!"

It was the first time we ever yelled at each other. Mom said Grandpa used to yell at lot when she was a kid but that he mellowed with
age, so I guess I caught a glimpse of the old Grandpa, before he was
Grandpa and was just a mean dad. I didn't like it. I felt sorry, though.
I had stayed out late and made him worry.

He seemed sorry too. He offered me dinner, and I accepted.

After a dinner of beans and white bread we sat by the windows
in the kitchen. That's where Grandpa kept his recliner, along with a
scratchy old chair he had dragged over from the seldom-used living
room when I first moved in. The windows faced the screened-in back
porch, but it was hard to see much through the screens.

After a bourbon and soda Grandpa said, "In the Army, to train
the medics, they had us do trachs on goats."

"What's a trach?" I asked.

"A tracheotomy. It's where when somebody's choking you stick a
pen or a straw into their necks."

"The goats were choking?"

"No." He got quiet, remembering. "It was just for practice."

I was shocked. "You practiced on goats? Live goats?"

Grandpa nodded.

"Did they die? The goats?"

"Yeah, but we could do few on each goat before it ran out of room
on its throat or bled to death."

It took me a while to notice Grandpa was crying, and when I did
I tried to pretend I didn't. But he knew I noticed, and he said he was
sorry. I wanted to tell him he didn't have to be sorry, but by then he
was telling me how by crying for the goats he was actually crying for
the men who died. But also for the goats. It was confusing.

"I have to keep up the fence for appearances," Grandpa said, "to make it look like I'm still raising them, to keep my Ag exemption."

I had lots of questions. Like why had the Army taken Grandpa's goats? Or were those different goats? Were there two sets of goats? But it would be better to change the subject, I decided, and seeing Grandpa cry made me feel like I could open up to him about my own life. But I didn't want to talk about Mom and Dad or Ruth-anne, and it was too soon to open up about my secret inner feelings on the subject of Trash Mountain, so I ended up just sort of sitting there until Grandpa started in on his story about the time he found a hobo bed in the converted garage ("A hobo bed atop an actual bed—whoever heard of such a thing!") so he had stripped the blanket and sheets and burned it all in the back yard as a warning to the hobos. He sat back and crossed his arms, like thinking of the burning still gave him a satisfied feeling, years later. But burning perfectly good sheets seemed pretty stupid to me. Probably those hobos, if they even existed, just needed a place to sleep and figured he wouldn't notice. He never used that part of the house. In fact, he used so little of the house except his bedroom and the kitchen that a whole squadron of hobos might have been living there as we spoke, which was creepy to think about so I didn't say it. Anyway, the whole thing made me wish Grandpa could get an Ag exemption for hobos instead of goats.

Chapter 10

HARD AS GRANDPA and I worked outside digging postholes and what-not, rainy days inside were worse. We just sat in the kitchen in our respective chairs, swatting mosquitoes and reading. Grandpa didn't have cable, but he had a VCR and fourteen VHS tapes, mostly erotic thrillers. The best was one called *Taxi Dancers*, where a gangster try-ing to turn his life around teams up with some strippers against an Asian street gang called the Yellow Dragons. There's decent motorcy-cle action, and the Yellow Dragons are pretty fierce pool cue fighters.

When I got through all the VHS tapes, I had no choice but to read. The only book I brought was *The Highest Mountain* by Bob Bilger, so I started reading it again. I skipped the childhood parts and went straight to the climbing parts. But Mount Everest got me thinking about Trash Mountain and about the fear I had felt while lying there with Boss as the workers passed by. I was a pretty half-assed adventurer, it seemed to me. Climbing Everest with your Sherpa buddy and a Betamax camcorder was pretty much the op-posite of sitting in your Grandpa's kitchen.

Grandpa, who read mostly historical fiction and presidential biographies, told me he tried to read *The Highest Mountain* but couldn't get through it.

I was shocked. Who couldn't get through *The Highest Mountain*?

"The man's a windbag," Grandpa said.

"Maybe," I said, "but he's also a great adventurer."

"Adventure is overrated." Grandpa went into his usual rigmarole about how adventure and warfare were closely related, the result of man's restless nature. He had no use for either. "And anybody who saw action in Vietnam," Grandpa added, "wouldn't glorify it."

"He barely even mentions Vietnam," I said, and I showed Grandpa in the book how it skipped from Bob Bilger's teenage years in Haislip to his disillusioning young adulthood on the streets of San Francisco.

"Maybe you're right," Grandpa said, "but I still think the book's for shit."

"Got another I can read?"

Grandpa looked at the stack of library books on the kitchen table and pursed his lips like he was thinking, but he didn't say anything.

A few days later we drove into town to buy groceries (cornflakes, white bread, onions, and a five-pound bag of dried pinto beans) and afterward we stopped at the library. The Komer/Haislip branch "didn't have books for shit," according to Grandpa, so he ordered them from the city through a loan service and picked them up once a month. This time there were more books for him to pickup than usual, and he sorted through them at the counter. I thought it was to make sure they gave him all the books he ordered, but then he handed half the books to me.

"These are some *real* books," he said, and I thought he meant "real man" books, or something like that, until I saw that half the titles had girls' names in them. I thanked him, though. It was the thought that counted.

I tried to put off reading the books, but it kept raining and raining and I had seen all the VHS tapes and finished *The Highest Mountain* so I had no choice. I started with the book that looked most like an adventure. It had a jungle on the cover. It was about an explorer named Henry Morton Stanley who navigated the Congo River and was the first white man ever to do so. The book started off pretty good, but the guy Stanley turned out to be a psycho. He was obsessed with gold and treated the Africans real bad. The ones he didn't work to death got sold as slaves. I told Grandpa about it and he nodded. "How's that for adventure," he said.

The next book I read was about some farmers in Nebraska. One of them was a girl who reminded me of Ruthanne, except she was way more useful on a farm than Ruthanne would have been. She saw a guy get sucked into a thresher and killed. Another guy ate a dozen melons in one sitting, like a sumo wrestler. The book was okay until the kids got older and moved to town and it got boring.

The next book I picked up was definitely for girls, though. It was about an orphan girl someplace in Canada who got adopted by a grumpy old brother-and-sister combo. The girl was a smartass and kept getting into trouble. Grandpa seemed to take a particular interest in that book so I wondered if the little orphan girl reminded him of me, which was embarrassing, but later he said it was Mom's favorite.

"But Mom doesn't read," I said.

"She used to," he said.

Even after the rain stopped, we spent more time indoors than we did before. At first I thought it was because Grandpa wanted me to read all those books, but his interest in them seemed to dwindle. More often than not he'd be in his recliner sleeping, not reading. I was worried he was starting one of his spells. I didn't know how seriously to take it. All I knew was it made things even more boring. I didn't dare sneak out to the dump again, but I did think it within my rights to visit Komer. Lucky for me, whatever made Grandpa sleep all the time also made him more pliable. When I worked up the nerve to ask if I could go into town on my own he said, "Sure. While you're down there pick up those candies I like."

"No problem," I said. He meant these coffee beans with chocolate on them that were sold at the drugstore. They were disgusting. "But, um, can you drive me?"

"Take the truck," he said.

"For real?"

"It'll take more than the likes of you to bust that old truck."

"But I don't know how to drive."

"I'll teach you."

"Don't I have to take a class from the city?"

"Nonsense."

"I think I have to take a class to get a license."

"Who said anything about a license? Mine expired six years ago." Grandpa explained how the Komer police had better things to do than to hassle good drivers, such as busting up dope rings and rustling hobos and illegals. He said the trick was to go five miles over the speed limit at all times.

"Wouldn't it be smarter to stay *under* the speed limit?"

"Everybody breaks it by at least five. Driving the speed limit is conspicuous, like you're driving dope up from Mexico, or human cargo for white slavery."

"What's white slavery?"

"Slavery of a sexual nature fueled by dope."

Learning to drive was pretty easy. Grandpa was a patient teacher. So patient I started to wonder if he was having a stroke or something. He stared out the window and breathed real slow, like a ninja. He didn't even mind when I backed the truck into one of the fence posts we dug. He said that was what bumpers were for.

We practiced in the driveway and then on the little road his house was on. There were barely any cars, but one time a truck got behind us and wouldn't go away until Grandpa reached over and pounded the horn with his fist until the truck pulled around. The driver scowled at us. The curving two-lane road was pretty blind.

Grandpa's truck was a 1991 Chevy Silverado with paint peeling off the hood, and it handled like a pontoon boat. I wouldn't have minded except I had a hard time telling where the perimeter of the car was. I stuck so close to the double yellow lines, from fear of veer-

ing off the road, that Grandpa sometimes tugged the steering wheel
in his direction.

We cruised up and down the narrow road, going faster and faster,
until eventually I was going five miles over the speed limit. Grandpa
told me to keep going instead of turning around. We came to a four-
lane highway, and he told me to stop.

"This is where you turn to get to town," Grandpa said, and that
was that. I was ready to drive.

Now that I could go to town on my own, I wasn't sure what to
do. I couldn't go to the dump again in case Grandpa smelled it on me
and flipped out. The dump would have to wait until school started,
when I'd have proper cover and could shower at the gym. I considered cruising around but decided it wouldn't be as fun as cruising on
my bike, because I'd be so nervous. I decided to call Pete.

Pete was glad to hear from me, which made me feel good. He said
he was bored and wanted to hang out, but that he didn't have a car so
we'd have to hang out in the woods behind his sister's trailer, where
there wasn't anything to do but smoke weed and shoot guns, and he
didn't have any guns. When I told Pete I could pick him up, he was
pumped. "It's on now, motherfucker," he said.

Pete's sister's trailer park was terrible. There wasn't the pride of
ownership one sometimes sees in trailer parks, with little flower beds
and trellises under the trailers and people sitting on lawn chairs and
grilling burgers. Half the trailers looked like they were sinking in
the mud. The only person I saw was an old man sitting in a rusty
chair on the porch of a whompyjawed farmhouse near the entrance.
The house was terrible, too. A couple windows were broken, and the
white paint looked like somebody had taken a sander to it.

Pete's sister's trailer was powder blue with a half-decent, makeshift porch. Pete shot out the front door before I could even park
the truck. He climbed into the passenger's seat and we bumped fists.
"Dang, dog," he said, "this is sweet." He started pressing buttons on
the radio and raising and lowering the window.

When we drove out of the trailer park, the old man on the porch was glaring at us. Pete said the trailer park used to be the old guy's farm, but he got too old to take care of it so he rented it for trailers. "He hates Mexicans," Pete said, "and forget about blacks—he won't even rent to the fuckers."

"What a motherfucker," I said.

Pete wanted to drive out to the old shooting range so that's what we did.

There were more cars in the field than I remembered, which didn't surprise me, since everything was turning to trash, and the Whitey Connors billboard said CONNORS FOR STATE TREASURER instead of for Comptroller. Unbelievable, I thought. Wasn't Comptroller enough?

Pete raised an invisible rifle to his shoulder and aimed it at Whitey Connors, squinting. "*Pew!*" he said, like a cartoon gun. "*Pew, pew, pew!*"

When Pete was done shooting we sat on the hood of a LeBaron convertible and Pete took out a cigarette pack that was empty except for a half-smoked joint, which he lit. He sucked on the joint for a while then passed it to me. I took a tiny hit, to be chill, but the weed was so strong I felt lightheaded immediately.

"That's Milk Dog's shit," Pete said, laughing. He took back the joint and sucked on it until it was so tiny he had to hold it between two long fingernails. He flicked it away and started talking about his sister and Milk Dog. He said they didn't show him any respect. "Ever since Milk Dog got a job with the cable company he thinks he's a big man," Pete said, "king of the castle. Yesterday he told me to get him a beer. Can you believe that shit? There I was, minding my own business, and he was like, 'Yo, Pete, get me a beer!'"

"Did you do it?"

"Hell yeah. Milk Dog's scary as hell." Pete said they treated him like a second class citizen even though he took better care of their kids than they did. "Milk Dog's always working, and Angie's always doing stupid shit with her girlfriends."

The thought of being in such close quarters with a drug dealer like Milk Dog, even a family man drug dealer, made me uncomfortable. But Pete never mentioned illegal activity. His complaints seemed pretty typical, the same kind of stuff I might have said about Ruthanne and Mom.

Abruptly Pete said, "Yo, dog, let's look through these glove boxes," and we stopped talking and started searching the glove boxes and center consoles of cars. The cars had been picked over for valuables, but a Toyota still had its owner's manual and a little kit with a tire gauge and a pen light.

"This is real leather," Pete said, stroking the kit with the backs of two fingers. He inspected the manual. "1999 Toyota Camry LE. Think we could sell this online?"

"Maybe."

"You got internet?"

"No. My Grandpa doesn't even have cable."

Pete let the kit drop to the ground, stunned. "You gotta get out of there."

"I don't know. I kind of like it. My Grandpa's acting weird, though." I tried to describe to Pete how Grandpa had changed: the sleeping, the lack of emotion. "I backed into a fence post and he didn't even care."

"Sounds like he's depressed," Pete said.

"No way," I said, but the idea troubled me. Were spells the same thing as depression? I remembered the pills in Mom's bedside table, the ones that weren't for diabetes. Mom slept all the time, too.

"He should see a doctor," Pete said, "so he doesn't kill himself or whatever."

"What?"

"Like Tom Talamantez."

"The weatherman? He killed himself?"

Pete nodded. "Hung himself, dog."

I pictured Tom Talamantez, the handsome smiling weatherman of my childhood, gesticulating in front of a cartoon map of Komer and Haislip while co-anchors Jasmyn Jones and Jerry Tidmore watched with feigned interest. The image was extra lucid from the weed I smoked. It was almost too much to bear. I thought about Grandpa. I pictured him hanging from the rafters of the living room like that old guy in the prison movie who got out of prison and hated it so much that he hung himself in a shitty halfway house.

"If he does it," Pete said, "you can crash with us."

"Thanks," I said, but I wanted to change the subject, to get those images out of my head.

Thankfully Pete was a frequent changer of subjects. He was already talking about a girl in the trailer two down from his who had unusual boobs. Then he said, "Yo, you seen Ronnie?"

"No," I said, and I felt kind of bad about that.

"Me and Red Dog got so drunk last weekend. Shit, dog, we called Ronnie all drunk and shit and Ronnie was like, 'Fuck y'all.' It's like he forgot who his boys are. He got all prude."

I nodded, but the word "prude" didn't ring true. I thought of how Ronnie had been stalking the seedy parking lot across from my old apartment, and his weird flaming skull Jesus tattoo. I didn't want to talk about Ronnie anymore, and I didn't want to talk about Grandpa or Ruthanne or any of the rest of it. I told Pete we should go home. I was tired.

The weed made the truck feel like a flying saucer, which wasn't something I was prepared for. Red Dog had smoked and driven all the time, sometimes intentionally. Pete asked why I was driving so slow, and I told him.

"If you go too slow they'll pull you over," he said, echoing what Grandpa told me about the Komer cops. I had to pick up speed. But we were already going so fast!

By the time we got to Pete's trailer I was freaking out. There was no way I could drive the ten miles back to Grandpa's house on country roads. It was starting to get dark.

Pete said I could crash with him. I didn't think Grandpa would mind, but I had to call and tell him so he wouldn't worry. But I sounded so high. I was sure he'd be able to tell I was fucked up. I started practicing aloud what I'd say to him: "Hey Grandpa, it's Ben. It got kind of late, and I don't really feel comfortable driving at night yet—how does that sound?" I was asking Pete, who thought I was crazy. He said I sounded perfectly normal. So I practiced my lines a few more times then called Grandpa on Pete's cell phone.

Grandpa didn't pick up, which surprised me. It was seven. Dinner time. Was he out in the garden? Was he already asleep? It was possible. I wished I were home to check, though, to make sure he wasn't hanging like Tom Talamantez.

I left a message that I was sure sounded nervous, like I was about to rob a liquor store.

Pete and I watched TV with his sister, Angie, until Pete heard a car in the driveway and stood up. I followed him into the tiny second bedroom where he slept on the top bunk of a bunk bed and the older of his two nieces, Gabby, slept on the bottom. Gabby was five but spent half the time at her grandma's, Pete said. Pete suspected this was because of him. The grandma, Milk Dog's mom, didn't trust him, even though it was Milk Dog, not Pete, Pete said, who "deals drugs and looks like a fucking cholo."

We sat on the bottom bunk talking—Pete was *always* talking!— and I tried to listen, but when the front door opened and closed I got scared. The Milk Dog of my imagination was massive and violent and hated white kids. I pictured him poking his head into the bedroom, seeing me, and throwing me headlong through the window.

The trailer felt like it sank a little as Milk Dog plopped down on the couch. I could hear him speaking Spanish. His voice was deep and lethargic. He started changing TV channels in rapid succession, and Angie complained in a mixture of Spanish and English that Milk Dog changed the channels too fast to tell what was happening in the shows.

Pete wanted to smoke again, but I told him I couldn't. I said I didn't want to be foggy with Grandpa the next morning, but really I just didn't want to freak out about Milk Dog any more than I already was. I wished I were in Dinwiddie's room, where I could turn off the bedside lamp and have peace and quiet and eight hours' sleep. Who cared about a few mosquito bites?

Pete told me I could sleep in Gabby's bed. I was tired and thankful for a place to sleep, but the bed had three teddy bears on it, and a stuffed unicorn. The sheets had cartoon princesses and wizards and talking donkeys. It felt weird to be sleeping in a kid's bed. Taking off my pants made it extra weird.

Pete turned off the lights, but I couldn't fall asleep. The TV was still on so I kept thinking about Milk Dog out there. What if he stumbled into the room looking for his daughter, whom he loved, and found a skinny teenaged boy in his underwear between her sheets? I wouldn't have time to scream before he twisted off my head.

I may have fallen asleep at some point, but I woke up soon thereafter. I had to pee. The bathroom was in the main part of the trailer, and I was afraid to go out there. The TV was still blaring. I almost peed out the window, but what if Milk Dog was out there smoking and saw the window slide open and a little white penis come out? I had to hold it in. I fell asleep again but kept dreaming about peeing then waking up worried I had peed all over Gabby's princess sheets.

The alarm on my watch went off at six. Pete was sound asleep, breathing heavily, but the TV was still on in the next room. I couldn't believe it!

I slid my shorts back on, feeling dirty for having taken them off in the first place, then crept into the living room. There, on the couch, was a fat man in khaki pants and an unbuttoned Bi-Star Cable shirt. A little patch on the right breast pocket said "Artemio." Was that

Milk Dog's real name? It seemed kind of dorky. The shirt must have belonged to somebody else, I decided, somebody who owed Milk Dog money, or a snitch he killed to warn other snitches. Milk Dog had a bag of corn chips open on his chest. I couldn't see any tattoos but there was a white tank-top undershirt over his torso and I was sure that under the tank-top was a big florid cross or maybe THUG LIFE in an Olde English font. Milk Dog's head was propped up against the couch arm closest to me so I couldn't see his eyes, but from the way his arm was flopped out, his meaty fingers resting on the carpet, I could tell he was asleep. I crept across the room as quietly as possible, and when I got through the door I shut it behind me and sped towards Grandpa's truck.

On the way out of the trailer park the old man was still on his porch. He glared at me, as if in warning.

I wasn't high anymore, but the drive was still tough. I was tired. When I got home I expected to find Grandpa in the kitchen, but he wasn't there. He wasn't in his bedroom either. I got nervous, remembering my conversation with Pete about Tom Talamantez and the old man in the halfway house. I walked around the house calling Grandpa's name, but I couldn't find him. Walking and hollering wore me out so I thought I might close my eyes for a minute. Maybe he'd be back when I woke up. When I went upstairs, I saw that the door to Mom's old bedroom was closed. I put my ear to the door and listened. I didn't hear anything.

"Grandpa?" I whispered.

If he was in there he didn't say anything, so I pushed open the door to take a look. The heavy curtains were drawn so the room was almost dark. The air was warm and smelled like cooked onions. Grandpa was curled in a fetal position on top of the covers of Mom's old bed. I got close enough to tell he was breathing, then went across the hall to Dinwiddie's room and took a nap myself. When I woke up, hours later, Grandpa was in the kitchen. He had a dazed look and seemed surprised to see me.

"I'll put more beans on," he said.

He did, and we ate some beans, but we didn't talk as much as usual. When we were done with our beans Grandpa said, "Well, I think I'll turn in early. Had a big day. You alright out here, partner?"

I said I was.

Grandpa piled the dishes in the sink without washing them and went to his bedroom. It was four o'clock in the afternoon.

I sat in Grandpa's recliner and tried to read for a while, but I ended up just staring out the window. The way the screens around the back porch blocked the sun made it seem like dusk. It always seemed like dusk in Grandpa's house, perpetual dusk, like winter in Alaska. Without Grandpa puttering, the house was so quiet, the soft light so creepy, that I could imagine the house to be a sort of abandoned hunting chalet deep in the forest. There was so much wood everywhere. The chair frames were wood. The walls had wood paneling. The floor was made of wood, and the floor wood was so old that there were little gaps between the planks. In the gaps the wood was flaking and looked like dirt. It made me think the house was crumbling, sinking slowly but irreversibly into the muddy ground, like those trailers. Like trash. Everything was becoming trash. It made me wonder how long the un-trash, like Grandpa and me, could hold out.

After two more days of Grandpa mostly sleeping and acting surprised whenever he saw me, I called Mom to ask her what to do.

"Sounds like one of his spells," she said. "It'll pass."

"I don't think he's eating enough."

"He's an old man. They don't barely eat."

"Usually he does, though."

"Oh, Ben, you're such a nervous nelly. Let me talk to him."

"He's asleep."

"Wake him up then."

"Isn't that rude?"

"Well, Ben, I don't know what to tell you. You wanted to live with Grandpa even though I told you how he is. He feeds you, don't he?"

"Yeah, but I don't know. It's kind of lonely here, Mom."

"Oh, Ben!" I could picture her clutching the phone to her breast like she did. It made me happy. The thing is, I didn't really feel too lonely, but I knew that saying it would make Mom treat me the way I wanted to be treated right then, which was with pity. I was a lone wolf, but I wanted someone to feel sorry for me. Mom said, "We been meaning to get down there and visit you, but Ruthanne's so busy with school, and—"

"I understand."

"Why don't you come up here? You got bus fare?"

"Yeah but I got work."

"That's right! I'm so proud of you, Ben. Ruthanne and I are always talking about how you got that good job at Bi-Cities, and for a boy your age." Mom seemed to have come around to my work, maybe thanks to Ruthanne, who could spin anything. Mom said, "That's the only business in town with any future. Everybody knows it. Why, you might end up the next Whitey Connors."

I was shocked to hear her say such a thing. Whitey Connors was a scoundrel and a gangster. He double-dealt with honest contractors like Leo. He raised the property taxes of hardworking retirees like Grandpa.

"Well," she said, "try to get up here before school starts. We'd love to see you, and you should see the pretty little apartment we got. There's a duck pond!"

Chapter 11

BY THE TIME junior year started I was sleeping at Pete's a few nights a week. It started off gradual, out of laziness more than anything. It was easy because Milk Dog and Angie spent half their time at Milk Dog's parents' house with their kids. Pete and I mostly smoked pot and played video games. There was a soccer game Pete liked but I hated (I didn't know anything about sports), and a game where we played a small-time drug dealer who had to work his way up by selling increasingly high-end drugs and robbing other dealers, but one time we accidentally played it in front of the kids so Angie made us stop. My favorite was an adventure game where we were an elf lord who got ritually sacrificed by dark magi but, unbeknownst to the magi, entered their magical netherworld in wraith form and had to infiltrate it by marshaling an army in secret and mastering dark magic to take revenge on the dark magi. We never got to the revenge part, though. The game was pretty hard, plus we were high.

When Milk Dog *was* around, he mostly ignored me. He seemed to make a point of speaking only Spanish to Pete and Angie when I was there. I thought he was talking bad about me, but Pete said Milk Dog thought I was homeless and felt sorry for me. I was okay with that. I barely saw him, like I said. But one day I drove up and Milk Dog was sitting shirtless on the makeshift porch. He didn't have a THUG LIFE tattoo like I expected. There were stretch marks on either side of his big fat belly. He was drinking a canned beer, which looked like a C-battery in his giant hand. I said hello and expected him just to nod, but he said, "What up, kid."

"What up," I said softly. I wanted to go inside, but Milk Dog's big body was blocking the way.

"Listen," he said, "I don't know if you and Pete be fuckin' or what, but I wish you'd rub off on Pete some."

I laughed uncomfortably.

"I saw them chips you bought." Milk Dog was referring to a night when Pete and I had finished a bag of chips. We were high and not really thinking straight, but I had seen Milk Dog eating those chips so I made a point of buying a replacement bag. It hadn't seemed like a big deal to me at the time. "You wash dishes and shit," Milk Dog continued. "You gotta teach that boy some *respect*, know what I'm saying?"

"I'll try," I said. "Thank you."

"For what?"

"The compliment."

"Wasn't a compliment, just a statement of fact. You bought chips. You wash dishes."

"Well, it's my pleasure."

Milk Dog laughed, which sounded like the word "humph!"

I tried to laugh too, but it came out so wretchedly meek that Milk Dog stopped laughing, like I made him lose his taste for it. He said, "Since you're sleeping in my little girl's bed half the time, it's the least you can do, right?"

"Yes. Definitely. Thanks for everything. You and Angie have been really generous."

"Humph!"

Milk Dog drained the last of his beer and crushed the can in his hand, but he didn't get up. I had no idea where the conversation was going. Thankfully one of Milk Dog's sullen friends pulled up in a noisy car, and I was able to make my escape.

From that point on I went out of my way to wash dishes and buy groceries. Mostly I bought snacks for Milk Dog and us, but I made a point of incorporating healthy snacks like these chips that looked like french fries but were made of vegetables. Milk Dog never touched them, but Angie did. She said they tasted good but gave her gas.

Helping out like that made me feel more welcome, but there was still the issue of Pete. How was I supposed to rub off on him?

School started that Monday, and I knew without asking that Pete had no intention of going. I couldn't blame him. He had missed so much time during his suspension that he failed a bunch of classes and was supposed to do them over. That was too much even for a laidback guy like Pete. He didn't want to have to sit there zoning out all day while teachers told him stuff he already heard, talked about books he already read or pretended to read. I had been meaning to get back to work at the dump but decided the dump could wait. I would set an example for Pete by getting to school on time and staying the whole day without even ducking out during lunch.

Sunday night I told Pete I would drive him to school the next day in Grandpa's truck. He seemed confused. "No thanks, dog," he said.

"Then how you gonna get to school?" I asked.

He shrugged.

"We're turning over a new leaf," I said. I was trying to sound serious and thoughtful. "We're getting us an education by any means necessary."

"By means of, like, showing up?"

"That and more. By paying attention. By doing work sometimes."

"Whatever."

Pete complained the whole way, but he did let me take him to school. And while I can't speak for Pete, I can say I paid better attention than I had in a long time. Part of it was all the sleep I was getting by not going to the dump in the morning. I felt laser-eyed, like I was dipping tobacco all day. I even talked sometimes. Principal Winthrope said hello to me in the hall.

The first week went well. We made it to school on time every day except Wednesday, when one of Angie's friends blocked the truck with her car so we had to take the bus. Pete and I even did homework while watching TV. Milk Dog made fun of us, but I could tell he approved.

On Friday I dropped off Pete then headed to Grandpa's for Labor Day weekend.

Grandpa seemed to be doing better. He asked me what I was studying, and I told him English, geometry, chemistry, parenting and paternity awareness, and US history. He asked if I learned about the Boston Tea Party, but I hadn't. We were still on pilgrim times.

We talked about school while brushing wood seal on the fence and porch. Grandpa said he wished he'd had my help during the week, with the power washing, but he understood school was important. He said he didn't mind me sleeping over at my friend's house during the week, to be closer to school, but he wanted me home weekends. I said that was fine by me.

On Labor Day proper Grandpa grilled a dozen hotdogs and we ate them with sweet potato fries. I didn't know I could eat so many hotdogs, but Grandpa said he wasn't surprised. He said a man in Japan one time ate fifty.

The next week at school went as well as the first, and I started feeling guilty. I guess I felt like school was only going well because I had sacrificed this other part of my life, the dump part, and what about my secret infiltration? And what about Boss? Boss didn't have the luxury of hiding out in school all day, or of wasting time getting high and playing video games.

One day after school I drove out to the dump, parked across the street from where the garbage trucks came and went, and slipped inside. I didn't see any garbage men so I crept along the fence to the spot where I usually found Boss. He wasn't there. I waited a while then walked along the other side of the hills that lined the big path we took, but I didn't find him there either. I thought about the last time we were there, how we hid in trash dugouts as the garbage men passed by, how my heart had been racing. I got nervous. The dump was so quiet. The only sound was the fluttering of garbage bags where the wind blew high across Trash Mountain. Not even the buzzards were circling.

I decided to check the bunker. I didn't like the idea of going in there without Boss, in case Leo was in a bad mood, but I had no choice, was the way I saw it. Maybe Leo and Candy would help me look for Boss, or would tell me he had been arrested.

I cleared the trash off the rough wooden door and knocked. No response.

I knocked again, waited a while, then pulled the door open a crack and saw it was dark down there. "Candy?" I whispered. "Leo?"

No response.

I swung the door all the way open so the room was partly lit by the low afternoon sun. I walked inside.

The room was empty. There was a toaster sitting on the table with its metal shell off to the side like the shell of a turtle about to be cooked. There was an open can of beans, half full.

With a feeling of dread I crept back out of the bunker and looked around me at the quiet landfill. What had been eerie turned sinister. I decided to leave.

The next day, I set my alarm early and headed back to the dump. I tried to keep a positive attitude as I drove. The day before had been a blip, I told myself, a sort of holiday they took off sometimes, or maybe a family emergency. Everybody had families, didn't they? Friends? Fellow scavengers?

But the dump was still empty. There weren't even garbage men. It was like a nuclear bomb had gone off and this was the forbidden blast zone with KEEP OUT signs. I walked around the features I knew by heart, not only Trash Mountain but the ancillary peaks I thought of as Lhotse and the South Col. The biggest shapes were much as I remembered them, but here and there were little gullies where trash had been dug away and compacted into cubes, stacked two and three high in a way that made them look like Aztec temples.

My search for Boss led me all the way over to the Haislip side, to the big metal hangar where I'd met him the first time. The excavator was parked inside with its scoop slumped down like the head of a sleeping dinosaur.

Since nobody was around, I climbed the fence and hefted myself onto the corrugated tin roof of the hangar. The sun was up so I could see all of Haislip stretched out before me, from Demarcus's house and the other little white houses scattered country-style, facing any which way, to the big Victorian rooming houses of Grande Esplanade. From far away those houses still looked like the mansions they had been. Beyond them was a little park. Though I couldn't see it through the tops of the pecan trees and scraggly live oaks, I knew that in the middle of the park stood a peg-legged statue of Colonel Llewellyn Haislip, the wizardy looking Civil War guy who built a toll bridge over the Ocmoolga River.

I walked across the slanted roof and lowered myself down to the rim of the dumpster behind it. I was close to the forest that went along the back side of the dump, and I decided to search it. I hadn't been through those shitty woods since the day I met Demarcus, years before—before we attacked Trash Mountain with Molotov cocktails—but I remembered the wadded up clothes, the empty vodka bottle, the crazed hobo of my imagination. There were still rumors of people sleeping back there.

The forest wasn't as dark as I remembered. Enough light came through the scrubby trees that I could see baby kudzu and all kinds of weeds on the ground, and little pink and blue mulberries. Mulberries were trash trees from China, Grandpa said, and he pulled them whenever he saw them. Whoever owned this patch of forest didn't take care of it, that was for sure. Probably the county, or Whitey Connors. That scoundrel Connors might have been using his power as Comptroller to let the forest to fall into disrepair so he could get it for a low price, bulldoze the trees, and fill the forest with trash. Just the thought of it made me spit.

As I wandered deeper into the trees, I tried to keep my bearings by way of the sun. I saw a dirty wadded up blanket or towel beside a sort of homemade dugout like war trench. There wasn't any food or empty bottles so it may have been old. I channeled my inner Ocmoolga Indian the way Grandpa showed me, by looking for crushed up leaves on the ground and tiny broken branches on trees. Grandpa had insisted Ocmoolgas were superior to ninjas, over my objection, because they could see in the dark and smell danger. I could do neither, so I was pretty much stumbling around looking for more hobo beds but afraid to call out because I didn't know what to do if I met an actual hobo. Though I disagreed with Grandpa on the predatory nature of hobos, his scary stories were swirling in my head.

I was beginning to lose hope when I spotted something bright blue in the distance. Closer, I saw it was a blue plastic tarp like they wrap around burned up houses to keep out kids and dogs. It was spread out and tied to tree trunks like a sort of picnic shelter, with blankets and coolers and cardboard boxes underneath. I didn't want to sneak up on anybody so I said, "Hello? Is anybody home?"

Nobody answered, so I crept towards the encampment and got a better look at what was under the tarp: big backpacks like explorers have, and boxes full of neatly stacked food. Maybe whoever lived there was on a long camping trip, I thought. The idea that it was campers, not hobos, gave me some comfort.

I wandered the forest for the better part of the afternoon, looking for whoever lived in that camp, in case it was where Boss and them lived (they could have done worse), but I didn't find a soul. I got all the way out to the tire shops that lined the road. Some were closed, and one had been torn down to make room for a strip mall with a pizza restaurant. I almost bought their cheap-ass pizza, I was so hungry.

I might have been halfway to Grandpa's house by that point, but I didn't feel like going there. I didn't feel like going to Pete's, either.

I wouldn't be able to sleep until I knew what happened. I remembered, dimly, what Boss had said about getting loaded into a van and
dropped outside of town. Like a goddamned raccoon, he had said. It
was abduction, I thought, like what aliens do, only instead of aliens it
was Whitey Connors and his secret crew. My mind was racing. One
time I saw an unsolved mystery on TV where a guy said he was made
to procreate with an alien woman on and off for twenty years. It was
rape, pretty much.

I turned around and headed back the way I came. I would make
one more pass, I decided, and I was glad I did.

When I got to the blue tarp there was a man beside it with a pretty black dog on a leash. The dog was the first one who saw me, but it
didn't bark; it just raised its front paws up and down like it wanted to
jump but knew it shouldn't. The man had his hands in a washbasin.
He was shirtless and had a hairy chest with tattoos on it. I thought
he was old because he had a big beard, but when he looked up at me,
he had a young face. He had dreadlocks like a black guy, but he was
white. He tilted his head, like he was surprised to see me, then he
smiled and said hello. I was nervous, but I said hello back to him.

"I'm Jon," he said, "but my friends call me J Star. This is Jericho."
He held his hand, palm up, towards the black dog. The black dog,
Jericho, rested its paw on his hand like an old lady about to be walked
across the road. It was a pretty cool trick.

I tried to think up a nickname for myself, but I couldn't do it fast
enough so I told him my name was Ben.

"Son of the south," he said.

"How do you mean?" I asked.

"Ben Jamin means *son of Jamin*, and Jamin means *right hand*,
which in eastern-oriented cultures means *south*."

I was impressed. "How did you know all that?"

"It's Hebrew. I'm Jewish."

"For real?" I had never met a real Jew before. I wondered where his
little hat was, and if he knew the Old Testament by heart.

"Well, I used to be," he said. "I don't really practice anymore."

"Is this where you live?" I asked.

"Sometimes," he said.

"Do you have, like, neighbors and stuff?"

"Sure. I live here with some other folks. And some others live down the way. People are always coming and going through these woods."

J Star had a friendly face and a warm voice, which was a relief after so many hours alone. I decided I could trust him. I told him who I was looking for.

"Sure, I know them," he said. "I met 'em at the shelter a couple times."

"This shelter? Do they sleep here sometimes?"

"I mean the food pantry. In Komer. You know, Saint Labre?"

I nodded, but I had no idea what he was talking about.

"It's pretty decent for a town this size, or at least it was." J Star explained how the Saint Labre place had served dinner five days a week last time he passed through town but now it was open only one night a week, and might be closing for good.

"I'm sorry to hear that," I said.

He laughed. "Me too."

"Then why are you laughing?"

"The way you said it. You're a funny kid."

"I'm no kid. I'm eighteen." I had just turned seventeen, but close enough.

J Star seemed surprised by my age, and the look on his face got more serious, as I hoped it would. He said, "I haven't seen your friends in a few days. Do you think they might have moved on?"

"Moved on where?"

"To another town."

"I don't think so. I don't think they're hobos like that."

J Star laughed again. "You don't think they're what?"

"Hobos." It occurred to me I shouldn't have used the word *hobo* in front of this man, in case he was a hobo himself, but he seemed more like a hippy college kid on a camping trip.

"What's a hobo?" J Star asked, smiling.

I shrugged. "A homeless wino who rides the rails and whatnot."

J Star laughed so hard he hunched over.

"What's so funny?" I asked.

"I haven't heard anyone say that in a while. The term *hobo* is a bit old fashioned. *Wino* too, for that matter."

"My Grandpa says it." This wasn't much of a defense, though; Grandpa was extremely old fashioned.

"It's pretty funny, but you probably shouldn't say it."

"Why not?"

"It's—I don't know—politically incorrect." He sighed. "Have you tried the jail?"

"No," I said. The idea was frightening, but of course it made sense. If Whitey Connors was cracking down, and if Leo and them wouldn't move, then he might have called the cops. He probably had the cops in his pocket, that scoundrel. There were always patrol cars in the Bi-Cities parking lot.

J Star sniffed, like he smelled something unpleasant. He lowered his head so it was closer to mine. He said, "You've been in the dump, huh?"

I was embarrassed. "Do I smell like trash?"

"Nothing in there smells like trash. Look, I know it's tempting: there's great stuff in there—the things people throw away, it's a shame—but that spray they use is poison." He fingered the sleeve of my t-shirt. "Can't you smell it?"

I sniffed the sleeve. I couldn't smell anything except mild body odor. But it occurred to me that I hadn't smelled the dump in years. "I used to smell it," I told J Star. "It used to smell like bowling shoe spray."

"It still does," J Star said. "You should shower off. You can use our water if you want."

I didn't like the idea of stripping down in front of a stranger so I told him I'd shower as soon as I got home.

"Where's home?" he asked.

I gestured vaguely towards the hills, where Grandpa lived.

J Star nodded. "Why don't you stay here tonight with my friends and me? They'll be coming back soon. Some of them are about your age."

"Thanks for the offer, but I should get back home."

We shook hands and J Star said, "God bless you, brother." I had no idea why he called me brother. He was weird, I guess.

Back at the dump I crouched outside the fence to listen for garbage men, but there still weren't any voices. I climbed back in the way I climbed out, then I wandered around a bit more, not seeing anybody. It was kind of fun to be alone because I could wander wherever I wanted. I wandered into the hangars where the loaders and excavator were parked. I even sat in one of the loaders and pretended to be driving it. Then I walked right up to the back of the headquarters building and tried to look into some windows, but the windows had burglar bars.

Time must have got away from me because the sun started setting. I decided to check the bunker one more time before I left. It was way in the opposite corner of the dump as the building, and by the time I got there the sun had disappeared behind Trash Mountain. I knocked on the door, just in case, then let myself inside.

The bunker was still empty, but they had left their camping lantern. I lit it so I could shut the door and be safer. There were some cell phone parts on the table, which gave me hope since Leo wouldn't have left that stuff unless he meant to come back for it. I sat in a chair and waited for a while, but then I started to get tired. I can't remember if I decided ahead of time I would sleep there that night, or if it just sort of happened. Boss had lined the floor with cardboard, which was dry and clean, and pretty soon it started looking good to me. I decided to lay down and rest my eyes.

When I woke up I thought I heard voices, something like whispering, but too rhythmic to be actual human whispering. I was curious but afraid to open the door, in case a security guard was making his rounds in a cart or something. I fell asleep again and woke up to a smell so sharp it stung my sinuses, high up in my nose. This time I was sure I heard something. It sounded like the truck that pumps the sewer, a rumbling sound with a *knock, knock, knock* on top of it. The smell wasn't anything like the sewer, though. The sewer would have been a relief. I pulled my shirt up over my nose and mouth so I wouldn't have to smell it, but the smell came through so strongly that my eyes watered. Forget about sleeping, I thought. Maybe I could burst out the door and make a break for it in the dark, but the noise was so loud I knew for sure there was a big machine out there. I pictured the slumbering excavator, alert and extended, ferocious. It might have scooped me up and crunched me for sport.

After a while the noise got softer and the smell got less bad, or I got used to it, and I was able to fall back asleep.

I woke up at dawn with a headache. I stood up and felt lightheaded, like I was high and hungover at the same time. The awful smell had persisted, but it no longer made my eyes water. Now my eyes were itchy and dry.

I opened the door of the shelter for a breath of fresh air, but there wasn't any fresh air to be breathed. I saw two men in white hazmat suits, like something from an A-bomb movie, and I ran the other direction, towards what I thought was the main entrance, but I got turned around. The dump had changed *again*. I peered through the fence to get my bearings in relation to Komer, and I saw the main street that went by my old house. I didn't see my old street, though, which should have been right there. There should have been an alley too. That's what had gone along the fence, when we lived there. In my confusion (or maybe it was the smell, messing with my brain) it took me a while to notice I was standing on firmer ground than usual. Beneath the thin layer of new-looking trash was a concrete slab. Twenty yards away was another slab, then another. A feeling of dread welled up inside me as I looked for signs of my old house, of any house, but all I found were an old bathtub and some bricks from a chimney. The rest of the house parts had been bulldozed somewhere else, I guess. Into one of those cubes, maybe, or up against the base of Trash Mountain itself.

I should have been angry, but instead I felt sad. I had avoided the house for years, not wanting to see another family in there, or to see it empty and filled with ghosts, and now it was gone. Vanished. The fact that it was indistinguishable from our neighbors' houses really bothered me. What if we had kept a family graveyard back there, like country people sometimes do? How would we visit our dead loved ones? But who was I kidding. We never even had a dog to bury, or a cat or a goddamn fish.

It was only later, on my way back to Grandpa's, that the anger came. I had a vision of other houses getting bulldozed. Schools and businesses too. I wondered how many busted up buildings could fit inside Trash Mountain, and what about gassed out bodies? What if Boss and them had fallen asleep and never woke up, and were tucked up in there dead? It made me think of Komer and Haislip and all their buildings and people as one big trash pile, the dumpster of the world!

I would buy the Red Dragon 400,000 BTU Backpack Torch Kit with Squeeze Valve, I decided. Hell, I had $2,013 in two shoeboxes wrapped in duct tape; I could probably buy a Stinger missile launcher from an out-of-work mujahideen. I could douse the place in napalm then shoot it from a distance like a sniper. I could fill Grandpa's truck with nitroglycerine, bum rush the gate, then crash the truck into the base of Trash Mountain and blow it sky high.

Turns out I didn't have to do that stuff, though. I got a call from Bi-Cities a few weeks later, and they pretty much invited me inside.

Chapter 12

TO THIS DAY I have no idea what makes a résumé stick somewhere, but I guess mine stuck. The call I got was from the guy who interviewed me for the Bi-Cities internship the year before, the one who loved self-starters. He said they had a new position for a self-starter such as myself. "The only caveat," he said, "is it isn't an internship. We can't offer college credit. But I'm guessing that isn't a problem?"

"No sir," I said, not even asking what kind of job it was. I didn't want to look a gift horse in the mouth.

"And your employer won't be Bi-Cities, technically," he said, "but Mister Connors himself."

"Hmm," I said.

"Expect an email from a woman named Marie Angiulo, to set up an interview."

At school the next day I checked my email between every class. The email from Marie Angiulo came during lunch. I was in the library with Demarcus, where the computers were.

Marie Angiulo said she wanted to meet me at an address that I knew at a glance wasn't Bi-Cities HQ. Demarcus looked it up and told me it was in a strip mall outside of town, which seemed weird to me. He did the satellite view and told me the strip mall was empty.

"Huh," I said, suspicious. This was Whitey Connors we were talking about. A gangster. "Do you think I should go?"

"You got to. Maybe it's a side business, and they need an off-the-books type character, like you."

I liked thinking of myself as an off-the-books type character, who could be relied upon for shady tasks such as arms trafficking, but I couldn't shake a dim feeling of dread. I pictured myself wandering into an empty storefront where the this Angiulo person was lurking in the back, waiting to spring out and bonk me on the head to kidnap me or steal my blood. What if the self-starter guy had passed my résumé to her with a note that I wasn't much of an employment prospect but might make a good eternal blood-slave?

The next morning I put on my western jacket and necktie and drove to town, or rather to the strip mall on the outskirts where the address was. The parking lot was empty except for a sagging burgundy Oldsmobile. The strip mall was empty too, except for one narrow storefront that had some posters in the window. The posters said CONNORS FOR STATE TREASURER.

My God, I thought. *This* was the side business?

I put my feelings aside and went in.

The swinging glass door set off a loud chime, but nobody came to greet me. The store, for lack of a better word, was gray and unlit. There was a table with some folding chairs, and a big wide counter where something had once been sold, or a service rendered. All over the table and countertop were posters and papers and greasy looking empty fast-food bags.

"Hello?" I said.

Nobody replied so I sat down in a folding chair and waited. A few minutes later there was a flush and a woman in a droopy sweater came out from the back. She had long grayish hair and big glasses like grandmas wear in movies, but she wasn't too old.

"Benjamin Shippers?" she said.

"Yes," I said, stopping myself from saying *ma'am*, recalling my conversation at the grocery store with the Darla Waddell, years before. I rose to shake her hand. "Miz Angiulo?"

"Call me Marie. Sit down. Alright, let's take a look at this thing."
It was more like *arright let's take a look at dis ting*. This lady wasn't
from Komer. She sat down and snatched a couple papers off the table:
my résumé and cover letter, the ones Demarcus had done up for the
internship. But a whole year had gone by. I couldn't even remember
what was on them!

"So," she said, "why do you think Christian Connors should be
State Treasurer?"

"Who's Christian Connors?"

"Whitey Connors."

"Oh, right." I didn't really know what a State Treasurer did, but I
had to think quickly. I said, "The way I see it, a man who can run a
big complicated dump like he does can probably run a state, or do its
treasuring at least."

"Never heard it put like that. Alright, what's this I hear about you
and William Mlezcko?"

"Pardon?"

"Bill Mlezcko, Junk Mlezcko. I hear you ran with him in high
school."

"I don't even know him. I swear. I knew his brother Ronnie."

She shuffled her papers and read something. "Ronnie, Ronald—
well, he's in jail too."

I couldn't believe it. Ronnie was in jail?

"You still run with him?" she asked.

"No, ma'am."

"Marie."

"Shit. I mean sorry."

"Don't worry about it." She eyed me over her glasses. "You got bigger things to worry about."

"Pardon?"

"The number for the leadership conference for gifted young people got me the voicemail of someone named Ruthanne Shippers. Any
relation?"

Shit, I thought. I had forgotten that Ruthanne screened her calls, like anybody ever called her, that shrew. "She's my sister," I muttered. The interview was going horribly.

"We couldn't get hold of Toni Mikiska, but I'll give you the benefit of the doubt on that one. The only reference that came through was"—she squinted, reading—"Mark Bauerman. He said you were a creative thinker, when motivated."

When motivated? Come on, Mr. B!

Marie Angiulo put down my résumé and slid it across the table far away from her, like it stank. "Ben," she said, "do you mind if I call you Ben? I gotta level with you. The sheer quantity of lying on this résumé is reprehensible. If it were up to me, I'd call the police. But lucky for you, Whitey is the type of man who can't see a thing without reading it, and he saw your so-called résumé right here on this table. Something about it must have struck him. He said to me, 'Hire this boy.' I tried to tell him you were a liar, but he wouldn't have it. He said to hire you as a shoeshine boy for all he cared."

I felt grateful to Whitey, then immediately tried to quash that feeling. The man was my nemesis.

"Welcome to Connors for State Treasurer," Marie said.

"For real?"

"Sort of. Nothing about campaigns is too real, really. We're bringing you on as junior administrative custodial."

"As what?"

"An office boy. We need somebody in here during working hours in case people drop in to give money or volunteer. Your first job is to sort all these papers." She waved her arm at the papers all over the room. "Scratch that. Your first job is to memorize this script." She slid a sheet of paper across the table. "It's stuff to say to people." She took out some keys and handed them to me. "At six o'clock, lock up, then come back tomorrow at seven. Think you can handle that?"

"Yes, ma'am—Marie."

"Don't spend all day on the internet jerking off. When you're done organizing, there's cleaning supplies in the bathroom. Make the place inviting."

Marie stood up to leave. I wondered when I'd see her again. And when, and if, I'd meet Whitey Connors.

"Any questions?" Marie asked.

"Yeah, um, why is this office way out here? Wouldn't it be more convenient for Mr. Connors if it was at the dump—Bi-Cities Sanitation, I mean?"

"Separate pies, know what I'm saying?"

I had no idea what she was saying, but I knew I couldn't infiltrate the dump from a strip mall two miles away. I would have to bide my time.

After Marie left, I studied the paper she gave me. If somebody called I was supposed to say "Connors for State Treasurer, may I help you?" then "Would you care to make a donation?" then "The core issue of Mister Connors's platform is improving education," which seemed weird to me, since he was a businessman and a sanitation expert, but the rest of the spiel explained it: "How, you ask? By redirecting the money wasted on government-run sanitation into schools and the arts. Bi-Cities children deserve an education, don't you agree? How will Bi-Cities children compete in the world economy without such skills as solar panel repair?"

Since when did we become Bi-Cities children, I wondered. Was Whitey Connors going to change it from Pansy Gilchrist to Bi-Cities Sanitation High School?

After I went over the paper a few times I spent the rest of the day straightening up. There was a file cabinet with hanging files, but the hanging files were empty. Instead, papers were piled up in the fronts of drawers, along with receipts, business cards, matchbooks, fliers, and knickknacks like a spoon commemorating the state bicentennial. I took my time sorting things into piles by category (e.g. "miscellaneous correspondence") and making labels for the hanging files. By six I wasn't anywhere near done so I stayed and kept going. When I got hungry there was half a can of peanuts in a drawer, and I drank water from the tap in the bathroom.

In the back was a storeroom with big metal shelves from floor to ceiling, but the shelves were empty. There were boxes of stickers that said CONNORS FOR TREASURER in red, white and blue. There were a couple thousand copies of a letter from Whitey Connors. It started, "*Dear Constituent,*" then said the same stuff that was on my paper. It was pretty boring. Anyway, there was a little couch back there too, one of those wood-frame couches with cushions you can take off, so I arranged the cushions in a line on the floor and went to sleep.

Marie showed up the next day around ten and was impressed by my progress. If she knew I had slept there, she didn't say anything. She said, "Anybody call?" and I said no. Then she gave me a big box of envelopes and a printout of a couple thousand addresses and told me to process the letters in the back room. By "process" she meant print the addresses on the envelopes, fold the letters, stick the letters in the envelopes, then put stamps on the envelopes since the meter was broken. Processing letters sounded horrible, but I could tell she was testing my mettle so I said, "You got it," in a real chipper voice and got started before she even left.

Processing the letters took me four days. Each day at lunchtime I drove to the post office to mail the ones I had finished. I did this without asking, hoping it would make me look like a self-starter who took the initiative.

I didn't see Whitey Connors that whole first week except once. It was early Friday morning. The front door chime went off, and Marie was in the back room before I could even stand up. I was worried about her seeing me like that, sleeping back there, but she was too preoccupied with the boxes to say anything. After she went through the boxes she turned to me and said, "Where's the goddamn stickers?"

I told her I had moved them to a drawer in the front, and when I led her out there, that's when I saw Whitey Connors, or at least

I thought it might be Whitey Connors. He was in the parking lot leaning against the side of the burgundy Oldsmobile with his cell phone in one hand and a thirty-two ounce styrofoam soda in the other. He looked small, and that smallness, combined with his curly brown hair, made me think he was young. I had expected an older man. He had a confidence about him, even just leaning there like that, a sort of compact energy that told you he was ready for action. I almost admired him, I'm ashamed to admit, and more shameful still: he reminded me a little of myself.

Chapter 13

THE OFFICE WAS supposed to be for potential voters and volunteers, I guess, but the only people who stopped by were Marie and deliverymen, and there were only so many envelopes to stuff and drawers to rearrange, so to pass the time I ended up reading some water-damaged paperbacks I found under the bathroom sink. There were romance novels like Ruthanne used to read, and self-help books with titles like *The Power of Positive Thinking* and *The Human Connection!: Pt. 2, Inference*. The AC was broken so I kept the front and back doors open for cross ventilation. October was hot that year. I was pretty miserable, I guess, and I hadn't seen Whitey Connors in two whole weeks, so what was the point? I wasn't infiltrating shit. I was thinking about quitting when one day Marie was sitting at the conference table marking some papers and started peering at me over her glasses. I thought it was to catch me standing still so I tried to look busy. I opened and closed some file cabinets like I was looking for something.

"Stop fooling around and come over here," she said.

I went over to her. She was looking at me like I had a rash on my face or a big spider crawling across it. She said, "Have you heard of Tom Donaldson?"

"Doctor Tom?"

"That's right, but I don't know what kind of doctor he is and I don't care. He was your congressman for years, but he lost his last bid. Now he's running for state treasurer."

"Against Mister Connors?"

"Right. Are you familiar with the phrase 'know your enemy'?"

"Sure." I didn't tell her just how familiar. "You need some info on him? I'm pretty good on the internet. Set me up with a computer and I'll dig up the dirt."

"We've done that already. We need more. Here's what I want you to do, if you're amenable." What she wanted me to do, she explained, was impersonate a reporter from the high school newspaper in order to interview Tom Donaldson and ask him a bunch of questions about himself. "Should be easy," she said, "since you're still in high school, technically. Use your school email address."

She slipped me a sheet of paper with my name and Pansy Gilchrist email address on it, along with erroneous details about myself: senior enrolling next year at Tech (Donaldson's alma mater), member of the Young Republicans, political editor at the student paper, etc. I told her I didn't think *The Pansy Eagle Times* had a politics beat, but she didn't care. The sheet also had some of the questions I was supposed to ask him, and they seemed harmless enough.

As instructed, I went to the Donaldson for State Treasurer website and emailed about setting up an interview. I read on the website about what a good doctor Dr. Tom was and how much he got done in Washington despite constant attacks from liberal elites who wanted to take away our freedom. There were photos of him shaking people's hands, holding babies, shooting baskets with some kids in wheelchairs. He was tall and had thick sculpted gray hair that was about half an inch away from being a pompadour. His face was smooth, and his teeth were white. He looked a lot more like a politician than Whitey Connors did, that was for sure.

Another place on the internet said Tom Donaldson used to be an OB/GYN doctor, which meant he delivered babies, and that he insisted on being called "Doctor Tom" even though he hadn't practiced in twenty years and his license lapsed. Some internet people claimed he did abortions in medical school, but Dr. Tom said he didn't. He was a Christian. He believed life started at conception and that the world was six thousand years old. That didn't sound right to me, but Dr. Tom was a doctor so maybe there was an argument to it.

Somebody at Donaldson for State Treasurer emailed back that Dr. Tom sent his regards but because of his busy campaign schedule he didn't have time for an interview—Go Tigers! (Ricky the Tiger was Tech's mascot.)

When I told Marie, she laughed.

"It's because you're in Komer," she said. "This is Whitey's territory. Ninety percent of high-school kids can't vote, and those who can, in a place like this, don't."

I thought that was the end of it, just a waste of time, but Marie said we were writing the article anyway. She gave me careful instructions.

The first thing I had to do was drive to the city and visit Dr. Tom's old med school. Marie warned that they were embarrassed he had gone there, because of the thing about the world being created six thousand years ago, so I didn't expect to have much luck talking to anybody about him. But the receptionist at the Dean's office called somebody and said what I was there for, and a few minutes later a pretty lady came out, shook my hand, and invited me into her office. She told me she was Associate Dean and asked if I had any questions.

I told her about myself (my fake self) and about the article and how excited we kids were that Dr. Tom, a big famous former congressman, was running for State Treasurer. The lies came easily. It felt good to be lying with permission. I made the article out to be a fluff piece. I said I was tentatively calling it "Dr. Tom: The Teenage Years," because teens like me were interested in what Dr. Tom was like as a teen.

"Sounds like a neat article," the Associate Dean said. "How can I help you?"

"Well," I said, "Doctor Tom likes to joke that he wasn't a very good student, but I don't believe it."

She laughed. "Nobody's perfect."

"But Doctor Tom seems like a genius to me. I bet he got straight A's. Do you know?"

"That was a little before my time, I'm afraid."

"Could you look at his transcript?"

The Associate Dean seemed surprised by this request, and I felt embarrassed, but then she started typing on her computer. When she got what she was looking for she said, "Yeah, nothing special. I'm not surprised. He gave it up for politics, after all." She laughed again, and I did too.

"But if you get bad grades," I said, "do you still get to be a doctor?"

"Yes. Just to pass med school classes and graduate is an accomplishment. If Doctor Donaldson hadn't gotten so many incompletes, things might have gone quite differently for him. He might have ended up in a more prestigious residency in a different city, maybe even a different state. He might never have run for congress."

"Wow. That's a lot to think about. But what's an incomplete?"

The Associate Dean hesitated, like maybe she hadn't meant to say that.

"Is it like an F?" I asked.

"No," she said.

I asked her if Dr. Tom had been in any student clubs, that type of thing, and she said she didn't know. I asked her a few more questions like that and got nothing. This lady was done with me.

When I left I called Marie to say I didn't get anything good, but Marie disagreed. She said the incompletes were a big deal, almost as bad as F's. Then she gave me the office phone number of Dr. Tom's old buddy, an OB/GYN in Komer who went to school with him. She told me to call this doctor and set up an interview.

The doctor's name was Dr. Matthews and his receptionist told me in a heavy accent that Dr. Matthews could see me any time I wanted. I guess Dr. Matthews didn't have many patients. I set up the interview for the next day, then I called Mom to tell her I was in the city on business. The idea that I was anywhere "on business" was confusing to her, but she was glad to hear from me. She gave me their address and told me to come right over.

Driving in the city was kind of scary, but I tried to be stone-faced in case Grandpa's truck gave away that I was a hayseed from Komer and people were watching me. I was on the north side of town in the ritzy neighborhood where the med school was and I had to get to the south side. I was afraid to take the expressway because I didn't like merging in traffic, so I drove the whole way through neighborhoods.

There were lots of nice ranch style houses with lawns and tall trees, parks with little playgrounds, strip malls where all the storefronts had stores in them. I enjoyed the drive. But as I approached downtown the traffic thickened. It was rush hour. The street I was on turned into a one-way the wrong way so I tried to turn and get on another street, but the street I wanted to turn on was one-way the wrong way too. I ended up circling downtown four or five times before I got spat out on a random street I never heard of before. The sun was on my right so I knew I was headed south, but that was about all I knew, unfortunately.

South of downtown, the houses got smaller and the strip malls more dilapidated, sort of like Komer but better paved. It stank a little too, and eventually I passed what looked like a chicken parts factory. I was starting to think I might have gone too far, but then I came to the street I was looking for. I turned onto the street and drove past fast food restaurants and tire shops, then I turned onto another street and pulled into the blacktop parking lot in front of Mom and Ruthanne's apartment.

The apartment was a horseshoe-shaped, two-story brick building with outdoor entrances. It looked a lot like our old apartment in

Komer, actually: the same little square windows, the same rust stains under the guardrails on the second floor, the same big, sad American cars. The only difference was a scummy pond in the middle of the horseshoe, where two Mexican kids were floating a milk carton boat. But if it was a duck pond, like Mom said, the ducks had flown somewhere better.

When I rang the doorbell Mom came to the door in tears, she was so glad to see me. She looked the same, which I was glad about, since I was worried she had gotten fatter. She invited me in and I was happy to see that the apartment had the same features as the one in Komer: the same TV, the same blue microfiber loveseat, the same watercolor of a bridge someplace in Italy, which was the only thing on the walls besides pictures of me and Ruthanne. Everything looked more crowded, though, because the apartment was smaller. It must have been cheap.

I asked where Ruthanne was, and Mom said she was working.

"At the library?" I asked.

"At a Burger Brothers down the way."

I was surprised. Ruthanne never worked a day in her life, let alone someplace greasy like a Burger Brothers.

Mom said Ruthanne worked two or three shifts a week to help with rent. "Your daddy lost his job again," she said, "and this city is *expensive.*"

"Sure," I said, but I didn't like the idea of Ruthanne spending half her time in a Burger Brothers when she should have been studying. I wished there was something I could do.

I fell asleep on the couch before Ruthanne came home, but she woke me up to talk. She kept hugging me and saying how glad she was to see me. She smelled terrible.

I told her about my job and she seemed impressed.

"But what about school?" she asked.

"It's an internship so it takes the place of school," I lied. "You could do one too, you know, and stop wasting your time flipping burgers."

"I do the register."

"For real?" I had a hard time imagining Ruthanne smiling at customers. She disliked old people, in particular. Nothing annoyed her more than standing in line behind an old lady fumbling through a coin purse.

"And what's it to you what I do with my time?" Ruthanne asked. "I'm getting good grades, which is more than you can say."

"Isn't there more to college than that? You know, like clubs and stuff?"

"Oh, yeah, the glee club."

"There you go."

"And the recycling club, and Amnesty International, and Chi Omega, and Agricultural Communicators of Tomorrow." She kept listing clubs until I knew she was jerking my chain. "It's a community college, Ben. Don't be an idiot."

We stayed up late talking about her classes and about my boring weird days at the campaign office. It was good to talk to her. It made me wish I hadn't waited so long to visit. When I left the next morning, after a big breakfast of bacon and eggs and white bread toast, I was sad to go. They wanted me to stay another night, but I told them I had a meeting back in Komer with a prominent gynecologist.

Dr. Matthews's practice was in a ratty old shingle building near the hospital. The waiting room was empty so the receptionist, a middle-aged Latino man wearing all denim, showed me right to Dr. Matthews's office.

Dr. Matthews had his chair swiveled around and was staring out the window at a parking lot. His face was reflected in the window, and his expression was somber, but when he heard us he spun in his chair and smiled real big. He had a grease spot on his necktie. He said, "Sit down, young man, sit down," and I sat down across from him.

While I told him about my article he kept smiling and nodding and sinking deeper into his chair. His body had a sort of looseness about it, like it was deflating. His eyes glistened with mirth or nostalgia, what Grandpa called Irish eyes. He said, "Tom is a dear friend, young man, a dear friend."

"Was he a leader?"

"Pardon?"

"Student government, that kind of thing?"

Dr. Matthews laughed. "Heck no."

I feigned surprised. "Really? We kids thought he was a born leader."

"A leader of revelry!" Dr. Matthews told a series of increasingly ribald stories about med school, where he and Dr. Tom used to cruise the city for girls by saying they were doctors instead of just students. "And we were barely even *students*. We were flunking!" He laughed.

"But y'all didn't flunk, right?"

"Well, I didn't." He winked. "It was easier back then. Med school was more like college. There were fraternities for gosh sakes. What mattered was who you knew. Me, I didn't know a soul. I was a country boy. Born right here in Komer, like you. But a professor took me under his wing." Dr. Matthews told me the story of this professor. It started off like his other stories, jokey and good natured—the professor was a coot, he said, an old country boy after his own heart—but then the story took a surprising twist. This professor had taken it upon himself to make sure all the future OB/GYNs learned to perform abortions. He did it at a clinic away from school, since it was a dicey thing and not everybody cared to learn, but most did, and if you wanted a letter from this old professor, you had to learn. "Because sometimes it was necessary," Dr. Matthews said, "a matter of life and death."

"He sounds like a good teacher," I said.

"He was." Dr. Matthews ran his big hand over his face. I thought he might be crying, but it was hard to tell; his eyes had been moist from the start.

"Did Doctor Tom know him too?" I asked.

"Everybody did. Knew him and loved him."

I felt sleazy asking the next question, but *abortion* was one of the target words on my sheet from Marie. "Did y'all feel bad about performing abortions?" I asked.

"Queasy at first," he said, "but not bad. Never bad." Dr. Matthews paused. He eyed me over his fingers, which were tented in front of his nose and mouth.

I knew I should ask more questions about abortions and whatnot, but I felt guilty. Dr. Matthews was a nice old man. If he wasn't a lady doctor I would have wanted him for my own doctor. I decided to change the subject: "Are y'all still in touch?"

He shook his head gravely. "We had a falling out."

"I'm sorry." I didn't know much about life, but I knew that friends were harder to come by the older you got. I didn't want to upset Dr. Matthews any further, even if it meant I had to stop digging up dirt on Dr. Tom.

"We joined the same practice after school was through," Dr. Matthews said, "but Tom kept getting in trouble."

I tried to stop Dr. Matthews by thanking him for his time, but he seemed lost in thought.

"There were young women about," he was saying. "That was the nature of the practice. And Tom, well, he always had a colt's tooth."

"A what tooth?"

"We were in a poor part of town and lots of the girls didn't have husbands. Tom wasn't even sly about it. He'd just ask them if they wanted to get a drink after he got off work. Sometimes they were flattered. He was a charming man, and handsome—still is, so you can imagine what a figure he cut back then, not even thirty—but lots of these girls were scared, you know. They weren't in the mood for that sort of thing. And sometimes they had their mothers or fathers in the waiting room and would tattle on Tom. It got to be a real problem. The doctor who owned the practice scolded Tom in front of the rest of us, which rubbed Tom the wrong way. He was a prideful person. Still, he would have stuck on if it weren't for the complaints of inappropriate touching."

I wanted to say "enough! enough!" but Dr. Matthews kept going. It was like he couldn't control himself, like he'd been waiting since Tom Donaldson first got elected to be interviewed, or uncorked, on the subject of good old Dr. Tom. Eventually he got to talking about an orthodontist in town who went to jail for groping women while they were "gassed out." He winced, as though embarrassed by his own story. After a pause he said, "I wonder why I said all that. He's an old friend, you know."

"The orthodontist?"

"Tom. That orthodontist was a scoundrel." He sighed. "I suppose I said it as a lesson. Yes. You see, young man, while I disagree with Tom on many fronts, there is no doubt he's a great politician and a powerful man. He's a verifiable celebrity, I suppose, which might be why young people like yourself look up to him so. I suppose I said all that to remind you he's human. He's just a man, and maybe a less decent man than most. I suppose I don't feel quite comfortable with him being celebrated in print. Why not celebrate someone like Bob Bilger?"

"I couldn't agree more," I said, thankful for the opportunity to change the subject.

We had a long talk about Bob Bilger. It turned out Dr. Matthews was a year behind Bob Bilger at Jeff Davis, which is what Pansy Gilchrist used to be called. They played on the football and basketball teams together. I told him I read *The Highest Mountain* three times, which was true, and that Bob Bilger came and talked almost every year at school. Dr. Matthews laughed. He said he went to see Bob Bilger talk at the VFW, hoping to get a moment alone with the man to relive old times, but Bob Bilger hadn't remembered him. "Can't blame him," Dr. Matthews said ruefully, "with his memory beclouded by such glorious adventures, why would he remember a small-town doctor like me?"

Dr. Matthews seemed sad so I told him delivering babies was more important than climbing a mountain with a Betamax camcorder, and that might have been true. I couldn't decide.

Before I left, I told Dr. Matthews I'd suggest to my editors that we present "a more well-rounded portrait of Doctor Tom than we first intended."

Dr. Matthews seemed satisfied. He told me he thought I was an impressive young man, and to let him know if I ever became curious about the medical game.

I was flattered. Now that I was back on the terrorist track, or at least infiltrating, I was tempted to think of medicine as yet another potential career I had to sacrifice to destroy Trash Mountain, but who was I kidding? I was a high-school dropout, pretty much. I wasn't a genius at anything anymore. Dr. Matthews was just being nice.

While I typed up my notes I felt bad, not because of what the notes said about Dr. Tom (I couldn't have cared less about Dr. Tom, that shiny-toothed gigolo) but because I had misrepresented myself to Dr. Matthews. What if Dr. Matthews read an article in the newspaper that had all the stuff he said? It wouldn't matter that the writer had a different name. Dr. Matthews was no dummy.

When I gave Marie the notes, she was impressed. I asked her what she was going to do with them and she said not to worry. "You're clean," she said.

"But if Doctor Matthews—"

"Don't worry about Matthews. That old glory hound was dying to tell you about his famous friend. You did him a favor. But it doesn't matter anyway. There won't be any articles, not in the conventional sense. We divide it all up." Marie explained that no legitimate newspaper would accept notes like mine from somebody in the Connors campaign, so what she did was give the notes to online news sites that wrote little articles for money. Nobody read the articles, she said, but they changed what came up when you searched for Dr. Tom on the internet.

"This stuff is perfect because of the irony," Marie said. "The smartass doctor congressman who almost flunked out of med school. The pro-life windbag who used to do abortions."

"But what do abortions have to do with being treasurer?"

"I don't know, kid, but what if he beat his wife? What if he called somebody nigger?"

"He'd be a jerk."

"Exactly."

"But Doctor Matthews said they had to do the abortions to pass med school."

"What you and I believe doesn't matter, Ben. This is the Bi-Cities. That shit won't fly."

The next day, Marie told me Whitey Connors was just as impressed as she was by my interview skills. So impressed, she said, that he wanted to meet me. She told me we were going to Bi-Cities HQ.

I drove us there in Marie's burgundy Oldsmobile (I hadn't bothered mentioning I didn't have a license) while Marie worked in the passenger seat, marking up papers then calling somebody on the phone and talking in a loud voice about an Elks Lodge where Whitey was supposed to speak. When we got to the dump, Marie directed me to a special entrance. She had to lean across me to wave a badge at a little gray box with a light on it that beeped.

The special entrance led to a little parking lot full of luxury sedans and shiny trucks with brush-guards and gun-racks that probably cost more than Marie's Oldsmobile.

Marie got out, still on the phone, and gestured for me to wait in the car.

I was disappointed to have to wait out there. Whitey Connors wanted to meet me, I thought, and I was ready to get the ball rolling in terms of casing the building for possible acts of terror. But I waited. And waited. It was pretty boring. When three guys in short-sleeve dress shirts and neckties came out to smoke cigarettes, I watched them in the rearview mirror for a change of pace. None of them said anything; they just smoked and stared off into the distance, like they had witnessed something unspeakable. Seeing them made me wish I could smoke to pass the time. Marie's cigarettes were in a cup holder in the center console. But I didn't dare smoke in Marie's car. It would have been presumptuous. I was afraid even to turn on the radio, because what if Marie came back all of a sudden and heard me blasting metal and asked if I was a future school shooter or what? It annoyed me to be worried like that, to want so badly to please her, but I did. So I just sat there in silence for an hour and fifteen minutes.

I was half-asleep when the back door popped open and somebody slid into the backseat. I thought it was Marie, but why would she get in the back instead of the side? In the rearview mirror I could only see the outline of a head, all black with the sun behind it. I remember thinking it was small, the head, then hearing the sound of liquid slurped through a straw and the rattle of ice in a Styrofoam cup. That's when I knew it was Whitey himself.

"I wanna thank you," he said. He had a higher voice than I expected, and a thick country accent.

"You're welcome, sir."

"Polite. I like it." He slurped his drink. "I hear you're a local boy."

"Yessir."

"Let me guess," he said, "Komer?"

I would have answered, but he was laughing. I wondered what was funny.

The straw made a honking sound as he knocked loose some ice. Then he popped the lid and poured the ice into his mouth and started to chew it. Through the ice he said, "Know the old joke about Komer?"

"No sir," I said, even though I knew lots of jokes about Komer, old and new, and jokes about Haislip too, which were the same jokes switched around.

"What's the difference between a Komer man and a carp?" he asked.

"I don't know," I lied.

"One is a bottom-feeding scum sucker, and the other is a fish." He laughed, so I laughed too, to be polite. He must have liked the way I laughed because he told another: "Did you hear about the Komer man who tried to blow up a school bus?"

"No, sir," I said, and that time I wasn't lying. I hadn't heard that one.

"He burned his lips on the tailpipe." Whitey laughed again and I did too, even though the image of kids getting blown up sort of complicated the punch-line. He kept going: "Did you hear about the Komer kamikaze pilot?"

"No, sir."

"He flew twenty-five missions." Whitey laughed harder this time. My own laugh must have gotten feeble because he didn't seem to hear it. "The pilot flew twenty-five missions because he didn't get it right the first time," Whitey explained. "He shoulda got killed that first time. He was a *kamikaze* pilot."

"I see," I said, and tried to laugh some more.

"Pretty good, right? Say, did you hear about the Komer man who won gold at the Olympics?"

"No, sir."

"He liked the medal so much he got it bronzed." Whitey laughed some more and I laughed loud enough to be heard this time. My face was getting sore from fake smiling so much, but Whitey kept going. He must have told a dozen. Lots of them had to do with hunting or sex. "A Komer man went hunting and shot two deer," Whitey said. "The taxidermist asked if he wanted them mounted. You know what he said? No, kissing will do fine. Did you hear about the Komer man hunting in the woods? He came upon a pretty lady laying naked in the grass. He asked her if she was game. She said yes, so he shot her. Why did the rapist move to Komer? In Komer, everybody has the same DNA."

I forced myself to laugh for so long that my laughter started sounding weird to me, like a crazy person's laughter, and I wondered if laughing like that was a way to go crazy. Whitey seemed crazy. His eyes were wild and his mouth hung open between jokes in a way that made me think of a hungry wolf, like the jokes were meant to lull me into a stupor so he could spring from the back seat and bite my neck. But he didn't. He kept telling jokes. "Did you hear about the jumbo jet that crashed into a Komer cemetery?" he asked.

"Yes. I mean no. I guess I—that doesn't sound familiar."

"Komer Search and Rescue has recovered three hundred bodies so far and they're still digging. No, wait, I screwed that one up. There could be three hundred bodies on a jumbo jet easy, so they don't gotta dig up no cemetery to get the bodies. It's gotta be a smaller plane. What's a type of smaller plane?"

"How about a helicopter?"

"That's it! Did you hear about the helicopter that crashed—" He repeated the entire joke then laughed like hell again, like he hadn't just told the same goddamn joke. By then I was through. I just couldn't laugh anymore. That's when he stopped.

It was like he knew he wore me out and was satisfied, or maybe he had worn himself out to the point of screwing up the plane crash joke, and the satisfaction he felt was like the feeling after a good workout. He said, "Let me tell you about Tom Donaldson. Call it a psychological profile, if you will." He raised his cup and sloshed the last of the ice into his mouth. "Tom Donaldson was a rich kid who got told he was special all his life. He aced high school, aced college, and when college was over he heard that all the special boys went to law school or medical school to ace that. He just wanted to keep being special, see? Only problem was he wasn't smart enough to ace it anymore. He had gone too far, beyond the limits of his natural abilities. That twisted him up inside. He started having personal problems. Urges. But he got through, even though he probably shouldn't have—money weighs the dice of fortune, I like to say—and he got into a nice little life for himself. But the urges wouldn't stop. He kept getting into trouble. So much trouble that one day he couldn't be a doctor anymore. Well, what was he gonna do?" Whitey paused. "What was old Doctor Tom gonna do, Ben? What would make him still be special? Why, politics, of course!" Whitey laughed, then sighed. "Politics is like business, Ben: it helps to start with a couple million in the bank, and it helps even more to start with the kind of trust a doctor gets, even the shittiest, grabbiest doctor in town. But you know what? Fuck him. Fuck him, Ben. When I'm done he'll be eatin' mud from a trough like a goddamn pig."

Whitey opened the car door, got out, and slammed it shut. I was startled. He headed for the building then turned around, came back, and stuck his face in the passenger window. He looked older up close, and meaner. His beady brown eyes were surrounded by fierce wrinkles. He said, "Whoever heard of a doctor tellin' people the world is six thousand years old? He's a liar or a goddamn idiot. You a religious man?"

"No, sir."

"Good, because there ain't no God. People talk that shit to get elected. They think we're a buncha goddamn rubes."

He turned and left, for good this time.

I wasn't as startled as I would have been if Whitey hadn't worn me down with all those jokes, but I was surprised by what he said about God. I didn't go to church but if pressed I would have said I believed in God. But maybe I only would have said it just in case: in case God *did* exist and would strike me with lightning for saying he didn't, or would wait until I died for payback via sending me to hell. The slim chance of being tortured in hell for eternity wasn't worth the risk, was the way I saw it. But maybe it was worth it to Whitey. Whitey seemed like a man of passion. A righteous man. I had to remind myself I was infiltrating him.

Chapter 14

WHITEY HAD THIS guy named Daryl, his buddy from high school, whose job was to follow Whitey everywhere and fetch him things and get people on the phone and refill his soda. Daryl had a combover and a big belly that hung over his khaki pants. Judging from Daryl, Whitey must have been about fifty years old, which surprised me. Whitey had a wrinkly monkey face, but his hair wasn't gray and the way he moved made me think of an elf. Not a handsome bow-and-arrow-type elf like in movies but an Old World elf, the kind who steal babies and switch them with dirty elf babies, or maybe Whitey was the dirty elf baby all grown up. Anyway, people called Daryl Whitey's "body man," and pretty soon they were calling me Marie's body man, Whitey especially, like it was some kind of joke. I didn't like it. It made me think of myself as a sort of extra body Marie used to do her bidding, like a zombie almost. It was kind of true, though: I drove her around, I answered her phone sometimes, and I went with her to meetings, where I sat down next to her and took notes nobody read. Marie wanted to get me a suit, but Whitey said no. He said my western jacket rubbed a little "hotshot Texas mojo" on the whole operation. He started calling me Tex.

I didn't see too much of Whitey except when Marie went with him to speaking engagements, but Whitey had a way of making you feel connected to him, like he was your buddy from way back. One

time we were at a community meeting where an old codger was holding court about how deer season should be longer, and I glanced over
at Whitey and he glanced back and rolled his eyes, then he slacked
his jaw like he was dimwitted, then he turned back to the old guy
and kept watching but nodding his head so earnestly that he looked
kind of crazy. When the old guy finished, Whitey raised his hand
and waved it around until the guy called on him and Whitey said,
"Sir, what you're saying is of great interest to me, and to everyone else
here, I imagine, but tell me this: what's your favorite thing about
killing an animal?" The old guy hesitated, like he thought maybe
Whitey was a secret tree-hugger. But then Whitey smiled and said,
"*My* favorite thing is the smell of blood. Nothing gets me out of
bed like the red promise of a bloody hunt." Then Whitey laughed
good-naturedly and everybody else laughed nervously, and the old
guy said yes, that the smell of blood was pretty nice in the morning.

Since I spent all my time going around with Marie, I started to
worry about the campaign office. Who was taking care of it? Who
was greeting people? Who was offering info on Whitey Connors's
questionable platform? Then in January a half a dozen real interns
started. They were college students who were supposed to work at
Bi-Cities HQ for college credit, but Marie said each could spend one-
sixth of his or her time staffing the campaign office. I showed them
the ropes. Most were from the suburbs outside the city and went to
good colleges, but one was none other than Kyle James.

I almost didn't recognize him, with short hair and khakis and a
coat-and-tie combo like a high school debater. He was handsome as
ever but had gotten a little thick around the collar. He said he had
rushed a fraternity and drank beer all the time, and he was trying to
get into a workout routine but couldn't fit it between his studies and
fraternity engagements. He was in his second semester at Tech.

"How about you?" he asked. "I didn't peg you for a college man—
no offense."

"I'm not," I said, then explained how I had dropped out of high-school to work full-time for Whitey and Marie. I was expecting Kyle to be shocked. I was kind of hoping for it, honestly, so I could play it hard like he was just a college boy and I was a man of the world, but Kyle nodded. He looked thoughtful.

"Yeah," he said, "if it wasn't for how we got in trouble about that stupid book, I might have dropped out too. But my parents sent me to military school. It was good for me. Taught me a little responsibility, you know?"

"Sure," I said, even though the only thing I knew about military school was from a movie where a truck driver kidnaps his own kid from one to teach him arm wrestling.

Kyle and I had that conversation alone in the campaign office, while I was showing him the campaign materials and telling him what to say on the phone. I was glad to see him. I thought we might be friends again. But when I saw Kyle back at Bi-Cities, he seemed afraid to let on he knew me. The other interns seemed to regard me with amusement. I heard one of them call me "little Whitey" to an-other, which just about made me spit. The only thing me and Whitey had in common was our size and accent, though I like to think I spoke better than he did. When I passed Kyle in the halls or had to speak to the interns as a group, I played it cool. I treated him brusquely. But the next time I saw him alone, at a makeshift desk in a Bi-Cities conference room where he was cold-calling potential donors, I came over to chat.

"Did you hear about Ronnie?" I asked.

"No," Kyle said.

"He's in jail."

"Big surprise."

That pissed me off. Ronnie and Kyle used to be friends. I said, "I guess your college buddies stay out of jail, huh?"

"Most people stay out of jail, Ben. The rest of the world isn't like Komer."

"The rest of the world? You mean that city two hours away?"

"I know it isn't much, but it's better than this."

"Then why are you here?"

"If Whitey wins, I can work for him in the capital next summer. If not, I'll work for Hoffer in DC."

"Who's Hoffer?"

"Our congressman."

"So you wanna be a politician?"

Kyle said he wasn't sure about the whole politics game, but it probably looked good on his résumé. "The safest bet would be to get good grades and go to law school," he said. "The money isn't as good as banking or if you own your own business, like Whitey, but it's lower risk. I'd have to start off at a firm in the city, but I could end up in-house. It's better hours. Hell, I could end up working for Whitey. I wouldn't mind that one bit. A guy from Haislip could do a lot worse than Bi-Cities Sanitation."

I didn't know what to say. Kyle had thought it all out. But I didn't like the way he talked about Whitey, like he knew him and could use him, like the world was a videogame and Kyle was playing it.

"What's the rap on Ronnie?" Kyle asked.

"No idea," I said.

"Well, it was only a matter of time."

"It could have been you. You said so yourself."

"I could have dropped out, not gone to fucking jail. Ronnie's a born loser. God knows why we hung out with that guy."

"Yeah, well, he never liked you either."

"Good."

I knew I should let it drop, but I couldn't. I thought about the night I saw Ronnie behind my old apartment, how he had asked after Ruthanne, shown me his flaming skull Jesus tattoo. "Ronnie isn't a loser," I said. "He has vision. A secret inner life."

"Deranged vision is what he has."

"You didn't think so back then."

"I was an idiot."

"You were his friend. So was I."

"If you like him so much, you should visit him."

"I do," I lied. The truth was I didn't know I *could* visit Ronnie. I didn't know how jail worked. "Maybe I'll drop by tomorrow."

"Go for it."

"Maybe I will, and maybe this time I'll pull a few strings."

"With the warden?" Kyle smirked. "Or maybe you know the governor?"

"I know Whitey."

I was bullshitting, of course, but it had the desired effect. Kyle seemed cowed: I was the one who knew Whitey, not him. When Kyle was in-house lawyer or whatever, he'd be answering to me too. Hell, I might have taken over Bi-Cities by then. That's what was going through my head at that moment. Later, I would remind myself not to indulge in fantasies like that. Bi-Cities was temporary. I was on a mission. A more important mission than the likes of Kyle would ever know.

Visiting Ronnie turned out to be pretty easy. The county sheriff's office website listed which unit people were in and what they were in for. The different units had different visiting hours. MLEZCKO, RONALD NMI was in Unit Five for POSS OF MARIJ-1OZ, POSS COCAINE W/INTEN, PROBATION VIOL, UNDERAGE POSS/FURN ALCH, and POSS/MAKING FALSE ID. His name was listed once for each crime so it was like there were five Ronnie's in there, which seemed pretty dire until I saw that one guy, PATTERSON, DUANE TYRELL, had his name posted twenty-six times. I clicked on Ronnie's name, thinking it would give me more information on his case, but it took me to his mugshot. He looked terrible. There were wrinkles around his nineteen-year-old eyes, and the whites were bloodshot. His mouth was partway open so the yellow tips of his buckteeth stuck out. He hadn't shaved and his black hair was greasy. His skin was so white it was green. After I got over the shock of Ronnie's appearance, I start-

ed to get mad. What was the point of humiliating him by posting
that photo? Even worse, his address was on there: "Park Place Homes
#13-B." Why did anybody need his address? It wasn't like Ronnie
was a sex offender or a spree killer. He wasn't even a burglar! I could
just picture a bored old lady pouring over this list for somebody who
lived near her, just to warn her old lady friends about that no-good
Ronnie Mlezcko down the block. It made me sick.

Anyway, all I had to do was call the jail and say I wanted to visit
Ronnie Mlezcko. The jailor looked at some kind of schedule on his
computer (I could hear him typing) and said, "Wednesday at three
p.m." He didn't even *ask* Ronnie.

After lunch on Wednesday I told Marie I had some personal business and she said no problem. We had that kind of a relationship.

On my way across town to the jail, I got nervous. It was the same
old building I had passed a thousand times, the same little court-
yard with inmates playing lazy games of basketball, the same tall
wire fence, the same sad looking gray bus parked outside. Whenever
one of the school buses broke down, the old gray jail bus used to be
brought in to replace it. The inside of the jail bus was exactly the
same as a school bus except for a cage around the driver and these
metal rings on the backs of the seats where they could shackle you,
if need be. Usually I sat alone, but if I was sitting with anybody else
I liked to tie my wrists to the ring by my shoelaces, as a joke. I used
to be excited to ride that bus, to pretend to be a jailbird, but now
that I was going to the jail to see somebody I knew, it felt different.
What if other jailbirds stared me down? What if Ronnie had got all
hard and wouldn't talk to me? What if he had a face tattoo? I almost
turned back, but then I thought about how they probably had told
Ronnie by then so he might have been expecting me. I didn't want
to disappoint him.

I parked in visitor parking and walked inside, where a corrections
officer looked at my driver's license (Marie made me get one) and
had me sign something on a clipboard, probably agreeing not to pass

Ronnie a saw, or that if Ronnie shanked me in the neck I wouldn't press charges. I don't know. I didn't read it.

I expected a long glass divider with old phones you had to talk through and people pressing their hands to the glass in solidarity or passionate love, but the visiting room looked more like the inside of a barbecue restaurant. Instead of tables and chairs there were picnic benches.

The room was empty except for a somber mustachioed man in coveralls talking softly to his wife or girlfriend, or maybe it was his sister; they weren't too affectionate. In addition to the corrections officer who had escorted me into the room, there was another standing in the far corner with his thumbs hooked over his belt. He had a big black gun and was wearing sunglasses.

I sat down as far away from the talking couple as possible, to give them privacy. I expected to wait a while, but Ronnie came right out. He didn't look nearly as rough as I expected from his mugshot; he looked like the same old Ronnie, except he was growing a beard and his coveralls fit. The little coveralls, unlike his droopy jeans and hooded sweatshirts, made him look wiry and spry. His face was real cold while he came towards me, so I thought he might be pissed I was visiting, but when he sat down he held up his fist and I bumped it. He said "What up, kid?" and I said what up. Then he glanced from side to side and leaned forward. "We gotta talk quiet," he said.

"Sure," I said.

"Thanks for visiting. It's good to see a friendly face."

"Doesn't your mom visit?"

"Not much. She's got lots of people to visit."

"Sure." I felt awkward. I wasn't sure what was appropriate to talk about with somebody in jail. I really wanted to ask how he got arrested, if the cops had busted through the door and stuff, but maybe that was rude? "So," I said, "how you holding up?"

"The black guys beat the shit out of me and the white guys ignore me. If it weren't for my uncles they'd beat the shit out of me too. One

guy, my uncle's buddy, is some kind of Nazi, swastikas and everything. I gotta choose sides, man."

"In what?"

"The race war." Ronnie explained how his theory of the coming
race war apocalypse had been confirmed by his jailhouse experience.
"I try to tell people, but it isn't a popular subject. There's this one guy,
Beauregard, who knows what's up. He writes letters to news outlets
and lets me read 'em as long as I promise not to tell anybody inside.
His idea is that the black people are gonna overthrow the white government and CEOs and put them on a secret shuttle to the moon.
He's says there's another NASA—*Black NASA*, he calls it—that's
got a shuttle and stuff in a cave in Tennessee, where there's thousands
of unexplored caves so nobody could find the shuttle even if they
knew it was there. I know what you're thinking: 'How they gonna fit
all the CEO types, let alone the government, onto one shuttle?' Beauregard says shuttle technology has made major strides, but we don't
know about it because the government, via NASA, *white* NASA, has
been holding out on us. It's like with cars. We could all be getting fifty mpg right now, but they won't let us. They got an agreement. Why
do you think Hyundai gets forty while the Jap cars get thirty? It's
because the Japs and the Americans are colluding but the Koreans,
they hate the Japs. They're like, 'No deal, motherfuckers,' and that's
why they build the cars down in Alabama. The workers there are
disenfranchised. They don't give a fuck. The Koreans will be on the
black side in the coming race war apocalypse, along with the Polacks
and Jews, and also the Lithuanians and former Yugoslavians—the
basketball countries. You ever wonder why poor people play basketball? Because it's cheap. The communists back in Poland or wherever,
they just nailed a few hoops to brick walls and said 'Here you go, kids.
Don't assassinate anybody.' It's an opiate, like religion. Beauregard
never plays and neither do I. Some say music's an opiate too, but I
don't know. Pop music? Sure. Soul music? Country? Anything you
can fall asleep or fuck to is an opiate, for sure, I hear you, but what

about the hard stuff? Gangsta rap, thrash metal—that stuff isn't opiating *anybody*. It's waking people up. I got these Corpse Christ bootlegs, I listen the hell out of 'em. The songs are the same as the album versions but each one's kinda different, like a separate work of art. Beauregard says art's another opiate. He thinks we're all doomed, but I don't know. I guess I don't see why we can't break free when the shit hits the fan and make our way to the shuttle. He says he can get me in with Black NASA, even though I'm white, but when we get to the moon all bets are off. Every man for himself. We gotta start thinking about the terraforming of other planets. The population is growing, that much is obvious, so what happens when we run out of oil? Water? Rare earth metals? Anyway, what you been up to?"

"Pardon?"

"You working or something?" He was eyeing my jacket.

"Oh yeah. Um—" Before I came, I had been debating whether or not to tell Ronnie I worked for Whitey, but now I was so dazed by his monologue that I didn't care anymore. "I work for Christian Connors for State Treasurer."

"Who's Christian Connors?"

"Whitey Connors."

"Holy shit. How deep are you?"

"You mean at Bi-Cities?"

"Yeah. I assume you're infiltrating?"

"Definitely," I said, though I hadn't taken stock of my progress in a while, infiltration-wise. I tried to tell Ronnie about my day-to-day, Marie, etc., but he didn't seem interested. He kept asking about Whitey: how many cars he had, how the dump made its money, if they brought in truckloads of guys from Mexico then hid the bodies when they died on the job. He kept going and going until finally he said, "You have to kill him."

"What? Come on."

"You used to talk about how you tried to blow shit up, how you're a terrorist at heart, but nothing changes until Whitey Connors is out. What happens if he becomes treasurer?"

"Nothing. He's just treasurer. Better to have him up there in the capital than down here bulldozing houses."

"The houses get bulldozed either way, motherfucker. He'll probably make a law so he can bulldoze the whole city. Can you imagine? Komer and Haislip, just one big dump. It might take a while to notice the difference."

Ronnie may have been exaggerating for effect, but the spirit of what he was saying rang true to me. It cohered with my own dim vision of the future. I started feeling kind of emotional, and Ronnie seemed to notice. He said, "Shit, man, you okay?"

"They bulldozed my house," I said.

"Fuck. Really?"

I nodded. I hadn't talked to anybody about it, not even Ruthanne, so it felt weird to be telling Ronnie. But I knew I could count on Ronnie to react with appropriate outrage, and he did, muttering about "fucking Whitey" and "fucking Bi-Cities" until the corrections officer in the sunglasses looked up at us. Ronnie didn't seem to care. "When Komer and Haislip are one big dump," he said, "they could use prisoners like me as workers, like a penal colony, and if anybody acts up it'll be trial by combat, gladiator style, prisoner against prisoner. That's good money right there." Ronnie laughed so I laughed too, even though it wasn't funny to me; it was disturbing.

"Let's be honest," Ronnie said, "Komer, Haislip, they're small potatoes. Nobody cares. But what if Whitey Connors is on his way to bigger things, know what I'm saying? It's like that movie where the guy can see the future and knows that this candidate guy is going to turn into a crazy fascist Hitler guy, so the one guy, the psychic, who's otherwise a pretty peaceful dude, takes it upon himself to stop the proto-Hitler guy by sniping him."

"Sure," I said, even though I never saw that movie. I just wanted to get out of there at that point. Ronnie looked good, and I was glad to see him, but listening to him put me on edge. It stirred up something inside me, something uncomfortable. "Listen," I said, "I should go, but I'll visit again soon."

"You do that. I enjoyed this talk." Ronnie leaned back and his face got hard. I wondered if he could tell I wasn't really listening anymore. I felt bad.

We stood up and bumped fists again, and I left.

Most of what Ronnie said was kind of crazy, sure, but the thing about Whitey stuck with me. Whitey wasn't a maniacal fascist Hitler guy, but he was definitely on the rise. I didn't have to kill him, necessarily, but I had to do *something*. I had gotten too comfortable, with the meetings and joking around and now the training of interns. I had to remind myself that I was there to do *my* job, not their job.

I thought about that on the way back to Bi-Cities, and I got pretty fired up about injustice and whatnot. But it was hard to stay fired up when I got there and saw Marie. She was so pragmatic. Right away she was telling me how the Haislip Kiwanis wanted money for a bingo ball machine, and could I find one on eBay? I told her sure I could, and there I was, just minutes after firing myself up, sitting in front of a computer weighing the pros and cons of manual versus hydraulic bingo cages.

The problem was I liked Marie. I liked running errands for her, arranging travel. I liked calling people on the phone and saying, "Hi there, I'm calling on behalf of Marie Angiulo, and she'd like to talk to so and so," then handing off the phone when the person she wanted was on the line. Sometimes it was Marie's sister in Rhode Island and the sister would joke that Marie was such a bigshot she couldn't even punch a few numbers anymore. Marie and her sister talked all the time. When I asked Marie about it, she said family was a choice.

I told Marie how Mom and Ruthanne were always bugging me to visit them but never visited me themselves. I told her they were lazy. Marie nodded. I expected her to say how lazy people were the worst, but what she said was that part of being an adult was taking responsibility for your relationships. She said, "It's decision time, Ben. If you want to keep having a relationship with your mother and sister, you gotta make an effort. Families drift apart all the time." I thought about that, how Grandpa was alone and Dad was with Geraldine, and Mom and Ruthanne were far away. I guess our family had already drifted apart, except for me. I was in the middle. I tried to think of myself as connected to all of them, like the hub of a wheel, but I hadn't talked to Mom in almost a month, Dad in three or four months. Even Grandpa I hadn't seen in two weeks, and I *lived* with him, or was supposed to. If I was the hub, then the wheel was broke; the hub had popped out miles back and been left in a ditch.

As if it weren't hard enough to stay fired up working with Marie, one day in February she told me she and Whitey had decided in the budget meeting to start paying me ten dollars an hour.

I was shocked. Minimum wage was one thing, but ten dollars an hour? That was good money. I thanked Marie again and again, but Marie said to thank Whitey.

"Free work is easy to come by in this game," she said, "but Whitey went to bat for you. Your new title is Assistant to the Campaign Manager."

I was dazzled. "Assistant to the Campaign Manager," I repeated. "What do I do? Do I do something different?"

"Keep doing what you're doing."

I felt emotional. It was like I had been working all my life for the promotion when really it was just a few months. I felt so thankful it was corny. I tried to remind myself that the one who was paying me was Whitey Connors, my secret nemesis, but it didn't make a difference. Whitey was the one who went to bat for me, like Marie said. I just didn't hate Whitey Connors. I wanted to, but I didn't.

"The question," Marie said, "is what you're going to do with that money. I'd warn you not to blow it on liquor but you're, what, sixteen?"

"Eighteen."

"You still sleeping in the back of the office?"

"No," I lied.

"Well, if you were, I'd say stop. It's like getting paid twice. Find a roommate and get an apartment, like a couple city girls. It'll be like a TV show except horrible. Sex in the Shithole. You could probably afford a mansion in this dirt-bag town."

"How do you find a roommate?"

She laughed. "I don't know anymore. Tell you what, I'll give you the number of the lady who found my place for me."

The lady who found Marie's place for her, meaning the furnished apartment she had rented sight-unseen when she moved down to run Connors for State Treasurer, was a realtor named Debbie McIntosh. I arranged to meet Debbie at an apartment in downtown Komer, and she showed up wearing high heels and a skirt-suit. She drove a hybrid car and had a businesslike air. The only thing about her that said Komer, not the city, was a colorful mask of makeup.

The apartment was in a new building where a parking lot used to be. It was four stories and each story had some terraces so overall it looked like a stucco ziggurat. Inside, the apartment had lots of windows and a shiny floor that looked like wood, but Debbie said was bamboo. The shower had two nozzles. The whole place was kind of creepy but I kept poking around to be polite and Debbie kept smiling and showing me the granite countertops, stainless steel appliances, linen closet, etc. Finally, when there wasn't anything left to show me, she said the apartment cost twelve hundred a month.

I couldn't believe it. "Twelve hundred dollars?"

"Quite a deal, I know."

"The last place we lived was three-fifty and it had two whole bedrooms."

Debbie looked at me quizzically. "You're from Komer?"

"Of course I am. Who lives in Komer who isn't from Komer?"

"Marie Angiulo, for one."

"For another?"

Debbie sighed. "Young professionals, is the idea, but they haven't gotten here yet. This building was supposed to be, like, an if-you-build-it-they-will-come thing."

"I'm sure it'll get filled eventually." I had my doubts, but I wanted to be nice. Debbie seemed to be taking this personally.

"What kind of place did you have in mind?" she asked.

I told her about the apartment where I used to live and said I wouldn't mind living there again, but she told me it was dangerous, which was true, and for about the same price she could get me a place much nicer and more centrally located.

"Central to what?" I asked.

Debbie sighed again.

I followed Debbie all the way to Haislip. I was excited. I thought she might show me an apartment in one of the old haunted houses along Grande Esplanade. But what she showed me was an apartment downtown, which wasn't much of a downtown, just a strip of shops in two-story brick buildings painted various colors. Most were closed. The apartment Debbie showed me was over a boarded up hardware store. She called it a loft apartment, but what made it a loft I had no idea. It was one long room with a toilet and a sink. The wood floor was pretty scuffed and had an unusual number of electric sockets along the baseboards. "It used to be a dressmaker's," Debbie explained. "The rent is five hundred a month."

I had done the math and knew I would make over four hundred a week, so I could afford the place, but five hundred for a creepy old dressmaker's shop where the toilet faced the kitchen sink didn't seem justified. I liked the idea of living in Haislip, though, and I didn't want to come off as a hayseed, so I said, "This place is nice, but can I think about it?"

"Sure," Debbie said. "Take all the time you need." Then she just stood there so I guess I was supposed to start thinking about it. I walked to the big front windows and looked down on Main Street, which was empty, but there were some kids throwing a football in the square. Beyond them were the mansions of Grande Esplanade. One had a long front porch with a lady in a rocking chair. Next to that one was the one with the round part like the tower of a castle. The windows on that one were broken, so I wondered if anybody lived there. I was looking for signs of life when a long-haired white man with a backpack let himself through a wire gate into the side yard. I watched for lights to come on, but none did. I wondered if he was living there in secret, what Grandpa would have called squatting. Grandpa would have called this man a hobo, but I didn't think of people that way anymore.

I told Debbie I just couldn't decide. I asked if I could talk to my Grandpa first, and she said yes, of course. "When you're ready to sign the lease," she said, "you'll need the first month's rent plus a five-hundred-dollar security deposit."

"A thousand dollars?"

"Cash or certified check."

I drove to Grandpa's, meaning to sound him out, but I ended up helping him pull the buckwheat he had planted to overwinter in the raised beds. "Buckwheat fixes nitrogen," he explained, "and it tastes good too." For dinner we had buckwheat pancakes. The batter was made from buckwheat flour he got at the store, though, not his garden. Maybe he was trying to convince himself of the usefulness of buckwheat. After dinner we watched *Traces of Red*, in which a Palm Beach detective runs afoul of a sensual heiress.

After the movie I went up to Dinwiddie's room and slid out my shoeboxes from under the bed. There was $2,013 inside, twice as much as I needed to cover the security deposit and first month's rent. A thousand was a lot of money, of course, but I had two thousand sitting right there, and what else was I going to use it for? I wasn't buying flamethrowers. I wasn't enriching uranium. I wasn't saving up for college, that was for sure. The money wasn't doing me any good sitting in a shoebox wrapped in duct tape. But to spend it felt like a violation. A violation of my ideals. Except what were my ideals anymore? What had they ever been? Destruction? Infiltration? And wasn't it also a violation *not* to spend the money? It was a waste, was what it was. The question I had to answer was if spending the money on a dumb apartment was the best way to spend it, or if there was another way that would do more good. I wracked my brain. A new bike? But I needed a car to get back and forth from Grandpa's. A new truck for Grandpa? But he never even used the *old* truck, preferring the smooth ride of his Crown Vic. New screens for the porch? A window unit for Dinwiddie's room? None of it seemed worthwhile. Grandpa and I were doing fine. But there were people in the world besides me and Grandpa. If Boss had been in that room with me I would have given him a hundred in cash right then and there, to ease his way. I would have given money to Leo and Candy, too. Maybe I could go around handing money to people, like some kind of Christmas movie. But I didn't like the idea of giving money to strangers. I wouldn't know what they might use it for. Even Leo, what if he just bought a sharper knife? What if Candy bought a moped? What if Boss, who wasn't too bright, let's be honest, bought a massage chair or box seats to the rodeo? No, I had to give the money to someone I knew well.

So the next morning I took the heaviest shoebox and wrapped it in one more layer of duct tape then dunked it in the toilet to make sure it was watertight (it was) and drove it to the post office in downtown Komer. I told the post office lady I wanted to send it the safest way possible, so for $23.30 I sent it priority mail with two-thousand-dollars insurance. She thought I was crazy to get so much insurance on a shoebox, but I insisted.

Ruthanne called two days later to ask if I was dealing drugs.

"Nope," I said.

"Then where did all this cash come from?"

I explained to Ruthanne that I had saved every dollar I ever made except for what I spent on the candy we shared.

"Keep saving it," she said. "I don't want it."

"I don't either. I don't need it. Use it for rent so you can quit the Burger Brothers and concentrate on school."

"What about you? What about college?"

"Well," I said, then explained my entire situation: how I started showing up late to school when I was scavenging at the dump, then missed a few days living with Pete, then stopped going altogether when I got my job at Connors for State Treasurer. The words came in a flood. It felt good to tell the truth, and what could Ruthanne do? She was a hundred miles away.

She didn't comment for a while. I expected her to rake me over the coals like she always did, then to tattle on me to Mom at the earliest opportunity, but instead she said, "Ben, you always did go your own way."

"What's that supposed to mean?"

"What it sounds like. You go your own way."

"Is that something Mom says or what?"

"It's something I say. I know you, Ben."

"So you're telling me to keep skipping school? What about college?"

"Seems like you're doing okay without college. Whitey Connors has been good to you. I don't hate him as much as I used to, now that I don't live there anymore. I mean, he's employing people like you, Komer people, which is good."

Ruthanne was so levelheaded!

"Look, Ben," she said, "it's you and me now, is the way I see it, and that's how it's always gonna be. It doesn't matter if you live down there and I live here or vice versa. There's this thing that happens, that's been happening to me, as I get older. It's like, when I'm apart from people—you—you continue to exist for me. Before, it was out of sight, out of mind. Now I think about you, I wonder what you're doing. I'll be on the bus to class and wonder if you're drinking a glass of water or combing your hair or what. It's kind of dumb, I guess."

"It's important not to forget people."

"That's right. You wanna talk to Mom?"

"No, I guess not. Don't tell her about the money, okay?"

"She's gonna ask when I pay the rent."

"Huh. Well, come up with something so she doesn't think I dropped out."

"I will," she said, and I knew she would. She was a genius at deceiving Mom.

The conversation was kind of sad in a way, but it gave me a good feeling, deep down. Ruthanne said it was her and me, and she was right. She would be my sister my whole life, or at least until she died. Ruthanne would probably die first, I figured, on account of her inactive lifestyle and possible side-effects from her weird spine.

"Ben," she said, "what the hell were you going to do with all that money?"

"I was gonna buy a Red Dragon 400,000 BTU Backpack Torch Kit with Squeeze Valve," I said, and that was that. I wasn't going to incinerate the dump. I wasn't going to throw my life away to murder Whitey Connors and end up in jail like Ronnie, gibbering about the race war apocalypse. I didn't even *dislike* Whitey Connors. It was a relief, honestly, except for the vague feeling that with the money went my chance at adventure. But maybe the life of an adventurer just wasn't for me. Or maybe it was but it would have to be somebody else's adventure, like Whitey's or Marie's, and I would get in on the action as a sort of Sherpa, possibly the superior climber but by virtue of temperament and circumstance more of a facilitator, a technician. That, or I could go my own way. Only time would tell.

Chapter 15

BY THE SUMMER, I was sending half my paychecks straight to Ruthanne and living in a squat beneath a mansion on Grande Esplanade. Squatting turned out to be pretty easy. The house upstairs was empty so nobody could hear me in the basement, and I came and went through a cellar door in the backyard, where the weeds were so tall nobody could see me. To get the water turned on all I had to do was show up at the county water office and give them enough money to cover the deposit and back bills. I didn't even have to pretend to be the owner of the house, a dead lady named Delores Jermyn. Electricity was harder, though. I had to show a title or lease and when I told the lady at the electricity office that Mrs. Jermyn was dead she went back to get her supervisor, so I left. I made do with camping lanterns, which I hung from the low ceiling by hooks. I had a camping stove too, but I didn't do much cooking since I didn't have a fridge. I kept milk for breakfast cereal along with some sandwich fixings in the breakroom fridge at Bi-Cities. I was working at Bi-Cities HQ instead of the campaign office because Whitey Connors lost the election.

After he lost, Whitey asked Marie to stay and be VP of Public Relations for Bi-Cities, but she said no. She told me privately that she thought hard about it, because she was getting sick of moving around all the time, but her mom had cancer back in Rhode Island, so that's where she went. I was sad to see her go. After she left, it fell

to me to take photos of Whitey at all the events he went to and spoke
at, and whenever a photo was really bad I emailed it to Marie as a
joke, like when the new PR guy convinced Whitey to wear a chicken
costume at a half-marathon sponsored by a sports bar called Chicken
Fingerz. I sent her a photo of Whitey sipping his soda through a hole
in the beak and she wrote back, "What a clown—lol."

Whitey was a clown, for sure, and a weirdo and a terror, but I
liked him. My job was to help his assistant, Carol, keep his schedule
and arrange his travel. So I was sort of like the assistant to the assistant, and also the assistant to the body man, Daryl, though Daryl worked strictly from nine to five so if anything happened early
or late, I was substitute body man. If we stayed past seven Whitey
would send me out for food and tell me to spare no expense. Then,
at the end of the night, he'd peel me off a couple twenties. Over-
time, he called it. Things might have gone on like that forever, and I
would have been fine with it, if it wasn't for this one thing that happened, which reminded me of my former life, and of the underbelly
of Whitey's success.

It happened at a fancy new grocery store on the outskirts of
town, where the campaign office use to be. I was buying groceries for
Grandpa and me (I still spent weekends at Grandpa's, where I could
shower and have some company), and when I came out of the store
with my groceries and was about to get in the truck, I noticed a man
bent over by the dumpster. He was picking through trash that had
overflowed from the top of the dumpster and fallen to the concrete
below. His gray overcoat looked familiar. His hands had a careful
quickness that was also familiar, tapping along the surface of the
trash like a pianist. When he held up a bag of romaine hearts to get a
look at them in the sunlight, I recognized his grizzled bird-like face.

"Leo!" I said. I was happy to see him. Enough time had gone by
that I didn't think about all the mean stuff he did to me.

Leo peered at me from under the brim of his hat, a stocking
cap on top of a baseball cap like some folks wear, but he didn't say

anything. Maybe he didn't recognize me, I thought, so I got closer. I waved and acted real smiley because I didn't want to spook him, but when I was close enough to shake his hand he still looked like he didn't recognize me. He had little red flecks on his cheeks, like shaving bumps, except he hadn't shaved in quite a while. He looked older than I remembered. On the other side of the dumpster was a shopping cart full of overstuffed black trash bags.

"Any cell phones in there?" I joked.

Leo seemed confused. He glanced back at his shopping cart, then at me again. I was starting to get offended, but I reminded myself that Leo was older; he'd seen many more faces than I had. Plus he probably loomed larger in my mind than I did in his.

"I tried to find y'all, you know," I said. "I tried to find you, but you were gone."

"Where?" His voice was raspy, like he hadn't used it in a while.

"The dump. Remember?"

"Where did we go?"

I was confused. "I don't know. You tell me."

Leo didn't say anything. He glanced at his shopping cart again. Maybe he was just being secretive, I thought. He had always been paranoid.

"How's Boss?" I asked, to change the subject. That's what I really cared about anyway.

Leo still didn't say anything. It occurred to me he might not know who I was talking about. He almost certainly hadn't called the man Boss, and I couldn't remember Boss's real name. I tried again: "How's Candy?"

At the name Candy, Leo looked down and grunted. "Candy," he repeated.

I'll never forget the sound of his voice as he said her name: a croak, but not like a frog's croak; like something halfway between a burp and the sound a machine makes on the fritz. The sound was chilling. It combined with his hollow expression for an uncanny effect that revolted me. I wanted to get away as quickly as possible, but I felt bad. I didn't want to hurt his feelings, in case he had any left. "Leo," I said, "are you okay?"

Leo turned without looking at me and started away, like I wasn't there. I felt sorry for him. I figured he must be fried on drugs, a bad trip or something. That would have explained why they left the dump: if something had happened to Leo, Candy and Boss wouldn't have been able to keep the operation going. But the idea of a bad trip didn't quite ring true. Leo didn't seem like the type who took enjoyment from the escape offered by drugs—unless something terrible had happened, something that changed him.

I watched him push his cart across the alley behind the grocery store, where the trucks came and went. The concrete slab backed up to some dirty thin woods. Leo pushed his cart between the trees and disappeared from view. I decided to follow him.

Where he disappeared turned out to be a dirt path, worn from use. I walked along the path, dodging tree branches, until I saw Leo up ahead. He was moving real slow so I kept my distance. My view of Leo came and went among the trees, but I could always hear his rattling grocery cart. There must have been cans in there.

We kept walking and walking. Instead of harder to follow, the path got wider. It made me think of the ancient buffalo traces, worn by animals and the hunters who hunted them. Now *we* were the animals.

I wasn't sure why I was following Leo, since he had made it clear he didn't want to talk to me. I guess I just wondered where—and how—he lived. Plus Boss might have lived there with him, though I hoped not, because if Boss was still hanging around Leo, *this* Leo, he couldn't have been in much better shape himself.

There was light up ahead. Leo had entered a clearing full of tall grass and weeds. Beyond him were the backs of three houses along a winding road of pristine black asphalt. Beyond the road was what looked like a dried up pond. One of the three houses looked incomplete. The top was jagged, like a dinosaur had come by and taken a big bite out of it. It looked new, though. All the houses did. I thought they might be brand new construction, but later I found out online that the houses had been aborted in 2008, around the same time as my first attempt on Trash Mountain. No one ever moved in. The new people, the people who bought groceries at the fancy grocery store, didn't like those houses I guess.

Leo pushed his cart up to the sliding glass door behind one of the houses, slid open the door, and went inside. If it had been anybody except Leo, I would have knocked on the door, but Leo had threatened me with a chef's knife the first time we met. For all I knew he still kept the knife in the pocket of his dirty cinched trousers. I imagined knocking on the door only for Leo to circle around the house from the front door, sneak up behind me, and stab me in the back again and again until I flopped face-first into grass and tossed around clutching my wounds, gasping for breath, then looked up at the sun through a death mask of terror and regret.

It wasn't worth it.

On the way back to the grocery store, I started feeling sorry for Leo again. Maybe he got senile from boredom, I thought. Grandpa once told me how old men who retire get senile because they don't have anything to do, but how he, Grandpa, had retired young enough to develop hobbies like growing sweet potatoes and dragging his property for hobos. If Leo was senile from boredom, I reasoned, it was because he got kicked out of Bi-Cities. It was because of Whitey. It was because of me!

When I got back to the truck and my bags of overpriced groceries, I felt low. The parking lot was full of fat people pushing grocery carts. The SUV parked in front of me had stickers on the back of stick figures representing the husband and wife and their three little kids. There was even a goddamned dog sticker. Were there hobo stickers? Jailbird stickers? Or how about a Sleeper sticker, where the Sleeper's stroking his veiny Sleeper dick while leering at the rest of those goddamned stickers?

Grandpa and I had a nice dinner of hot dogs and baked sweet potatoes, which made me feel better, but I couldn't sleep that night. I kept picturing Leo shuffling around behind that dumpster, and me coming up behind him, coming closer than I had in real life. The way I pictured it, half dreaming, I put my hand on Leo's shoulder and he turned to face me but his face was slack. He was looking at me without seeing me. His eyes were dead. The brain they led to had been hollowed out like a dried-up beehive.

It was then that an even darker thought occurred to me: what if it wasn't drugs or drink or boredom that had changed Leo, but the dump itself? I remembered the noxious smell of the dump spray the night I stayed there, and the peculiar smell of the metal shavings Leo scraped from the circuit boards. *Rare earth.* It sounded so strange now. They mined it in China, Grandpa said, and Dad said the Chinese didn't care what happened to the working man. Maybe in China there were thousands of old wrecks like Leo wandering zombielike through the streets.

I had to say something to Whitey, I decided, but what could I say? Whitey hadn't done anything directly, or maliciously, and he could spin what he did as a favor to Leo. Leo made money, after all, and he did the work by choice. Whitey was a smooth talker. I had to practice what I would say to him. I would start off slow, something like "Mister Connors, may I have a word? I ran into an old friend of mine, and he wasn't looking too good. His name's Leo. Maybe you remember him?" But Whitey might say no, he didn't remember Leo, and where would I go from there? And how would I make it clear, without being rude, that I blamed Whitey; that, in my opinion, Whitey should bear some responsibility for Leo? And for Ruthanne's weird spine? And for bulldozing my childhood home to make room for more trash?

"Listen, motherfucker," I said, staring at my own face in the bathroom mirror and karate-chopping the air for emphasis, "here's how it is: you bulldozed my goddamn house, and now you're gonna pay!"

When I got to work, I felt awkward asking Carol for an appointment to see a man I saw every day, but Carol didn't seem fazed by it. Maybe she figured I was asking for a raise. She said Whitey could fit me in at 4:15, and I agreed to it.

For the rest of the day I rehearsed in my head what I was going to say. I even wrote it down, pondered it, revised it: "*You bulldozed my home, Mr. Connors. You ruined my sister's spine. Yeah, she's okay now, thanks for asking.*"

At 4:10 I was sitting on the loveseat across from Carol's desk, waiting. It reminded me of Principal Winthrope's office, like *I* was the one in trouble, not Whitey. I tried to think of Leo, Ruthanne, the noxious dump spray. But then Whitey poked his head out to say something to Carol and saw me sitting there.

"Goddamn, girl," he said to her, "don't keep this man waiting." I knew he was just saying that to flatter me, at Carol's expense, but it felt good anyway.

Whitey ushered me into his office and we sat down on either side of his desk. There were framed photos of him all over the walls, smiling among bigger and older men in suits, breaking ground with golden shovels, snipping ribbons with big novelty scissors. I knew I needed to dive right in, before he got the best of me, but Whitey was too quick: "Ben," he said, "I'm glad you're here. I've been meaning to talk to you about something."

"Me too," I said.

"Me first! Listen, school's about to start, and I know, I know, you don't wanna go. School's for dummies. I hear you. I dropped out myself and would do the same again, so I can't stand here and tell you to go back to school. And I don't *want* you to go back to school. What would I do without you? 'Specially now that Marie's gone. But listen—" He launched into a spiel about the importance of education while I sat there, stunned. I had come into the office ready to tell him off, but he was bombarding me with fatherly advice. "Which is why," he concluded, "I want you to take night classes for a GED."

"What good would that do?" I asked. "I have a job already."

"We got a good thing going, for sure, but businesses don't last a lifetime, not even for Russian oil tycoons. What if you gotta do a résumé again? You can't keep lying on your résumé, Tex."

"But why would I pay for night classes if I can go to school for free?"

"Opportunity cost. Besides, I'll pay."

I couldn't believe it. Whitey was pulling me deeper than ever. I tried to refuse the offer, but he insisted.

"Never look a gift horse in the mouth," he said. "Ever heard that one before?"

"Sure."

"Ever thought about it?"

"Not really."

"The meaning is twofold. The first meaning is obvious: if a horse is given to you as a gift, don't look in its mouth for a horse disease such as distemper or horse gingivitis, at least not in front of the fella what gave you the horse. That's the way everybody takes it, and that's good advice, let me tell you, on the campaign trail especially. But there's a second way to take it. That's where the horse isn't the gift but the giver."

"A horse that gives gifts?"

"Yep."

"There's horses like that?"

"Sure there are. Santa's reindeer, for instance."

"A reindeer's a type of horse?"

"For sure."

"I thought it was a moose."

"You're missing the forest from the trees, Ben. A bird in the hand, is what I'm saying. A stitch in time. I don't want you to make the same mistakes I did."

"What mistakes?"

"Choosing too soon. You don't have to choose between work and school. A boy can do both, and anyone who says different is a pansy. The way America is today, it coddles the young person. Go to high school, it says. Go to college. Spend a couple years after college waiting tables so you can get to feeling unfulfilled and wind up in grad school for social work. But some people, they don't have to noodle around like that. They're like arrows shot from a quiver. Take Ben Franklin, for instance. Did you know Ben Franklin was apprenticed at the age of thirteen?"

"No, sir."

"To his brother, as a printer. And Ben Franklin became one of the greatest printers in the history of the United States, and a writer and a diplomat. An inventor, too. He invented the lightning rod, the bifocals, and a glass harmonica for which Mozart and Beethoven composed. Now, would Ben Franklin have ended up where he did if he were left to noodle around a few more years before getting into the printing game? Maybe. But why risk it, is what I'm saying. And that's the way I feel about Bi-Cities Sanitation."

I didn't follow. Was Whitey Ben Franklin in the analogy, and Bi-Cities the glass harmonica? Whitey had a way of overwhelming you with words. For a moment I forgot my purpose in meeting with him. Then he said, "Ben, how do *you* feel about Bi-Cities sanitation?" and it all came back to me. Now was my chance to tell him what was on my mind.

I looked at Whitey, who had been pacing around. He had stopped, though, and was waiting for me to speak. "I don't know," I said. "I guess I kinda felt more comfortable working for your campaign than for Bi-Cities, you know?"

Whitey withdrew slightly, crossing his arms. "More *comfortable*?" he repeated. "So you're saying you're *uncomfortable* working here at Bi-Cities?"

"No, sir."

"Bi-Cities puts money in your pocket. Mine too. Good clean money. And that's hard to come by nowadays." He started pacing again, like he was looking for something. "Where's my drink? You seen my drink?"

He meant his giant soda. It was on the floor beside his desk so I picked it up for him. It smelled kind of funny, like cough medicine.

"Thank you kindly," he said, then sat down and started slurping the warm drink through a straw. When he stopped, he leaned back and sighed. He said, "It's the trash, isn't it?"

"Sir?"

"The stigma of working with trash. I wouldn't have figured you for it, Ben. A Komer man. A man who made it by the skin of his boots. I wouldn't have figured you for having secret delicate sensibilities."

"I don't have sensibilities," I said, feeling defensive. "I was picking trash before you even knew me. I probably spent more time in that dump than you have. I definitely spent more time looking at it. You can't even *see* Trash Mountain from this office."

Whitey spun in his chair to look at me. "What mountain?"

"Nothing," I said. I didn't want to talk about Trash Mountain, to besmirch my memories by sharing them with Whitey, who, like any other adult, might have turned them into something they weren't, some kind of boys-will-be-boys, oh-you-kids bullshit. So I cut to the chase: "Remember Leo?"

Whitey smiled. "Of course I do. What's that old rascal up to?"

I almost told Whitey how I saw Leo behind the dumpster, but I didn't know how to describe what I saw in Leo's face, or what I failed to see, and I didn't want to hear Whitey say something glib about the man. Leo deserved some dignity, was how I saw it. "He isn't doing too good," I said.

"How about his girlfriend, that black lady? I always liked her."

"Candy. I didn't see her."

"What about the other one? Tall fella? Harelip?"

"Boss. I haven't seen him either." I was surprised Whitey remembered Leo, let alone Boss and Candy. I wondered if he knew more than he let on.

Whitey forked his fingers and pointed at his two eyes. "Ben," he said, "my office may not face it anymore, but I see everybody who comes and goes from that dump. Hear me?"

"Yessir," I said, "but why'd you fire them?"

"Fire them? They never worked for me."

"They recycled for you, the rare earth and whatnot."

"They screwed me is what they did. I told them they could pick over the trash for recyclables, but they got greedy. I got another guy, Ramón, who salvages the electronics. Not that it matters anymore."

"Why doesn't it matter?"

"The Chinese are paying for all of it, and they don't want it picked over before it gets to China. You seen those dozers making it into cubes?"

"Sure."

"That's to ship it. I didn't kick your friends out, just tightened up security. I do it every few years anyway, to keep kids out more than anything. There isn't a kid in this county who hasn't snuck into Bi-Cities and made himself a trash fort. But you wouldn't know anything about that, would you?" He eyed me across his desk, a smile creeping up his cheeks. "You never snuck in and messed around, huh?"

For a moment I panicked. Did he know I tried to blow the place up? Had he been keeping track of me all those years? Keep your enemies close, is what they say. But no, that was impossible. He would have had to be omniscient to keep track of all those people. Godlike. Hundreds of kids snuck in to stack beer cans and pull apart rusty appliances and poke dirty condoms with a stick. The ovens and refrigerators had been hiding places for a whole generation.

"You know the insurance I pay on this place?" Whitey asked. "All kinds of ways for a person to die in a landfill. One of the deadliest jobs in the country. There was a TV show on it. But the Mexicans, it's this or the chicken factory for those boys. I put ads in the newspaper down there and they come. Why you looking cross, Ben? Who's gonna do it if they don't? You? That old criminal Leo and his crew?"

"I'm not cross."

"Don't lie to me. You got a face like an open book. That's why I can trust you. Goddamn, Ben, people try to make it so simple. They try to make like there's this evil dump that's poisoning everybody and everybody's innocent. They never write about how people be climbing in and out of the dump like goddamn monkeys. But you know what? It's been three years since anybody died here, including Mexicans."

"I guess I don't see why you care so much about safety inside the dump when there's people getting sick from it and stuff. Rashes and stuff." My voice was cracking. My face felt warm so I knew it was red. I was too embarrassed to look at Whitey so I looked at my hands.

"I know about Ruthanne," Whitey said.

I looked up. Whitey's face was kind of pinched, like he was trying, and failing, to manufacture the appropriate expression. He said, "I know and it breaks my heart. And I know she's in school right now and doing fine. And I know I *don't* know a damned thing about airborne particulate waste matter, and nobody else does either. As for Leo, that old drunk, he had some good years, right? Why you looking at me that way? Listen, Ben, there's something I'm gonna say to you. People pretend it ain't true, and maybe it ain't, but we act like it is so what's the difference. Here's the thing: some people's lives aren't as valuable as other people's." He raised his hands, like he was sorry to say it but somebody had to. It made me wonder if it was a speech he had given before. "Unchristian? Sure. But we don't live in a Christian world, Ben. Religion is a Band-Aid. Think about war: how do we go off and fight other people if we think their lives are as valuable as ours? And what about the clothes we buy? Would we let our own kids work in the sweatshops that make them clothes? Hell no. We won't even let 'em work in a goddamn dump. That's for the Mexicans. Only reason we let our kids fight in wars is the ones who fight are like you, Ben: poor kids, city kids who'll never get a job otherwise, country kids who'll waste their lives on couches, eating junk food, raising fat little babies just like them. At least the Chinese are honest. They throw bodies at projects like you wouldn't believe: construction projects, mining projects, engineering projects like that three-forked dam they got. One time I was in a Shanghai hotel and woke up in the middle of the night. I couldn't sleep so I went to get my soda like I do, and my soda was on a table by the window. The hotel was in this tower, see, and when I looked out the window the sky was black—there weren't no stars, from the smog—but the ground was covered in clusters of twinkling lights. Do you know what those lights were, Ben? Those little white lights like stars?"

"No, sir."

"Blowtorches. Men were down there working construction all through the night, every hour of every day, every day of every week. Those men went home to see their families maybe once a year, too tired to do anything but sleep." It was exactly what Dad had said on the subject of the Chinese working man, which made me wonder if Whitey had really been to China or if he saw the same TV show Dad did. Whitey said, "They call it human capital down there, and that's what it is. We could learn a thing or two from China, let me tell you."

"Seems like you already have," I said.

"I'm not telling you how the world should be, Ben, just how it is."

"But what's the point? Why build all those buildings so fast? Why mine so much rare earth? Just to make more cell phones?"

Whitey rubbed his fingers together and smiled. He didn't speak, like the answer went without saying. But I wasn't satisfied.

"What's it for?" I asked. "Look at you. I mean, no offense, but you don't spend it any way I can tell. You don't have a fancy car or go on vacation. You don't have shiny teeth like Doctor Tom, or an expensive haircut. You don't even wear nice clothes. No offense."

"None taken. You're right, Ben. I didn't get into this business for money. I didn't get into this business to recycle anything either, let alone some doohickey for cell phones. Where I grew up, we burned our trash." He swept his arm vaguely. "If it was all the same I'd burn it still. Burn every single piece of trash in Bi-Cities Sanitation. That would speed things up."

"Speed things up for what?"

"All I'm saying is I didn't buy this place for trash. I bought it as a long-term real estate venture. This is prime real estate. I did my research. You know where Staten Island is?"

"New York City. That's where Fresh Kills is." Fresh Kills was a famous dump that got clogged up with chunks of the World Trade Center. I knew about it because I'd made a study of dumps during computer class, years before.

"Exactly," Whitey said, "and you wouldn't believe how much they make on the little pieces of that place they carve off and sell to developers. What I didn't expect was to make such a killing on the trash part. The people who ran this place before—the government people, before they had the good sense to privatize—they must have been goddamn idiots. They didn't make a dime!"

"You said it wasn't about the money."

"It isn't! Oh, Ben, it isn't! Look here." He sprang from his chair and opened the closet. On the back wall was a safe with a combination lock he quickly spun. He withdrew what looked like a thin coffee table book. He turned to me, clutching the book to his chest. "Have I ever told you my thoughts on racism?"

"No sir," I said, bracing myself for another speech.

"Racism is a species of suspicion of one's fellow man. So are sexism and gerontism, which is hatred of the elderly. The slow separation of Komer and Haislip, first by class, then by race, is the legacy of hatred, the devil in man's heart. But one day the two will be reunited as a glorious whole. Ever heard of Budapest?"

"Sure, up north somewhere."

"Hungary. It's a glorious city, but it's actually two cities, Buda and Pest, with a lovely river between them."

"But we've got a dump, not a river."

"One day, not too far in the future, the dump will be the single spot of undeveloped land in the middle of a great metropolis."

I found that hard to imagine, but I played along. "So you'll sell it?"

"I'll donate it, but not before I flatten it and make it into a municipal park. You heard of Central Park, in New York City?"

At first I thought he was kidding, but Whitey proceeded to lay out a vision so grandiose, so elaborate, that he had to be serious. With whispering care he described groves of crepe myrtles and azaleas, hills of native grasses, an outdoor café, a Shakespeare garden, decorative boulders rolled in from the piedmont. The park would be an inclusive space, he said, a neighborhood anchor, a focal point for the daily rhythms of the lives of its users, promoting ecological, programmatic, experiential, and social diversity. I couldn't believe the stuff that was coming out of his mouth. I never heard him talk like that before.

"Ben," he said, "I'm gonna show you something I've hardly shown anybody else in this world. It's precious to me, so be gentle if you think it's corny." He knelt beside me and opened the thin book so we both could see it. On the cover it said it was a Proposal for Landscape Architecture Services by Vokler Associates LLC. Whitey said Mr. Vokler was the best in the business, a real gentleman, then he started turning pages in the book for me. There were sections and plans, mockups and photos. The photos were done up on a computer so you could see people lounging and cavorting in a park that didn't yet exist. Sometimes there'd be a photo of the dump on the left-hand page then a photo of the exact same spot on the right-hand page but with, say, a man walking his dog while talking on a cell phone. There was an outdoor café, just like Whitey said, and a bunch of big boulders. There were little cartoon people eating lunches on blankets, kids riding dirt bikes, a dog high up in the air catching a Frisbee.

After turning all the pages in reverent silence, Whitey explained how he was going to sell the outskirts of the dump to real estate developers in order to create "a self-perpetuating endowment that will last for eternity."

As I listened I was stunned but also relieved, and a little confused by this turn of events, this re-jiggering in my mind of Whitey's motivations and, by extension, his character. Only minutes before, I'd been angry, thinking about Leo and Ruthanne and everybody else who suffered because of this man, but now I felt different. It was a beautiful park. I guess I felt proud of Whitey, and a little bit sorry for him too. I thought about the empty unfinished subdivision where I found Leo, and about the weird ziggurat apartment Debbie showed me. The man walking his dog, the people eating lunch, the kid on the bike—where would they come from?

"Thanks for sharing this with me," I said.

Whitey stood up and tucked the book under his arm. "It felt good to show it to somebody like you," he said, "somebody young and full of ideas. The kind of person I hope this town can keep, down the line." He glanced around. "You seen my drink?"

"I think it's empty."

"Shit. Anyway, what did you want to see me about?"

"Pardon?"

"You're 4:15 on my calendar and it's damn near five."

"Oh, nothing. I just wanted to touch base."

"You want a raise, but you lost your gumption, didn't you?" He wagged the book and smiled. "It was the park, wasn't it? You think I'm a philanthropist now. Nobody wants to swindle a philanthropist."

"Yeah," I said. "I guess that's it."

On the way home I was relieved. I didn't have to confront Whitey quite like I thought I would, and I didn't feel bad about it because Whitey really did have a vision that went beyond money. I admired it. So what if the vision was self-aggrandizing and possibly delusional, built as it was on a hypothetical Komer/Haislip metropolis? It was more vision than anybody else had in Komer, or Haislip, or in Buda or Pest, probably. I was relieved, like I said, but a little dispirited too. I guess I wished it was my own vision, not his.

I parked down the block and was walking to my squat when a lady in a tracksuit came towards me smiling and waving. I thought she was just being friendly, but she stopped. She said, "You the boy who lives down there?"

"Yes, ma'am," I said, since she was old enough to be called ma'am.

"That's the old Jermyn place," she said.

"Delores Jermyn?"

"That's right. You knew her?"

"No, ma'am, but I tried to contact her next of kin."

"Good luck." She rolled her eyes. Then she said how she had known Delores Jermyn, who was "just the nicest little old lady you ever met." This woman, whose name was Barbara, had been "school chums" with Delores's younger sister, Pearl McCaskill. Pearl never married, Barbara explained, which was why she still had the last name McCaskill. Delores had married a serviceman by the name of Lawrence McCoughtrie, then somebody else whose name Barbara didn't remember, and then, finally, the dentist Arthur Jermyn. "Everybody around here knew Arthur Jermyn," she assured me, "and was his patient!" She laughed. I smiled. Then she told me about her own sister whose sister-in-law had married into the Donaldson family, and the Donaldsons were cousins to the Jermyns. "So we're all related, you see? Why, Doctor Tom Donaldson and me go to the same family reunion. Can you beat that?"

I told her I couldn't.

She smiled again and said, "Well, young man, I'm glad to meet you!" Then she walked away fast, swinging her hips with her fists tucked up near her shoulders. It was some kind of exercise, I guess. She seemed like a nice lady.

Downstairs I sat in a camping chair and tried to read one of the dusty *National Geographic* magazines somebody left behind. There was an article from March 1985 that showed some wrinkly Mongolian guys hunting with eagles. The hardest part, the article said, was racing on horseback to get to the dead rabbit or mountain goat before the eagle ripped it to shreds.

After I finished reading about the Mongolian eagle hunters, I couldn't find another article that piqued my interest. All of them made me think of adventure, and here I was in a basement squat reading a magazine. It was pathetic.

I felt hungry so I could have passed the time cooking, but I didn't really feel like it. I guess I felt lonely.

I called Ruthanne, but she didn't pick up her phone. I called Pete, but he didn't pick up either. It had been a couple months since I saw him, and he hadn't graduated. I hoped he was okay. I couldn't call Ronnie, though I made a note to visit him again in jail. I could have called Grandpa, I guess, but our conversations always involved errands or directions and only lasted about fifteen seconds. It wouldn't have been satisfying. So I decided to call Demarcus. He had graduated and it was almost time for school to start, but I had no idea where he was headed. Tech, probably, or somewhere out of state for smart people. I would call him and find out, I decided, but his number wasn't on the phone I got from Bi-Cities, which meant I hadn't talked to him since I started there. Actually, I hadn't even seen him since then. In all the years since I met him I never hung out with Demarcus even once outside of school, never even *saw* him. But why? He was my friend, wasn't he?

I left the apartment and got back in the truck. It was six o'clock, a decent hour because it was late summer and still light outside.

The little white house looked the same, though the porch might have been sagging a bit more. Even the gray cat, Ghost, was still behind the screen door, so fat and old he barely raised his head when I came creaking up the stairs onto the porch.

I knocked on the doorsill real softly, in case Demarcus's dad, Gerald, was asleep between shifts. But when I heard a man's voice call out "Who is it?" I knew I woke him up despite my effort.

"Sorry to bother you, sir," I said. "It's Ben, Demarcus's friend. He around?"

"He's at work."

"Oh yeah. Right. Where does he work again?"

"Hold on."

The floorboards creaked, and the man I'd seen years before emerged in the same blue bathrobe. He wasn't quite as tall as I remembered, and the puffs of hair over his ears were completely gray. He said, "I remember you."

"Yessir," I said.

"It's good you came around. Demarcus is leaving soon."

"Leaving, sir?"

"Yep. Made his decision. He can tell you all about it. He's down at the Lounge."

"The Motown Lounge?"

"That's right. Go in the back, since you ain't twenty-one. It's the door by the dumpster. It'll do him good. Pretty slow in there at this hour."

When I got to the Motown Lounge there were a few cars in the parking lot, but some of them might have belonged to people inside the title loan office next door. As per Gerald's instructions, I walked around back to a metal door beside a dumpster. I would have knocked, but I didn't want to draw undue attention, so I let myself inside.

The inside of the Motown Lounge was dark except for some dim lights behind the bar and a lamp hanging over the pool table. The lampshade was stained glass with a Schlitz logo. There was a man leaning over the bar and another man in the corner at the table. Both looked at me then looked away. Demarcus was behind the bar fiddling with his phone.

I went to the side of the bar, not daring to sit down, and whispered "Demarcus? Demarcus?" until he looked up at me with surprise.

"Ben?" He came towards me. "You can't be in here. You have to be twenty-one."

"Your dad said I could come see you."

"Oh. Well, if Dad says it's okay."

The man at the bar croaked, "Can't be in here if you ain't twenty-one."

"Can if my dad says you can," Demarcus told the man in a different voice than he used with me. The voice was stern, and it made Demarcus seem pretty old.

"Your dad told me you're leaving town," I said.

Demarcus nodded. "The army."

I couldn't believe it. The army? Demarcus didn't seem like the type. But he explained how the army would pay a hundred percent of his college tuition if he served on active duty for thirty-six months. "That way," he said, "I can go wherever I want. I don't have to go to Tech or some community college. No offense."

"I don't go to community college."

"But Ruthanne does, right?"

I nodded, touched that Demarcus remembered her. He was a considerate person. I couldn't imagine him marching around, hefting a gun, cleaning latrines and whatnot. I didn't *want* to imagine those things. I said, "But what if, you know . . ." I didn't know how to phrase what I was trying to ask. I didn't want to jinx him.

"What if I get my ass shot off?"

"Yeah."

"With my grades, I'll get a desk job. Plus I got a skin condition." Demarcus explained how he got rashes ever since he was a kid, and how it was probably related to the spray they put on the trash at the dump. There was a class-action lawsuit pending and his dad was looking into it on his behalf. We were discussing whether or not Ruthanne could get in on it, what with her weird spine and all, when it occurred to me I worked for the man Demarcus was planning to sue. I let the subject drop. Demarcus talked some more about the Army and how he was sure he'd get his ass kicked in boot camp since he was "pretty wimpy," he allowed, but he looked forward to seeing other countries.

"Like Iraq and Afghanistan?"

"More soldiers are stationed in Japan and Germany, believe it or not. How about you, Ben? What you been up to?"

I decided to come clean. I told Demarcus how after the campaign was over I stayed on at Bi-Cities. I explained what I did as succinctly as possible, not wanting to sound like I was bragging in case Demarcus thought I was a sellout. But he didn't. He was smiling like he couldn't believe my good fortune.

"My man," he said. "My man!" He gave me an elaborate handshake. "That's the American dream right there. That's sit-down work for sure."

I wanted to tell him more, about the not-so-nice thing I did to Tom Donaldson, about what happened to Leo, about how strange Whitey was, but it made me feel good that Demarcus seemed proud of me. And anyway the man at the bar was asking for a refill and another bowl of goldfish crackers. I said I should probably go. I said it was good to see him, and Demarcus said the same about me. I said I'd see him around, but I wasn't too sure.

After leaving the Motown Lounge, I felt nostalgic. I drove out to the west side of the dump, where Demarcus and I had snuck in, years before, and I walked along the strong new fence until I got to the outbuilding I used to climb. The dumpster was still behind it, so I climbed up the dumpster and onto the corrugated tin roof of the building. I didn't care anymore if a garbage man saw me, since I worked there and some of them knew me by sight.

It was a clear day so I looked all the way across the dump and tried to approximate where my house used to be. In the distance were some houses I recognized, but I couldn't remember which street was which anymore. I was still looking for my house when I noticed something different about Trash Mountain. It was still a mountain by any stretch, still as tall as it had ever been, but the trash all around it had gotten so high that Trash Mountain didn't *seem* like a mountain anymore. More like a bluff or something. The flattened expanse of trash made it easier to imagine the park Whitey envisioned, the weird Central Park of his dreams. In my mind I could overlay the landscape of trash with rolling green hills of similar shape. I tried to see it like Whitey did, to see the picnickers and dogs, the outdoor café, maybe a fountain or two, kids running through fields of cut grass instead of picking through trash. But there was something sad about that. Picking trash was more fun than running in circles like an idiot. That vague sadness must have colored my thoughts, because the field I was seeing began to transform. It got spooky, less like a park than like a graveyard. A graveyard without headstones. I began to see dark figures emerge, first hands then heads full of foul yellow teeth, then whole pale rubbery bodies. The Sleepers. One of them might have been Leo, I thought. Another might have been Boss, bigger than the rest, a real Frankenstein. Yet another might have been Ronnie, the true seer of these horrors. Ronnie was alive, of course, but he was also dead. He was forgotten. You didn't have to be dead to be forgotten, see? And if you were alive, you could still be partway dead. The trash was all mixed up with us. Trash Mountain could be flattened, sent to China, and replaced by a park, but it would loom out there forever, and inside us too.

Biographical Note

Bradley Bazzle is the recipient of the 2016 Red Hen Press Fiction Award, judged by Steve Almond, for *Trash Mountain*. His short stories have won awards from the *Iowa Review* and *Third Coast*. They also appear in *Epoch*, *Copper Nickel*, *New England Review*, *New Ohio Review*, *Web Conjunctions*, and elsewhere. Bradley grew up in Dallas, Texas, and has degrees from Yale, Indiana University, and the University of Georgia, where he taught writing. He remains in Athens, Georgia, with his wife and daughter.

In Gratitude

Many people contributed to this book, and I thank them. I thank Cheryl and Wayne Bazzle, my parents, who let me leave my drawings and weird projects all over the house when I was a kid, and who continue to encourage me. I thank Andrea and Lenore, my family, who support me and bear with me through the ups and downs of the writing life. I love you both. I thank Maceo Montoya, my friend and tireless reader. I thank my uncle, Tim Coveney, for his wisdom and excellent web design. I thank the rest of my friends and family for their kindness and support. I thank my collaborators in the comedy groups I've been part of (Trophy Dad, the Viola Question and Improv Athens, among others), who have guided me over the years towards what's funny and/or interesting. I thank Stuart Dybek, who selected a portion of this book to win the *Third Coast* Fiction Contest. I thank *Third Coast*. I thank the good people at Red Hen Press, and I thank Steve Almond, who selected this novel to win the Red Hen Press Fiction Award, and whose comments helped me shape the book into its final form. And I thank the other writers and teachers who have encouraged me, especially Judith Ortiz Cofer, who died too young, and whose praise for an early version of the first chapter started me down this road.